*Before th... ...
he pau...
a br...*

She could feel the warmth of him, heard the sound of his quick breathing, which so matched her own.

"Should I stop?" he whispered, his voice husky. "Tell me now, Sarah."

She could stand it no longer. She stood on her tiptoes and kissed him. It was like nothing she'd ever experienced, not in any dream. His mouth was soft as he pressed gentle kisses to hers. Their bodies still touched nowhere else, and she ached to lean against him, found herself arching—

And then what would happen? What would he think?

She broke the kiss but didn't flee, simply stood there and stared wide-eyed at him, her fingers twisted together to keep from pulling him back. Warmth had swept from the crown of her forehead clear to her toes, intensifying deep in her belly. Oh, this was desire . . .

Julia Latham

Wicked, Sinful Nights

AVON

An Imprint of HarperCollinsPublishers

AVON BOOKS
An Imprint of HarperCollins*Publishers*
10 East 53rd Street
New York, New York 10022-5299

Copyright © 2010 by Gayle Kloecker Callen
ISBN 978-0-06-178346-3
www.avonromance.com

First Avon Books paperback printing: January 2010

Avon Trademark Reg. U.S. Pat. Off. and in Other Countries, Marca Registrada, Hecho en U.S.A.
HarperCollins® is a registered trademark of HarperCollins Publishers.

Printed in the U.S.A.

10 9 8 7 6 5 4 3 2 1

To my sister-in-law, Joanne Hall.
I've known you since you were a teenager,
watched you blossom
in marriage and motherhood
through determination and love.
Thanks for becoming my sister.

Chapter 1

Oxfordshire, 1487

She was brazen, for a murderer.

From horseback on a nearby hill, Sir Robert Hilliard looked down upon Drayton Hall, where nursemaid Sarah Audley walked hand-in-hand with her charge, five-year-old Francis Drayton, whom she'd made a viscount by killing his father.

No one suspected the truth but the League of the Blade, the secret society born long ago in a time of darkness to bring justice to innocent victims. Robert was a member, although not by the usual methods.

Viscount Drayton, the murder victim, had once been a Bladesman, too—Robert's mentor—and had risen to the Council of Elders. Such a man's death would always be scrutinized. The symptoms of slow arsenic poisoning could look like many other illnesses to the innocent, which explained why it was often employed. But the League was not easily misled, and they had informed King Henry, who'd agreed that a nobleman of his court must be avenged, in court if possible; but if not, Robert knew where his duty lay.

"Do not be misled by Sarah Audley's beauty." Sir Walter, Robert's partner, gave him a penetrating glance.

Like all typical Bladesmen, Walter's last name was a secret. He was a veteran of the League, of average height but impressive strength, his whiskered face lined with care and duty, his gray hair cut short.

"Beauty often disguises ugliness," Walter continued. "Her beauty was an enticement to Lord Drayton, who could not resist taking her as his mistress. 'Twas a fatal mistake."

Robert knew why Walter would feel the need to instruct him in even life's most basic lessons. Robert's last mission hadn't begun as a sanctioned League assignment. The fact that it had restored Robert's brother Adam to the earldom of Keswick gave it credibility. But the League seemed to have forgotten that success, as well as Robert's previous accomplishments as a Bladesman. Now they only cared about his behavior during the last year. They should not blame him for enjoying himself, when the League was the reason he'd known so little of his own heritage and the pleasures of the outside world. He'd been revealed as the brother of an earl, with money to spend. Women had flocked to him, men had enjoyed his company, and there had been more than one wild night of impropriety.

But now he was on probation, expected to prove himself, when he'd spent his life doing everything the League asked of him. Anger simmered within him, and he wasn't used to feeling that way toward the League, which had saved and molded his life.

Robert squinted, noticing that Sarah's red hair was bared to the late spring sun. She was holding hands with the little boy, dancing in a circle. "I cannot tell if she's beautiful," he said to Walter with practiced ease. "And 'twill not matter to me. Viscount Drayton was a man who took interest in my education and in my well-being. I will not allow a woman to sway my purpose. She will pay for her crimes."

"As we gather proof against her, you may instruct me as you see fit."

Robert shot a glance at Walter.

"You are in command of this mission, Sir Robert."

Robert met the man's gaze, and if he saw a hint of irony, it was faint. "So the League has decided to evaluate me?"

"We are all evaluated on occasion, Sir Robert. There is no shame in that."

Robert's eyes narrowed as he studied his partner.

Did Walter approve of the League's plan—or not? There was no way to tell if he was an ally or an enemy. Which meant Robert could only rely on himself. It had always been that way. The Hilliard brothers were alone in the world, after all.

As he straightened in the saddle, his horse Dragon gave a whinny and tossed its head. "Do your best, Sir Walter. There will only be impressive things to say about me." Robert gave him a carefree smile. It came naturally, and could hide so much. He remembered the way Drayton had sought him out whenever he had visited the League fortress. He'd shown an interest in Robert's studies and training when others only wanted to examine him as an experiment. Robert would never forget the nobleman's kindness.

"Both the League and I want to trust you in all things," Walter said. "But I feel you need to know that I did not approve of the League's experiment with you and your brothers when you were children."

"I appreciate your honesty."

"Then we understand each other," Walter said.

For several minutes, silence reigned between them as Robert considered his position as commander of this mission. Sarah Audley and the young viscount were now kneeling, looking at something on the ground. She touched the boy's shoulder gently, with obvious fondness.

"We will be hiding our purpose here," Robert decided.

Walter only nodded his agreement.

Robert grinned. "Then follow my lead." He urged his horse down the hill, trotting toward the woman who would be defining the next few days—perhaps weeks—of his life.

She looked up as they neared, and he watched her pleasant expression change into curiosity. She rose to her feet with a natural grace, and he let his gaze drift down her body. She was short and sweetly plump, with rounded, feminine curves meant to make a man feel well comforted in bed. Her gown was plain and unadorned, as befitted a servant rather than a lady. That red hair he'd noticed from afar was pulled back with a simple ribbon, not hidden by a headdress or wimple. He could see the curls she'd attempted to train into submission, but imagined that if she loosened the ribbon, her hair would be wild and untamed.

And then he realized that he was evaluating her as a potential bed partner rather than a murder suspect, the same way he'd evaluated every woman he'd met since he'd been allowed to see women. Though the League thought they'd prepared him for everything, he was unprepared for—her.

Her face was as petite as the rest of her, faint freckles scattered across her upturned nose. She was a woman who did not hide herself from the sun. Lips as deliciously plump as her body were already forming into a generous, though polite, smile. Her eyes were brown, warm in the golden afternoon, almost too large for her face. They should either be cold with death, or veiled to hide her true thoughts. Instead he saw a wealth of sadness, determination, and intelligence. He usually allied himself with uncomplicated women who were full of joy and seeking pleasure. But Sarah Audley was an enigma, a widow, and already he found himself distracted from what he knew her to be. Was this how she had seduced Drayton? She would not find him so easy a target.

While her brilliant eyes assessed both men in return, she put her hand on the boy's shoulder as if she could protect him from the world—when she was the one who'd made him an orphan.

Robert deliberately gave her the appreciative smile he always offered a beautiful woman, ignoring Walter's curious glance at him.

"Good afternoon, mistress," Robert said, letting pleasure ripple through his voice. "Tell me we have come to Drayton Hall, for it has been a long day of traveling."

"Aye, you have, good sir."

Sarah Audley felt the spell of the stranger's voice almost immediately. It was deep and soothing, carrying hints of laughter and secret amusement, well cultured and polite, the voice of an educated man.

But she knew a voice could easily hide the truth of a man.

He was a knight at the very least, although surely not much higher, by the plain, functional brigandine he wore over his tunic to protect his torso, and the woolen breeches that covered his legs. He had the broad, muscular body of a man well trained. He was but a knight—so why did she feel a touch of unease?

And then she realized that she was still staring at his body. She quickly lifted her gaze to his lean, angular face, with its square jaw imprinted with a cleft in the middle. He had black, wavy hair cut to just below his ears. His eyes were as bright blue as cornflowers, and regarded her lightly, teasingly, with a hint of admiration, she thought with disbelief. She almost looked over her shoulder. He could not possibly be focusing that look on her. Men did not look at her with possibilities in their minds, as if they could sense all the ways she was a failure as a woman.

But this man didn't know her. She lifted her chin, her hand still on Francis's shoulder; the little boy often forgot caution when he could be near a new horse.

Or at least he used to, before grief had claimed his spirit.

"I am Mistress Sarah Audley of Drayton Hall," she

said. Feeling a bit vulnerable, she was not ready to reveal to strangers that the boy with her was the young viscount. "We welcome weary travelers. Unless you have business here that I may help you with?"

"I am Sir Robert Burcot, late of the king's court," the younger man said, his smile so warm and knowing.

"And I am Sir Walter Gravesend." The older man nodded, his face grizzled even as his body displayed that he was yet a warrior.

Sir Robert looked from his companion to her. "We are traveling on the king's business, so we appreciate your generosity."

She withheld a shiver. *The king's business.*

Sir Robert's too intelligent gaze dropped to the boy, and Sarah resisted the need to pull him closer.

"And who is this fine young man?"

Francis giggled, even as Sarah knew she could not keep his identity from such men. "He is my charge, Francis, Viscount Drayton."

To her surprise, Sir Robert dismounted and while holding on to the reins, bowed before Francis. "'Tis indeed a pleasure to meet you, my lord."

Francis covered his mouth against another giggle. He had curly brown hair and more freckles than she did. It was good to see laughter in his eyes rather than sadness. He missed his father terribly. He didn't remember his mother so well after a year, but the grief from his father's death weeks before was yet fresh. He had taken to hours of long silences, when he would look at her with his great wounded eyes. Lately, it was difficult for her to capture his interest and distract him.

Yet she understood him well, for once upon a time she'd suffered through her own grief.

Sir Walter dismounted as well, his face grave as he regarded the boy. "We heard of the viscount's passing. You have our sympathies."

She nodded, then found her gaze on Sir Robert again. "Sir Anthony Ramsey, the viscount's guardian, is not in residence at present."

" 'Tis a shame," Sir Robert said. "I had heard of him at court, and looked forward to an introduction."

"You can come in," Francis suddenly said.

Sarah gaped down at the little boy, and she knew that the two men might misinterpret her expression. But how could she explain her shock at Francis's ease of speaking?

Sir Robert's smile was blinding in the sunlight. "You are gracious, my lord. I accept your offer."

Before she knew it, she and Francis were leading the way through the gatehouse. Inside, the courtyard opened up, surrounded by lodgings built into the castle walls, along with shops and sheds for the various craftsmen. The old keep rose before them, with its high turrets, which had been keeping watch over the castle for centuries. There were windows cut into it now, an attempt to make it more modern, but it still looked forbidding to her—yet safe. She'd so wanted to be safe there, and she had been, until Lord Drayton's death.

The houndsman nodded to her as he led his dogs toward the gatehouse in a happy pack. Knights continued their practice on the small tiltyard near the barracks, the sound of their swords ringing in the air. Laundry women carried baskets from the main keep and away from the courtyard, where chickens scratched in the dirt and fluttered out of everyone's way.

"'Tis a fine castle," Sir Robert said, coming up beside her.

"Aye. 'Twas a welcome place for me when I arrived." She almost winced. Why was she rambling about something that was not this stranger's business?

"You have not spent your life here?"

"Nay, I was raised elsewhere." She said nothing else, hoping he would understand that she considered her life private.

"So you must have come here to be the boy's nursemaid."

She was surprised to find him watching her with such interest. Sir Walter behaved as other men usually did, staring about the courtyard as the servants and craftsmen attended to their duties. Francis only let his gaze wander back and forth between the newcomers.

"I do not remember telling you my position," she said, hoping to dissuade his unsettling interest.

"You called the boy your charge," he said, shrugging. "I pay attention to everything a beautiful woman says."

She almost snorted with amusement at that. Even Sir Walter looked away, as if he couldn't watch. Did Sir Robert make a habit of charming women wherever he went? And it must work, if he continued to employ it. But she was not a woman used to succumbing to a man's charms—my goodness, men seldom tried.

There *was* Sir Simon Chapman, she amended guiltily, remembering the knight from Sir Anthony's household. He had been paying sweet attention to her in the last few weeks, and lately he'd begun to touch her, taking her hand or putting an arm around her waist. She had flinched the first few times he'd done so, embarrassing herself and him. She wanted to be past the memory of her husband's cruelty and the way it had touched her for too many years.

She didn't know if she should respond to Sir Simon's courtship or not. Would Sir Anthony release her from service, now that Francis was his ward? She tried not to shudder at the thought, reminding herself that he seemed in no hurry to lose her. But Francis would grow older, of course, and someday soon would no longer need a nurse. Would she be an outcast, alone and friendless again?

"'Tis late in the afternoon," she said. "Shall I show you to lodgings for the night? You would be welcome to join us in the great hall for supper."

"That is gracious of you, mistress," Sir Robert said, sweeping his cap from his head.

"I will tell Cook," Francis suddenly said, then raced off toward the keep.

Sarah hesitated, then glanced at Sir Walter before saying, "Forgive my surprise a moment ago, when the young lord invited you inside. My expression had nothing to do with either of you. It is just that . . . he has spoken little since his father died, and with your arrival, he has said more in an hour than he has in a day of late."

Sir Robert smiled. "You have my thanks for the explanation."

She gestured for a groom to come tend their horses, then led them to the guest lodgings built into the curtain wall, where several stone staircases led up to the first floor of each lodging.

"There is an inner and outer chamber on the first floor," she said, gesturing within to the room sparsely furnished with a table and benches, a cupboard and a chest. "There are two bedchambers above this. If you take the interior stairs to the ground floor, you can follow the passage into the keep itself, rather than walk outdoors on a stormy day. I will send chambermaids to see that your rooms are aired and well supplied with linens. Supper is at five of the clock," she added, gesturing to the clock on the mantel. She curtsied and departed.

Sarah hurried across the courtyard, smiling at servants and friends, shrugging at their questions about the new guests. She resisted the temptation to look back where she'd left Sir Robert and Sir Walter. Besides their names, she didn't know who these men were, or what business they were about for the king.

But they'd looked at her too closely. She was a woman many men treated as almost invisible. Why did she suddenly merit notice?

Chapter 2

"**Y**e look skittish."

Sarah jumped, almost dropping the vase of flowers she was carrying to the head table on the raised dais in the great hall. Margery Platten, the chief seamstress at Drayton Hall, gave a snort and crossed her arms over her chest.

Margery, tall and willowy, with black hair and dark blue eyes, gestured with her head toward the intricately carved hearth at the far end of the great hall. "Ye're skittish because of those strangers."

Sarah sighed, placing the vase on the tablecloth, near where Lord Drayton had once sat, and now Francis did. She did not look at the hearth—she didn't need to. She knew Sir Robert and Sir Walter stood talking with Master Frobisher, the steward of the Drayton estates. She'd brought them ale herself.

"I am not skittish," Sarah said, knowing she sounded too prim.

"Well, ye're not yerself."

Margery stepped closer until Sarah had to look up at her friend's impressive height.

"That handsome one is lookin' at you," Margery whispered.

"I wish he would stop," Sarah said. "He's making me nervous."

"Nervous to be admired?"

"I know you do not feel that way; you're used to the attention of men."

Margery's amused expression softened. "Sarah—"

"Nay, do not pay any attention to me. 'Tis nothing."

"But it is. Ye're lettin' the past take hold of yer mind. Don't be doin' that. Men are not all like yer cruel husband."

"And women are not all like me," Sarah answered brittlely. "I have certainly proven that I am not the sort of woman to make a man happy. I cannot even do what nature intended and give a man a child."

"Sarah—"

She sighed. "I am not feeling sorry for myself. I am finished with that. I am barren, and 'tis something I've long ago accepted. I have a good life here and do not need—"

"A man's attention? Sometimes that makes life worth livin', gives a spark to yer day ye'd not get otherwise. I think ye're makin' like an old lady in her dotage, when there is Sir Simon sniffin' round ye, and now this stranger eyein' you with admiration."

Sarah told herself to be admired was a good thing, but it was suddenly so overwhelming. And a man's attention had once only meant she'd soon see his hand, raised in violence.

"But Francis needs my attention now," she insisted, feeling like a coward for using a child as a shield from frightening emotions.

"But there will come a day, far too soon, when he does not."

Sarah shuddered. "I never feared that Lord Drayton would dismiss me when Francis was too old for a nurse. But now Sir Anthony is in command."

"And he appreciates yer work," Margery soothed. "And he will see how ye run the castle as if ye were its lady. Ye're takin' the place of Lady Drayton—"

"Shh!" Sarah said, lowering her voice. "I am not taking that good lady's place. I am not a noblewoman; I am just helping where I can, in gratitude for my keep. Now I must finish my duties, Margery."

The seamstress raised both hands, smirking. "Far be it from me to bother you."

Wincing at her own poor choice of words, Sarah reached for her dear friend. "Margery—"

The woman laughed, her voice deep and husky,

causing more than one male head to turn. "Go on with you now. We will speak again later."

Sarah smiled and turned away, but it wasn't long before she again felt like she was being watched. She well remembered the feeling from two years before, when she'd been cast from the home of her husband's family. The suspicion, the anger, the way eyes had followed her—

She looked over her shoulder, but saw only the valets and grooms setting up the trestle tables and positioning benches in preparation for supper. No one looked at her, not even Sir Robert, whose gaze seemed to pierce her when it touched.

She couldn't just wait around like an ignorant fool. She'd made that mistake before, and it had almost ruined her life. She was in charge of Francis, especially while his guardian was elsewhere. It was up to her to discover if the king's men had anything to do with him. He was under her protection. The trust placed in her by his late father, and now by his guardian, meant more to her than life itself.

"Mistress Sarah!"

That little voice touched her heart as no other could, bringing a smile to her face and a sweet softness in her breast as Francis came running toward her, sliding through the rushes scattered across the floor.

"Sir Robert said I could eat at his side," Francis

said. "He's going to tell me about his horse. He calls it Dragon. Isn't that funny?"

So many wonderful sentences, all said with more excitement than he'd shown in weeks. How could she caution him? How could she say no? She nodded. "May I eat with you, too? I would love to hear about Dragon."

He rolled his eyes as if she were being ridiculous. "Of course you may. You always eat with me."

He wanted her at his side, and the joy of that was enough—for as long as it lasted.

Robert sipped his ale and watched Sarah when she wasn't looking. He knew he himself was being watched by Walter, so he understood how Sarah felt, he thought with grim amusement. Walter did not care for Robert's method of getting to know their murder suspect. He'd hinted at it when they'd unpacked their few possessions in their lodgings. But they hadn't talked, not when chambermaids were coming and going, chambermaids who gave Robert saucy grins. He was certain Walter had seen that, too. Women always flirted with him thusly. Yet he didn't need to have Walter—and thereby the League—constantly reminded that he enjoyed women, and that the women seemed to *know* he enjoyed them.

After talking to Francis, Robert watched the boy

run toward his nurse. He studied Sarah's expression and saw more than simple tolerance. Did the boy love her in return? Did children know when an adult was patronizing or using them? Robert didn't have any experience with children, so Francis's eager friendship intrigued him. Perhaps children naturally liked him, too.

He was using Francis's offer of friendship to assess Sarah's devotion to the boy. But even he could tell that Francis showed no hesitation at being with his nurse—no fear, no resignation. The boy did not sense that his nurse had killed his father. She was very good at hiding her true nature.

Before Robert's arrival at Drayton Hall, other Bladesmen had completed the initial investigation. The viscount's death wasn't related to the League or to the Crown. It only had to do with his personal life, and this woman he had taken as his mistress. The League had claimed no one else had as good a motive to want Drayton dead. Surely that made him a saint, if no one else had reason to be angry with him.

But the League had uncovered rumors that Sarah had killed her first husband. That made her the prime suspect.

If Sarah was leery about Francis eating his meal with Robert, she didn't show it. When Francis came to drag him to the head table, Robert realized that Sarah must sit there with the boy every day. From Francis's left, she gave Robert a simple smile as Francis patted the chair on his right.

"Sit here," Francis said. "Your friend may sit next to you."

Even Walter appeared reluctantly amused.

Over Francis's head, Robert sent a special smile to Sarah, but she only nodded briefly and looked away. He did not think overly of himself or his skill, but usually women were more responsive to his attention. This one might prove more difficult. She let her gaze search the hall. Servants moved about with platters of beef and lamb, bowls of salad, fresh white bread ready to be broken into chunks. Supper was a simple affair compared with dinner. Without words, the servants looked to Sarah for confirmation that they were doing their work well. The steward, Master Frobisher, had admitted that Sarah ran the household in his place. There had been reluctance in the man's voice when he'd spoken of her, but Robert hadn't been able to place the emotion behind it—yet. Master Frobisher, too, was sitting at the head table, although with too many people separating them for a conversation. Walter was speaking to the person on his right, so Robert turned to Francis. He noticed that although the boy carefully cut his own meat while Sarah watched with pride, he didn't seem to eat much of it.

"Your nursemaid is a busy woman," Robert commented to the boy.

Sarah's sharp gaze met Robert's, but other than incline her head, she did nothing.

Francis straightened with importance at being spoken to. "She's good at things."

"Women are," Robert wanted to ask about what "things" she was good at, but knew it was too soon to be so curious.

Sarah bit her lip, eyes downcast, but he sensed that she might be hiding a smile.

"She's in charge of me, and Master Frobisher says I can be a handful."

The steward's round face reddened, but he didn't turn their way, as if he hadn't heard.

"All boys are a handful," Robert said.

"Were you?"

"Of course."

"Did your mother have to scold you?"

He would use as much of the truth as he could to keep his lies straight. "I never knew my mother. She died when I was a little boy."

Francis grew solemn. "My mama died when I was little, too."

"I regret that we have that in common."

"Did your father scold you?"

He almost wished he could make up a better childhood than he'd had. "I don't remember my father either. But the people who took care of me say that I was incorrigible."

"In—in—" Francis scrunched up his face. "What is that?"

Robert leaned closer, as if imparting a secret. "Incorrigible means I was very persistent in doing what I wanted, even if it was the wrong thing. Sometimes I did not always listen to my foster father. I had to learn many lessons before I behaved correctly and no longer needed to be scolded."

"So you were a handful, too?"

"I was," Robert said solemnly, then smiled at Sarah who was regarding them curiously. "I can still be incorrigible sometimes."

Her only response was a raised eyebrow.

"Where do you live?" Francis asked.

It was second nature to Robert to use the story he and Walter had created for their lives. After breaking off a piece of bread from the loaf, he said, "London."

"I have never been there," Francis said. "Mistress Sarah has not either."

"Your nurse would enjoy the excitement of the king's court. King Henry is a young man, newly married, and there are many young people."

"Not an easy place to raise a child," Sarah said calmly, as if needing to discourage the boy.

Robert noticed how precisely she cut her own meat, all the while glancing at Francis's plate, as if wishing he'd eat more. Francis was scrawny, but he was a growing boy after all. Perhaps after his father died, he had not eaten well. Robert cut a piece of lamb and ate it with relish. After a moment, Francis mimicked him.

"Sarah was raised in a manor," Francis said between chewing.

"Was she?"

"Her father was a knight, but his liege lord was not my father."

"Then how did she come to be with you?"

The boy frowned and turned to his nurse. "I don't think I know. Do I?"

Sarah chucked him under the chin. "I came to help tend your mother, remember? Then you and I liked each other so much that your father allowed me to be your nurse."

When the cook intruded for a moment of Sarah's attention, Robert quietly said, "Mistress Sarah seems like a good nurse."

Francis nodded. "She's almost as good as having my mama. I think Papa was very sad when Mama died, but having Mistress Sarah with me cheered him up."

And of course, Mistress Sarah cheered up the viscount in other ways, Robert thought cynically.

After supper, as several musicians tuned their instruments, the servants cleared the tables, then dismantled some of them, hiding them behind the tapestries.

Walter and Robert stood alone, watching the smooth way everyone worked together. For a household whose lord had recently died, they all seemed confident in their futures with their new young viscount. His guardian must have given them all assurances that life would go on as usual, which was a gracious thing to do.

Robert was not the only one watching Sarah.

Walter said, "The same young knight has talked to her several times."

Robert nodded and regarded the tall, slim, brown-haired man who bent over Sarah and spoke without a smile. "He seems rather earnest to me. Serious."

"Something elusive for you," Walter said dryly.

"Oh, your barb struck home," Robert said, clapping his partner on the back. "I did not think you had a sense of humor."

Walter arched a brow.

"We'll have to discover the man's name," Robert continued.

"Sir Simon Chapman, a knight in Sir Anthony Ramsey's household."

"Ah, Sir Anthony the guardian. He must have left men here to keep watch for him."

"A guardianship is an important position, one taken with the utmost seriousness. Unlike your guardians," Walter added softly.

Though Robert gave him a glance of surprise, inside he felt a moment of anger. "My foster father, Sir Timothy, was a good man, who disagreed with those above him but bowed to their wishes because he had no choice."

Walter looked away. "We should not be discussing this here."

"I agree," Robert said. Once again, Walter was pointing out his disapproval of Robert's childhood. The knight was a calm man who showed little of what he was feeling, so he must be decidedly bothered if he kept bringing it up.

"Back to the subject of Sir Simon," Robert said in a quiet voice, smiling at a maid who sauntered near the musicians and boldly eyed him.

"Perhaps you have things more pressing," Walter said dryly.

This was too much. "Sir Walter, my methods are not yours. We can discuss your concerns later tonight."

Walter's wintry gray eyes held him. "Aye," he said slowly. "Your words are wise."

That was as close to an apology as Robert was going to get, but it satisfied.

"About Sir Simon?" Robert prodded.

"My dinner partner mentioned that the knight has begun a flirtation with Mistress Sarah."

" 'Tis not much of a flirtation," Robert said, then took a sip of his ale as he watched the knight drone on to Sarah. "He's not even asking her to dance. I shall have to rectify that."

Walter opened his mouth as if to speak, then closed it.

"Good man," Robert said, handing him the tankard and sauntering away.

But he didn't begin with Sarah. He went to the maid still waiting by the musicians who'd now begun a lively country tune. Her eyes brightened at his approach, and she glanced at her friends with subtle triumph.

Athelina was her name. She was a lively dance partner, and Robert found himself turning within the crowded floor, lifting her high into the air, then linking arms with her to process within the dancers. He was pleasantly heated with exertion by the time he danced with his third partner, who pouted her disappointment when he bowed and took his leave.

As he approached Sarah, he studied her. If Simon Chapman didn't flirt well, then Sarah was a good match. She did not bat her eyes or grin, although her smile was pleasant. She seemed personable, not like a murderer would be, but then he'd never known any female murderers. Women were mothers, nurturers; this crime went against everything he'd always imagined a woman to be.

Beneath that personable smile, what was she? Everyone had a deeper side of themselves not shown to many. But only facts and proof of her guilt mattered to the League.

He wanted more from her; he wanted her secrets.

Sarah seemed to notice his approach at last, and he thought she stiffened.

Chapman turned his head slowly—perhaps he did everything slowly, including courting a woman. Robert didn't believe in wasting time.

"Sir Robert Burcot," Sarah said, "allow me to present Sir Simon Chapman."

They nodded to each other, and Robert felt in Chapman the wariness of a man whose territory was being encroached on. His somber eyes studied Robert.

"Good evening," Chapman said.

"And to you as well," Robert answered. Then he bestowed his most charming grin on Sarah. "It seems a shame for a beautiful woman to spend the entire evening conversing. Shall we dance?" He took her hand and gently pulled.

Her brown eyes widened in surprise. Was she offended by his boldness? Did she wish for a man who plodded through his courtship? He usually preferred women as carefree as he was, but there was something well hidden within Sarah. She'd been married, she'd been a man's mistress—why the restraint? Perhaps every man she encountered was intrigued by her cool façade.

Although she glanced at Chapman, she didn't resist as Robert tugged her away from the knight.

Robert was strangely jolted by the sensation of her hand in his. For a small woman, she had long, delicate fingers, strong but supple. Her skin felt smooth, soothing, and in his imagination he explored more of her skin, moving up her arms, dipping his tongue in the hollow above her collar bone—

And then he restrained his wandering thoughts. Had he spent so many years longing for female companionship that even after a year of debauchery in London, he could not control his thoughts about this one woman—who happened to be the logical suspect in a murder?

She was looking up at him in confusion, her lips softly parted, her pale, freckled cheeks touched with a blush. His body's response only strengthened. To distract himself, he launched into a vigorous dance as the beat of the music sped up.

Chapter 3

Sarah didn't know what had happened. One moment she was calmly assessing Sir Simon, flattered by his attention, since the only man she'd been able to trust after her father's death had been the viscount. She was logically considering that Sir Simon met her husbandly requirements of hard work, future security, and decent common sense—

And the next moment, she was in the arms of Sir Robert. She knew little about him except that just his touch jumbled her thoughts, made her feel hot and cold as if unaccustomed to the restraint of her own skin. She could feel the muscles in his arms, the very firmness of his chest when she was forced to support herself to keep from stumbling in this maddening stupor that consumed her mind.

And those chambermaids she'd thought silly when she'd watched them fall all over themselves to dance with him? She silently offered them apologies. If he affected every woman in the castle like this, little would get done until he departed.

She forced herself to focus on the dance so she wouldn't make a fool of herself by falling. But that made her aware of the uninhibited way he moved her among the other dancers. He was so strong he could position her at will, could probably pick her up, and she wouldn't even notice that her feet were dangling inches from the floor. To guide her, his hand occasionally touched her hip or her back, but always returned so that he could hold both her hands in his—big hands, rough with the calluses that came from holding a sword in battle.

And then he did pick her up, his hands gripping her waist, but without pain. In that suspended moment, when she was above him, her hands clutching his arms, her hair came undone from her simple ribbon. Her wild red curls cascaded down her back and forward over her shoulders.

And that wide, white smile of his faltered, but not with dismission, even as he set her back on the floor. Her unmanageable hair affected him in some way, and for the first time in her life, she didn't want to self-consciously tame it back into submission. Then his smile widened again. She'd seen him bestow it on so many women in just these scant hours, yet now it seemed just for her. Men didn't smile at her like this! And if they did, she was able to ignore it.

Not this time. Now she was caught in the spell of this stranger, her gaze locked to his bright blue eyes until she felt she could lose herself in them.

She was not a woman who lost herself, she thought, jolted back to the reality of the situation. She didn't know Sir Robert, didn't know his mission or why he was focusing this intensity on her. He was too free with his hands, and she'd long ago thought she was done wanting a man's touch.

He bent over and picked up her ribbon, presenting it to her almost formally, but with a twinkle in his eye. And now he made her want to laugh! Instead she gathered her hair at the back of her neck and tied it into place.

He pressed a goblet of wine into her hands.

"Drink this," he said, chuckling.

She did, taking several deep gulps, hoping the cool liquid would put out this hot, confusing flame inside her.

"You are a lively dancer, sir," she said, embarrassed by the breathlessness of her voice.

"'Tis *one* of my favorite things to do."

His gaze slipped briefly down her body, and she realized he meant her to think of his other favorite pastimes. Good Lord! She took another drink, then choked.

He laughed, a good-natured, merry sound.

"Where did you learn to dance like that?" she asked.

"My brothers and I were well trained."

"How many brothers do you have?"

"Two, and I am the middle child. Sadly, we had no sisters to tease."

She almost snorted at that.

"Did you have siblings?" he asked.

She shook her head. "'Tis a bond Francis and I share." She paused, listening as the musicians chose a more sedate tune. Others were doing as they were, refreshing themselves, catching their breaths.

People were watching Sarah and Sir Robert with interested speculation. All those eyes made her uneasy. She didn't even search for Sir Simon, mortified by what he might be thinking of her.

Though Sir Robert was watching her, too, it was a different sort of feeling, one she had to fight hard to ignore. She turned her thoughts back to Francis and wondered why this man paid such attention to a lad of only five years.

"You were good with Francis at dinner tonight," she said, watching his expression. "Do you have children of your own?"

He blinked in surprise. "Nay, I do not. But there is something about the direct way a child's mind works that fascinates me."

"So you like people to be direct?"

She thought she saw a hint of amused wariness flash and then vanish in those deceptive cornflower blue eyes.

"Aye, it makes things simple," he said.

She hesitated. It was not her place to question a traveler, a guest of Drayton Hall. But he'd been so forward with her . . .

"Are you often assigned duties by the king?" she asked.

He grinned as if he had expected her to say something else. "Not often. The king chooses the man for the assignment."

But he wasn't telling her the assignment, she thought, frustrated. "You must feel very proud that he has chosen you."

He gave a self-deprecating shrug. At least he was not a boastful man.

"Do you have to be somewhere soon?" She was trying to find out if he meant to stay, which might imply that his business was here.

"Are you asking me to remain at Drayton Hall?" His voice was quiet, intimate.

She glanced up at him in surprise, only to realize that he was teasing her. She felt a blush heat her cheeks.

"Nay," she said quickly, "I would never dream of something so forward."

"But you would *like* to be forward?"

"Sir Robert, you are turning around my every word!" she cried in frustration. Suddenly, she felt a tug on her gown and looked down to see a yawning Francis regarding her with sleepy eyes.

"Mistress Sarah," the boy said when his giant yawn had finished, "are you scolding *him* now, too?"

Sir Robert chuckled.

"Of course not, Francis," she said, feeling like the evening had gotten away from her. "We were just having a silly conversation. But I can see that you have stayed up far too late this night. 'Tis time to find your bed."

Though Francis frowned, he didn't protest when she took his hand. He tugged back briefly as he looked up at Sir Robert. "A good night to you, sir."

That little voice could even work magic on a large knight, for the man came down on one knee and gravely said, "And to you, Lord Drayton. May dreams not disturb you in the night."

It annoyed Sarah that she found Sir Robert's treatment of the boy charming and sweet. She gave the man a perfunctory smile, then led Francis down the corridor, taking the circular stairs up to the family lodgings on the next floor. Francis's bedchamber had adjoined his parents'. He hadn't wanted to move into the rooms that he had inherited, and she couldn't blame him. When his mother had been ill, she'd moved Sarah into chambers that adjoined Francis's, so that Sarah could easily move between the boy's room and the viscountess's bedside.

As she helped him change into his nightclothes, she remembered his father with respect and gratitude. He'd given her a life when she'd been abandoned and hopeless. Yet always her memories of him were marred by the way he'd died.

And now her life was all about his son. She tried to forget that in only a few years, Francis would probably go to another family to be fostered, as every child of a great family did.

Would Sarah be able to continue her role overseeing the household? Or would Lady Ramsey, wife of Francis's guardian, have something different in mind?

In the outer chamber of their lodgings, Robert closed the door to the courtyard and watched Walter. He didn't know his fellow Bladesman at all. Would he be an angry pacer? An arguer?

For a moment, he considered that in his future with the League—and they *would* grant him one—he would always have a partner who might rebuff or resist his methods. Was that worth the satisfaction he felt when he was able to be of help?

Walter poured himself another ale and sat down at the table near the hearth.

"I will make certain we are not overheard," Robert said. He searched their bedchambers, the privy, even went downstairs to the torchlit corridor that connected all the lodgings with the main keep before closing that door behind him. He sat down across from Walter, saying, "All is secure."

Walter's eyes were hooded as he studied Robert. "Your methods today were . . . interesting."

"A more flattering word than I thought you'd use," he said dryly.

"Your flirtation is not something I personally would employ." Walter arched a brow, a touch of amusement in his voice as he added, "In my younger days, I could have successfully pulled it off."

Robert grinned. "You could flirt in your younger days?"

"Let us not go too far with this cockiness, boy," the man responded gruffly.

Robert tamped down his amusement. "Today was a good beginning. My methods put people at ease. The men assume I'm not serious, that they have no reason to be defensive toward me. The women think I only have one thing on my mind, and that either makes them feel flattered, or dismissive."

"I would have thought Mistress Sarah the latter, but now I'm not so certain."

"Nor am I," Robert said. "For a woman who's been a wife and a mistress, she is strangely virginal in her approach to men."

"Or so she makes it seem."

"Then she makes it seem that way all the time, for no one thought she behaved out of the ordinary. More than one person appeared grateful that I was showing her the same interest I showed the other women."

"This definitely makes it seem like her crime was one of emotional response, a fit of rage, rather than a calculated murder. She was Drayton's mistress; he probably wouldn't marry her, and she could not accept it. Unpremeditated, but still a crime."

"A 'fit of rage' sounds like it would lead to a sudden crime, such as pushing him down the stairs. A slow death by poisoning is a cold, cruel anger."

"We will discover the details about how her first husband met his death," Walter said. "Then we'll know."

Facts mattered the most, and they did not have enough of them. Too much was at stake—a dead man's justice, a child's future.

"She is female," Robert said, "and emotion is part

of her. You have seen her with the young viscount. She holds nothing back from him."

"Perhaps she loved him too fiercely, and the late viscount thought it inappropriate," Walter said, looking at him from beneath his furrowed brow.

Robert relaxed back in his wooden chair. "I am not a parent, but I do not think I would be offended if someone loved my child deeply."

"You miss my point, Robert. There is such a thing as obsessive love."

"Nay, I understood what you were saying, but her relationship to the boy does not seem unhealthy." He frowned briefly. "And then there is her role as mistress of this household."

"Such a position of honor might be worth killing for."

Robert shook his head. "She had it *before* the viscount was killed. Tell me why a mistress would be openly elevated to such a position of authority, especially if there were rumors she killed her first husband."

"Respect for the viscount?" Walter mused, rubbing a hand through his cropped hair. "And we are not sure the rumors ever reached here. Either I or another Bladesman will journey to her late husband's home for further details."

"A good reason not to marry." Robert smiled. "Are you married, Walter?"

The other man only arched an eyebrow.

"Of course we must never exchange anything personal. 'Tis just a shame that with the way I was raised, you know everything about me."

"Not everything," Walter said dubiously. "You have yet to prove yourself to me."

Anger flared in him, but he ignored it and widened his grin. "And you have yet to prove yourself to me."

The silence between them was momentarily tense.

"Did you notice the steward's hesitation about Sarah's role?" Robert asked, returning to the subject of their investigation. "*There* is someone who might feel threatened."

"Yet 'threatened' is not exactly the word that describes his reaction," Walter said. "He mentioned that Sarah is well-controlled in both thought and emotion. And yet she has only five and twenty years, one year beyond you."

Another barb to his youth, Robert thought, but all he did was smile.

"In a man such control is deemed appropriate," Walter continued. "In a woman 'tis often interpreted as cold."

Robert only arched an eyebrow.

"I shall attempt to earn Master Frobisher's trust and his secrets—with your permission, of course."

Robert laughed. "You do that. Who else were you charming at supper?"

Walter harrumphed. "I do not need to charm. I question."

He was saying that "charming" people was unnecessary. Robert relished the challenge of proving him wrong. Robert might be furious that after an entire life of service to the League, they were requiring him to prove himself, but that didn't mean he didn't enjoy showing Walter that different methods could still yield good results.

"My thanks for your making clear your interrogation methods," Robert said flippantly. "So whom did you question?"

"My dinner companion was the Drayton treasurer, Sir Daniel."

"The man holding the purse strings of a young viscount—under the guardianship of Sir Anthony, of course. We will see what kind of guardian the man is with his ward's money and holdings." It was too early to rule out the motives of others where the viscount's death was concerned. "We will speak with the other upper servants, to gather more information."

Even as Walter acquiesced and retired to his own chamber, Robert sat looking into the fire. At first, all he could remember was the wild red tumble of Sarah's hair as he'd held her in the air above him. It had made him think of having her in his bed, where she could rise above him as she took him inside. He clenched his jaw and closed his eyes.

He must firmly ignore those thoughts, or he'd never be able to sleep that night. He turned instead to the next step in his own plan for Sarah, the one he had not chosen to confide to Walter.

Chapter 4

Sarah was surprised when she saw both knights, Robert and Walter, at daily mass in the chapel the next morn. She had spent a restless night worrying about them, and had hoped for a moment's peace to pray for guidance, but even that would be denied her. She did the best she could, bowing her head and not looking at them—oh, she could not delude herself. She was only trying to avoid looking at *one* of them.

The handsome Sir Robert was the picture of innocent piety at mass, those blue eyes raised to the heavens when appropriate, then lowered to the stone floor with humility. If he noticed the female stares cast his way, even in the chapel, he did not show it. But he did take a moment to smile at Francis, who grinned back with happiness. The boy had an entire castle full of men to look up to, but somehow he'd chosen this stranger, a flirtatious man with a mysterious mission.

When they went to the great hall to break their fasts, Sarah made it a point to oversee the meal rather than sit at the head table, so she could watch Francis from afar. Again, the elder knight spoke to other men at the table, but Sir Robert answered Francis's questions with ease and grace. His kindness should please her—

It bothered her.

Margery sauntered over to her, standing at her side to look over the hall. Sarah sighed.

"Ye made a lovely dancer last night," Margery said softly.

Sarah closed her eyes and stifled a groan.

"'Twas a good idea to make Sir Simon jealous. He watched you with no expression, but he was thinkin' somethin', I know for sure."

"I would never deliberately try to make a man jealous," Sarah said, turning her back on the room to look out the mullioned window. As if she were really looking at anything.

"'Tis sad, that is. It can be a good strategy. So ye didn't want to dance with the stranger?"

"If you noticed, I had no choice."

"Ooh, a bold man. I like that."

"Then *you* should dance with him. Men should not make free with a woman without her permission."

Margery's gaze softened, but she didn't respond to

the lessons Sarah had learned in life. "If he asks me to dance, I will. Or should *I* be the one to ask *him* to dance?"

"You probably will not get the chance. I assume he is leaving today."

"Probably? Ye do not know for certain?"

Sarah grudgingly shook her head.

"Those are not travelin' garments they're wearin'," Margery mused.

Sarah looked back across the hall. Their clothes were simple tunics and breeches. And then Sarah realized why, when together all the men of the garrison gathered to leave the hall for their morning practice of arms at the tiltyard, and Sir Walter and Sir Robert mingled with them.

"They're stayin' at least the morn," Margery said, covering her mouth.

"Do not laugh." Sarah felt like grumbling.

The seamstress's amusement faded, and she gave Sarah a curious look. "Why are ye so against them?"

She wanted to wring her hands together, but stopped herself. "I do not know," she said in a low voice. "He said he was on the king's business, and I do not know if 'tis here or somewhere else. But if he's not leaving, then that is an ominous sign."

"Ye don't know that, dearie." Margery's voice was kind. "Be patient."

Francis ran to Sarah and did his usual skid to a stop. "May I go to the tiltyard with the men?"

She frowned. "'Tis a dangerous place to be, my lord. You know that."

"But Sir Robert said I could watch him, if I was quiet and respe—respe—"

"Respectful?"

"Respec'ful of the dangers."

So the knight had thought of everything.

"Regardless, you must wait for me," she said. How could she tell the boy that they didn't know this stranger? How could she even know if Sir Robert were telling the truth about having the king's ear?

Oh, she would make herself crazy with all of these thoughts.

But a session at the tiltyard would tell her more about him, so after wishing Margery a good day, she only made a wiggling Francis wait a few minutes before following him out into the courtyard.

Sarah gave the boy some freedom, not forcing him to remain at her side. He showed good judgment, staying well back as the men began to don partial armor and helms for protection before beginning their sword work.

She told herself to pay attention to the armor that concealed Sir Robert, but she didn't need to. He wore only chest and back plates, leaving his arms unprotected—and bare, since the leather jerkin he'd donned was sleeveless. Was he trying to say he thought no one here could harm him?

She'd seen many a man's arms; it should not bother her. But he was so tall, so impressively muscled that she felt flushed. And she had to look his way, because there was Francis, bringing Sir Robert his helm although he had to drag it behind him, offering a horn of ale before they'd even begun to train. Sir Robert grinned and accepted it.

She thought Sir Robert would spar with one of the Drayton men, test his skill against theirs, and several looked rather hopeful for that, even stepping forward, ready to call him out. But instead Sir Robert's and Sir Walter's gazes met and held. Sir Walter squared to face him, Sir Robert's grin hardened, and then both lowered their helms and lifted their swords.

Sarah realized she was holding her breath, even as the Drayton knights and soldiers paused to watch.

The clash of two swords meeting high in the air was impressive, ringing on for a long moment, breaking the stillness. Both men's arms held, vibrating, then the men jumped back and began a slow circling. Sarah couldn't see their faces, but she could see the grace in Sir Robert's light step, and the deliberate, careful tread of Sir Walter.

She realized she'd almost forgotten Francis, but he was standing on a bench away from the combat, his hands clasped together, his mouth open in awe, as if he'd never seen men spar before.

But he hadn't seen *these* men, she thought with a shiver, for suddenly they both attacked, hacking, thrusting, parrying each other's sword aside. When Sir Robert jumped over a low slash across his legs, she gasped aloud, thinking this was far too dangerous for training.

And both men seemed to realize the same, for they took a step back.

Sir Walter raised his helm. "My apologies, Sir Robert," he said, breathing a little heavier. "Challenging your impressive skill made me far too competitive."

Sir Robert lifted his own helm to reveal his sweating, grinning face. "I'll accept your apology if you accept mine. Shall we go at it again?"

They attacked with renewed, ferocious vigor, as if they hadn't even apologized. Sarah found herself wincing, stiffening, even beginning to duck once as if she were the one fighting. Sunlight reflected off a particular slash of Walter's sword, dazzling her eyes. By the time she could see again, she saw the small drip of blood on Sir Robert's upper arm, beginning a slow trek to his elbow from a thin gash.

Sir Robert tipped off his helmet again, bowing to his opponent. "I concede defeat," he said.

His voice implied anything but, yet Sir Walter bowed and accepted the concession.

"There are other disciplines at which you might excel," Sir Walter said graciously, with a bit of gruffness.

"Age and wisdom would still win out."

Sir Walter arched a brow. "Then shall we get on with the testing of that theory?"

Sir Robert's grin was wolfish, and Sarah felt a sudden chill sweep across her skin.

"But you're hurt!" Francis cried, jumping from the bench and running toward the two men.

Sarah gasped and dashed across the tiltyard, seeing the men fighting on all sides. But all were watchful of Francis, and moved aside when they saw him coming. Both Sir Walter and Sir Robert turned to face the boy.

"Fear not, Lord Drayton," Sir Robert said. "'Tis but a scratch."

"Mistress Sarah says we cannot let wounds get dirty," Francis insisted. He reached for Sir Robert's gauntleted hand and began to pull.

"Where are we going?" Sir Robert asked, grinning back at Sir Walter, who only shook his head in amusement.

"To Mistress Sarah, of course."

Sarah came up short in surprise. Her gaze met Sir Robert's.

"Now that you mention it, it does sting," he said.

Several nearby knights stifled their laughter.

Sarah felt herself blushing again, something easily noticeable with her fair complexion. Why didn't Sir Robert bluster a refusal, like any normal man with such a paltry injury? But he allowed Francis to lead him to a bench, where he sat down so the little boy could peer at the cut, which had already stopped bleeding.

"It doesn't truly hurt," Sir Robert offered.

"Good." Francis turned his head. "Mistress Sarah?"

She felt foolish still rooted to the spot, and briskly approached the bench. Sir Robert's gaze seemed to move up her body far too slowly before reaching her face.

"Mistress Sarah!" Francis poked her arm. "You must bandage his wound."

"I do not have my tray of medicines with me," she said, trying not to look at the patient man before her.

Francis put his hands on his hips. "Do you not have a clean handkerchief up your sleeve?"

She closed her eyes for a moment. "Aye, I do."

"Can you not use that?"

She produced the handkerchief in resignation, then

bent forward to look at the cut. She felt the heat of exertion coming off Sir Robert. "The sword made a clean slice, of course."

"But a sword isn't clean!" the boy said.

Sir Robert was silently laughing now, his face too close, his gaze as heated as his body.

Francis looked around him, as if her healing supplies would magically appear. "We need something to wash the wound with, too."

Sir Robert plucked the handkerchief from her hand and neatly tore it in two. Francis grinned and took one piece over to the bucket set aside to quench the men's thirst.

In a low voice, Sir Robert said, "I am sorry my clumsiness at training has caused you such problems."

"'Tis no problem," she said, trying to sound indifferent. "Francis is a caring boy."

"Does he keep you on hand to bandage every injured knight?"

She sighed. "Nay, he is usually at his studies with the chaplain this time of day."

"Ah, then I am fortunate to be receiving such tender ministrations."

"We shall see if you think the same after I have bandaged you," she said dryly. "I will probably have to use *great pressure* to stop the flow of blood."

"And here I thought the bleeding had stopped." He chuckled. "I look forward to your care."

Thankfully, for her composure, Francis returned to hand her the dripping handkerchief. She wrung it out and bent to wipe the blood from the wound. As she'd discovered the previous night dancing in his arms, Sir Robert was in fine training form. With his head turned, he watched her, making her far too uncomfortable. She scrubbed a bit harder. He only arched a brow and smirked.

She straightened, wearing a frown. Usually she employed a leather hair tie to hold impromptu bandages on a little boy, but for some reason today she'd chosen a pretty blue ribbon to hold back her curls.

Francis looked from one to the other in confusion. "Mistress Sarah?"

"I have nothing to hold a bandage in place," she said. "Is there a piece of rope or leather somewhere about, Sir Robert?" She expected him to get her out of this mess by refusing to use such a clumsy, awkward restraint.

"I know not, mistress."

He innocently blinked those big blue eyes at her. She told herself to remember to breathe. She wanted to give him a shake, to tell him to stop behaving like this.

Why did he not play along with her instead of dragging out this farce?

Francis pointed at her head. "You can always fetch another hair ribbon, mistress."

She glanced at Sir Robert from beneath raised eyebrows. "Do you want a blue ribbon wrapped about your arm, sir?"

She expected him to defer on account of his partner, Sir Walter, or the other knights loitering nearby.

But he only looked at Francis. "Whatever you think is best, my lord."

She rolled her eyes when she knew Francis wasn't looking, then yanked the ribbon from her hair. The morning heat had already sent her curls into a frenzy, and soon they would be plastered against her neck and cheeks.

"I think her hair looks like fire," Francis commented to Sir Robert.

She stiffened.

"A very different hue, 'tis true," Sir Robert answered back.

Sarah frowned at the two of them. "'Tis not appropriate to discuss a woman as if she's not here, Francis."

Francis winced. "I'm sorry, mistress."

Sir Robert showed no repentance as he said, "'Tis not the boy's fault."

She wanted to be finished with his foolish playacting. She brusquely lifted the knight's arm up so that the bandage wouldn't slide down, pressed the dry half of the handkerchief into place, and neatly tied a blue bow around the whole thing. The ribbon was barely long enough to fit around his arm muscles.

She put her trembling hands on her hips. "When you are ready to travel today, I will replace this with a more appropriate bandage."

He rose up before her until she was forced to tilt her head back. He stood too close to her, saying quietly, "But we are not leaving today, Mistress Sarah. I hope this will not inconvenience you."

His breath touched her face softly, the heat of his body still bathed hers, and he didn't move away, as if he didn't care who saw him.

She took a step back. "You have decided to rest from your travels, Sir Robert?"

He cocked his head. "You might say that, Mistress Sarah."

She cursed silently to herself, the effect of his nearness forgotten. He definitely had another reason for being at Drayton Hall. Was he challenging her to discover it?

"My thanks for your healing abilities, mistress."

She wanted to scoff at him and his secrets.

He gave her a polite nod of his head, then held out his arm to Francis. "How do I look, my lord?"

"Silly, but better. We don't want you sick in bed,

Sir Robert, do we, Mistress Sarah? Then you'd have to tend him."

Surely she could blame her red face on the sun, she thought miserably, folding her arms across her chest.

But she could not escape the fact that her last hope that he was leaving today had died.

"What are you doing next, Sir Robert?" Francis asked.

He tousled the boy's hair. "So I have your permission to continue training? Then I imagine I shall practice jousting."

"You will ride Dragon?" Francis said eagerly, clapping his hands together.

"What is the name of your pony?"

Sarah saw the boy's hesitation and felt pity for him. He had not taken to horseback riding like other boys his age. That was why she was so surprised he was interested in Sir Robert's horse.

"I do not have my *own* pony," Francis confessed, glancing at the group of boys on the far side of the courtyard, who were using sticks to roll a hoop to each other. "But I'm practicing, so that I get better and deserve my own."

"While I'm here, if you ever want to practice with me, I will be glad to help you."

"Oh, aye, we could do that!"

Sarah closed her eyes. It sounded like he meant to

stay for a long time. That was something that would have to be taken up with the steward, of course, and through him, Sir Anthony. If only she could demand the truth from Sir Robert!

Now that her eyes were briefly closed, Robert took a moment to study Sarah. He'd flustered and teased her, and she bore it all with an innocent reluctance. She did not seem like an evil woman, but the League's theory was that she'd committed murder when highly emotional.

Emotional? She seemed like a woman in such control of everything except the blushes she could not hide. Yet a woman so normally composed would behave far differently when provoked too far.

After he'd saddled Dragon, he went to the lists at the far end of the tiltyard, where the knights rode their horses and practiced piercing metal rings with their lances. Francis was already there, standing on a bench, jumping up and down as each horseman took his turn at the joust.

Simon Chapman was ahead of him in line, and if Robert expected the other man to maneuver as slowly as he did when courting a woman, he was surprised. Chapman moved as one with the horse, and his lance perfectly speared several rings in a row. Young Francis cheered each knight so loudly that Robert could almost hear him as he galloped down the lists.

Later, Sarah allowed the boy to ride one of the Drayton ponies with Robert walking at his side. Francis was obviously nervous, and naturally the pony could feel that, which didn't help his learning.

Francis said, "My father used to walk with me like this."

Now Robert understood. "You must miss that."

Francis lowered his gaze to the pony's mane. "I never worried that I would fall when he was here. But after he died, one of the grooms made me try again, and I fell."

Why would anyone insist that a grieving boy ride? Robert knew he himself had not been raised as other people, but it didn't make sense to him.

"Everyone falls," Robert said.

"You do, too?"

"Of course. When I was younger, I once hurt my leg so badly in a fall that I couldn't walk for days. My foster father put me back on the horse as soon as I was able, because if one lets the fear take over, one might never want to ride again."

Francis seemed to be considering this. "So the groom wasn't being mean to me?"

"I was not there, my lord, but I would assume not."

After that, Francis's worry seemed to ease, and he allowed Robert to gradually increase his pace.

Robert was amused by his own behavior with the young lord. He'd already discovered much about the relationship between Sarah and Francis. But the more time he spent with the little boy, the more Robert laughed. That bit with the bandage, and the look on Sarah's face when she realized that Francis meant her to tend him—Robert had almost guffawed out loud. But it hadn't been so funny when she'd been touching him with those warm, smooth fingers, and he'd had to pretend that he wasn't feeling more than amusement. She'd smelled like sweet lavender. And he still sported the feminine ribbon on his arm for Francis's benefit— and Sarah's.

He glanced at her where she sat primly on a bench, having searched for shade to protect her skin. She was focused on Francis, which meant focused on Robert.

But Robert found himself studying the boy almost as much as Sarah. There was something about this little orphan, left alone in the world with great responsibilities he didn't understand, that made one feel protective. He was much like Adam, Robert's brother who'd known from childhood that he was the true earl of Keswick. Unlike Francis's circumstances, Adam's identity had to be kept a secret. A killer had also taken Robert's parents, so he and his brothers had even more in common with Francis.

At last Sarah took the young lord inside for his studies, leaving Robert near the stables. He watched the nursemaid and her charge disappear into the great hall.

Walter approached him.

"Come for a rematch?" Robert said idly, his mind still on Sarah and the boy.

"Only if you insist on proving yourself."

Robert glanced at the older man, whose look was bland, as if there was no deeper meaning beneath his words. Or was this his attempt at humor? Robert chuckled, and then said, "Our sparring will have to wait, although I regret it. I have our regular duty to perform."

"You will leave now?"

"I will return quickly."

After retrieving the small leather packet from his bedchamber, Robert crossed the courtyard again and went out through the gatehouse. The Oxfordshire countryside was wooded between rolling hills, with plenty of streams. He chose the nearest to the castle, then followed it into the forest.

He knew almost immediately that someone was following him, and after backtracking once through a series of trees, he saw the red of Sarah Audley's hair. Intrigued, he wished he could deal with her immediately, but he first had to finish his mission. He increased his pace into the woodland, following the stream into the first clearing, as every Bladesman was taught to do. He left the message between rocks, positioning sticks, leaves and pebbles in the League method to subtly point out the hiding place for his first report to his superiors.

And then he blended back into the trees and waited for Sarah's approach.

Chapter 5

S arah felt like a fool as she worked her way slowly into the forest, not following a path, only following her ridiculous intuition and Sir Robert. Sticks poked at her hair, yanking strands of it, slapping her in the face if she let go of them too quickly. Her gown kept getting caught on prickly bushes, and more than once she thought she'd lost sight of him.

What was he doing out here alone, away from the castle?

She went through an overgrown clump of ferns and low-hanging branches, pushing at dangling leaves and her own wild hair, when resistance gave way and she stumbled into a clearing.

Sir Robert was watching her, legs braced wide, bare arms folded over his chest.

Waiting for her.

A cold sweat broke out across her skin, and she shivered, fighting back fear. She had thought of nothing but discovering his secrets, protecting Francis and her home. She'd become complacent, confident in her new life.

God above, could he have known she'd been following him?

She was a different person now, she reminded herself. She would not so easily return to the cowed woman she'd been. She forced a smile. "Sir Robert, what are you doing here?"

He only arched a brow, his small smile hinting at amusement.

When he said nothing, her words seemed to just tumble out, sounding more and more foolish. "Francis and I enjoy walking through the woods. I point out birds' nests in the trees, and frogs beside the stream. I was trying to find a new path for one of our lessons, and suddenly, there you were!" she finished brightly.

He began to walk slowly toward her, each stride covering much ground. She remained rooted to the spot, even as her frantic brain urged flight. He was a stranger who'd been paying too much attention to her. Now she was alone with him—how could she not have learned from the past?

But if she ran, he'd know she'd been lying, and she'd never discover the truth of his mission.

He stopped in front of her and spoke in a low, even voice. "Following men is never a good idea, mistress."

She blinked as if in confusion. "Well, of course I know that. I was not following you. 'Twas an accidental meeting."

"I've been watching you following me since we left the castle."

How could she answer that? She trilled a laugh and fluttered her lashes as she knew other women did. "Oh, please, Sir Robert. If you must flatter yourself, then—"

He gripped her upper arms, and her words died on a fearful gasp. Even the birdsong seemed to stop.

Some strange look passed through his eyes and he just as suddenly released her. She took a shaky breath.

"You do not need to pretend to be other than yourself for me," he said.

"And neither do you, Sir Robert." She inhaled deeply, calming the butterflies in her stomach. "'Tis not my place to ask, but I can no longer hold my tongue. What king's business brings you to Drayton Hall?"

A wry smile twisted his lips as he regarded her. "My mission has concerned you much?"

She nodded. "The young lord is in my care."

"And you felt the need to brave the woodland alone?"

She bit her lip, then softly confessed, "I had to know."

"I am here to investigate the viscount's death on behalf of the king."

She gaped at him for a moment, knowing this was so much worse than she'd imagined.

Arsenic. The subtle whisper of a word invaded her mind, and the guilt rode hard behind it. She couldn't believe it—didn't want to believe it.

She forced herself to look surprised, then shocked. "But—but—the physicians thought his illness the black death. All left him alone to keep it from spreading to the rest of the household—"

"All left him alone?"

"I—nay, of course not. Someone had to care for him."

"And who was that?"

"Myself, of course. I am the Drayton healer."

"So they all risked you to the illness, but not themselves."

She stared at him, confused. "'Tis my chosen skill. I care not how or why someone is ill. I attempt to heal them."

"And you tried to help the viscount."

"Of course I did! Oh, surely this conjecture is all madness," she said, throwing up her hands and pacing away from him. She couldn't think beneath his intent gaze. "Why would the king investigate Lord Drayton's death?"

Sir Robert followed her, stepping back into her line of vision, forcing her to look at him. "Because Drayton was murdered."

Hearing such words aloud was truly terrifying. Her mouth sagged open, and all the fears she didn't want to confront rushed through her mind.

He caught her elbow. "Mistress Sarah? Are you ill? If you swoon in my presence, I'll be forced to carry you back to the castle, and you won't like how that will look."

"I am not going to swoon!" She pulled her elbow out of his grip and almost stumbled. Her stomach clenched with grief and nausea as she was forced to at last realize that Lord Drayton had suffered terribly for a cruel reason. "M-murdered?" she said, wincing as she stuttered. "Who would do such a thing to a kind, decent man? He had no enemies."

"So it once appeared, yet that doesn't change the fact that the symptoms of his illness were of arsenic poisoning."

She covered her mouth with both hands. How could she tell him she'd suspected the truth, but that it had been too late? She had been closest to Drayton at the end; she knew what it felt like to have unjust suspicion fall on her. If she told Sir Robert that she'd suspected poisoning, it would look like she was turning suspicion away from herself.

She had whispered her fears to Margery, and even her own dear friend hadn't believed her, had told her to be quiet instead of risking her safety and position with unfounded rumors.

Sarah despised herself for succumbing to her own fear. She'd once felt the hopelessness of abandonment and hunger, had been too afraid to experience it again, so she'd kept quiet. She was telling Sir Robert the truth when she said she couldn't imagine who wanted Drayton dead.

"His symptoms of long-term poisoning seemed clear to the king's advisors," Sir Robert continued.

She knew she continued to gape at him, but he seemed to easily ignore her white face and haunted gaze.

"The headaches and vomiting, the loose bowels—"

She shuddered, hugging herself, tears stinging her eyes. "But those are the symptoms of so many illnesses!"

"But his red face? The peeling of the soles of his feet?"

She gasped. "I had never seen the latter before, didn't understand . . ."

Didn't *want* to understand, she amended silently.

She was a failure at so many things in her life, but had always thought she was a competent healer. And now she didn't even have that illusion any more.

She couldn't hold back the tears that leaked between her tightly closed eyelids. Lord Drayton had suffered needlessly, and she hadn't been able to help him. She felt overwhelmed and hopeless, and when Sir Robert patted her back, she didn't think about who he was. He was trying to comfort her, when no one ever had. Since her father died, she'd always been alone.

Without thinking, she turned into him, desperate for solace and absolution, and knowing she would never have it. And then she felt the warmth of his arms around her, the heat of his body against her cheek. She inhaled the scent of him, of manly things like horses and the clean sweat of training.

And for just a moment, comfort swept through her.

Horrified, she immediately pushed away.

She stared up at him and winced at his impassivity.

"Sir Robert, I didn't—I never meant—" She tried to gather her thoughts together, knew that she was now in a precarious position at Drayton Hall, especially under the eye of the king. "I would never play on your sympathies," she continued gravely, trying to keep a quiver from her voice. "What will you do now?"

"With you?"

Her eyes widened with confusion. "I—nay, that wasn't what I meant."

"But you are a part of my mission."

A shot of fear burned her from the inside out. "What do you mean?"

"I need your assistance."

She put a hand to her chest as relief flooded through her. For just a moment, she'd thought he was about to accuse her of murder. "My assistance? I am a healer, a child's nursemaid. What do I know of a king's mission or a murder investigation?"

"You know Drayton Hall, and all its inhabitants. Someone here murdered your lord. Do you not wish to help me find and bring that person to justice?"

She felt unsteady, as if her world turned upside down. "You think someone *I* know killed him?" she whispered, appalled.

"You yourself said he had no enemies. The king's men have agreed. So that leaves someone close to him."

"But he had no enemies within the household, either!" she cried, then covered her mouth as her voice rang through the clearing.

Sir Robert solemnly said, "But obviously he did."

She couldn't imagine anyone wanting such a good man dead, felt stunned and heartsick and terrified all at the same time. Who among her friends could do such a thing?

"Nay, I cannot believe that someone I know—someone the viscount knew . . ."

"He was a powerful nobleman, Sarah. He had command of life and death over everyone here."

"But he would never use it! He believed in fairness and justice!"

"Perhaps someone didn't agree with his version of such noble beliefs."

She took a deep breath. "I understand what you're saying, but no one ever spoke of such a thing. Who would question our lord?"

"Perhaps not aloud, but that is what I am to determine."

"But why me? Why not Master Frobisher, a man far more knowledgeable than I could ever be? Or the sheriff?"

"Those men will be of use to me, of course, but they might also make people too fearful or intimidated to answer my questions. But although I have only spent a day at Drayton Hall, already I can see how much you are respected and loved."

She blinked at him, feeling her throat tighten and her eyes sting. She'd had none of that just two years before.

"People feel comfortable around you, Sarah," he said in a low voice.

The informal use of her Christian name seemed too familiar, too personal, but how could she correct him? And now he wanted her to work closely with him, help him find a murderer?

"I am hoping that with you at my side," Robert continued, "your friends will speak more willingly."

"Why *wouldn't* they speak willingly? All will want justice for our lord."

"Not all," he reminded her.

She shivered and rubbed her arms.

"Will you help me?"

She hesitated, but already knew what her answer would be. She owed it to little Francis to discover who murdered his father. She owed respect and loyalty to the memory of the man who had saved her. "Aye," she finally said, lifting her gaze to Robert. He was watching her calmly, closely, as if he wasn't sure what her answer would be.

It was almost as if such a look questioned her loyalty. She straightened, feeling a sense of purpose wash through her, strengthening her. "Aye," she repeated, her voice louder. "I will provide all the assistance you need."

His eyebrows rose as he studied her, but that slow

smile showed his approval. "You have my thanks, mistress, and my gratitude."

"You do not need to thank me. I admired Lord Drayton as a man of principle and loyalty and goodness. The fact that someone cut short his life sickens me. This person deliberately took away a little boy's only parent. We need justice here at Drayton Hall; therefore I am at your disposal. What do you need of me?"

"I need you with me as I question people. I need your observations and reactions. You know the castle and its layout. Everything and anything will be helpful to me."

She nodded. "And this relationship between us—I will report to you as if you are now my lord?"

The seriousness in his eyes softened, and once again the charm peeked through. "Your lord? That is a powerful word, Sarah. Can we not be partners?"

"Partners? How can that be? I will take orders from you, assist you as any underling should, but I know nothing about the methods to find a murderer. You do. You represent the king in this, and have his trust, which is a great honor and worthy of my respect."

His frown was too playful. "Now you make me sound like a wise, doddering ancient. I am not those things, Sarah. I am just an investigator who needs your help."

It was her turn to frown as she strove to keep their conversation focused. "You seem rather . . . young, for such an important task. How old are you?"

He laughed softly. "Twenty and four years."

"Younger than I!" she said in surprise.

"So 'tis you who are doddering and ancient."

"Sometimes I feel that way," she muttered, shaking her head. "But why you? Why were you chosen?" Before he could speak, she snapped her fingers. "Ah, I see. You are here with Sir Walter."

"He answers to me," Robert said smoothly.

There was something unusual about their partnership, but she sensed she would get no clear answers. And he owed her none, of course.

"I have assisted the king on other matters," he said, "but of course I cannot betray their true nature."

"And obviously, you've been successful, since he's entrusted you with the investigation of a nobleman's demise."

Robert's nod was almost a bow.

"So how shall we begin?" she asked.

He led her to a boulder beside the stream, and she dutifully sat upon it while he stood before her.

Robert looked down at Sarah, her skirts spread

around her, her lovely, freckled face lifted to him in expectation. After displaying surprise and horror about the viscount's murder, she'd settled into a resolute determination to help him.

Yet he could not forget her look of fear when he'd first confronted her. She was worried that her crimes would be discovered.

He linked his hands behind his back. "The murderer poisoned the viscount slowly, slipping arsenic into his food or drink over a period of several weeks. So the murderer would have to be here during this time."

"Or have someone in his employ do the terrible deed."

He smiled, even though she could be deliberately misdirecting him. "Very good. Perhaps you will prove an apt pupil."

She lowered her gaze with apparent modesty. "I am good at my studies."

"Your studies?" he asked, arching one eyebrow.

"I did not have much education in my childhood beyond the simple things a woman is taught. But during my marriage, my husband's family allowed me to study with the tutor of his brothers. I discovered I enjoyed languages and poetry and the sciences. Learning is something I am good at."

She said it with quiet conviction, as if discovering such a thing about herself gave her peace.

She was a healer, a woman of learning—a woman capable of figuring out and undertaking a secretive murder. He wanted to know about her marriage, what made her delve into studies rather than simply making a home for her husband. But he could not be too obvious.

"Then you will learn and understand my methods as we go along," he said. "So talk to me about the people here. Do not try to think about their guilt or innocence. I want to see them as you do."

After a moment's hesitation, she began to speak of the people that formed her world, her gratitude that they'd accepted her. She must not have felt welcomed in her late husband's family, and he would eventually have to explore that. She spoke of the steward and treasurer with respect but no true friendship. There were bailiffs overseeing each of the viscountcy's numerous properties, men who came regularly to Drayton Hall but did not live there. Yet she'd already realized they could still be suspect, and so had named them to deflect even more attention from herself. By her explanation, the cook was a man gifted with food, but not with the management of his kitchens—and arsenic was the main poison to kill rats in a kitchen.

That was mostly likely where she had procured her weapon of choice.

When she spoke of the household staff, it was obvious she was closest to one of the seamstresses, Margery, for she mentioned her with fondness.

"Should I talk to you about the dairymaids? The stable grooms? There are so many people . . ." Sarah trailed off, her expression distant.

"That is enough for right now. We don't want to make anyone suspicious by our absence."

"Oh good Lord!" she cried, jumping to her feet. "Francis will be wondering where I am."

"And where is he now?"

"With the chaplain at his studies, but surely 'tis time for dinner. We must go."

He caught her arm when she would have hurried away from him. "Sarah, wait."

But touching her had been a mistake. Her garments contained the warmth of her body, and her sweet lavender scent rivaled the flowers scattered in the clearing. Her eyes watched him solemnly, yet he sensed a faint nervousness about her.

"Our partnership must remain between you and me," he said, staring down into her wide, dark eyes with their pale brown lashes. "I do not want to see you in danger."

"Danger?" she scoffed.

He didn't smile. "Someone is hiding a terrible secret at Drayton Hall, and they think they've gotten away with it. That person will feel trapped and defensive when he or she discovers that their crime is known. Desperate people lose their ability to act rationally. I expect this person to focus his ire on me. But I do not want it to spill over onto you. So we will be friendly, you and I."

"Friendly?" she said with doubt, her wary eyes studying him.

"Friendly—and flirtatious, so it will seem as if we have a reason to be together. Will that bother you?"

She opened her mouth, then seemed to rethink her answer before speaking. "Nay, I understand your concerns."

"Is there someone who will be offended if I pay such attention to you?"

"Are you asking if I have a suitor?"

"I am."

"Nay, there is no one," she said slowly.

"Not Sir Simon?"

Her gaze flew to his in obvious surprise. "Why would you think that?"

"Men understand one another where a beautiful woman is concerned."

"Stop saying that." Her pale skin showed her every blush. "You do not need to flirt with me when no one is watching." She stepped away from him. "And my friendship with Sir Simon is none of your concern, Robert."

She was already calling him only by his given name. That was a good start.

"A friendship. That is a good word. Then I shall not worry that I am intruding on another man's—"

"Another man's what?" she interrupted stiffly. "I do not belong to any man."

He wondered at her attitude, and what it said about her marriage, and her husband's mysterious death. And she'd been a man's mistress—hadn't that meant she belonged to Drayton? Or had she resisted that notion so forcefully that she'd killed him? Yet the League believed that she'd murdered the viscount *because* he didn't offer marriage.

"But Sir Simon has shown an interest in you first, and might not appreciate my . . . attentions." Now he gave her his wickedest smile.

She only lifted her chin. "If I agree to accept his courtship, it does not mean that I cannot be courted by other men." Turning away, she added almost under her breath, "As if that ever happens."

"What was that?" he called.

"'Twas nothing of importance. Act as you see fit

toward me, and I will understand the reason, though I will tell no one the truth. Now may we leave, before Francis worries about what has happened to me?"

"Of course. Do you wish to return before I do, so that it will not be known that we were alone together for so long?"

She blinked up at him, and her tension eased. "Aye, thank you for thinking of appearances. I imagine you are not known for that," she added dryly.

His eyes widened in feigned astonishment. "Why, Mistress Sarah, what can you mean?"

"I sense you are a man who does not much care what others think of him."

"I care what *you* think."

She tsked and shook her head. "There is no one to see you flirt in this glade, so you don't have to bother."

"'Tis no bother, mistress."

But she showed him her back and walked away, saying over her shoulder, "We shall speak again, Robert."

"Aye, we shall," he added meaningfully, even though she could not hear him.

Without sound, he followed her back through the woodland, making sure she reached the castle grounds. He admired the sway of her curvaceous hips, the bounce of her breasts, the way her hair looked like fire in the sun. He told himself that thinking of her in such physical terms would help him flirt with her. Once she'd gone through the gatehouse, he made his way inside the cover of the trees toward the lane to the village, then appeared on it as if he'd gone for a walk. He was within the great hall in time for the midday meal, and the next step in his plan.

Walter, who was standing near the hearth with a tankard in his hand, caught his gaze. Walter lifted another tankard from a passing maidservant's tray and brought it to Robert, who gladly took several long swallows.

"'Tis warm outside," Robert said, after wiping his mouth.

"Perhaps our sparring exhausted you for the day."

He gave Sir Walter a broad smile. "Hardly. But I did enjoy the challenge. Did you?"

He thought his partner showed a faint hint of amusement, but it was hard to be certain.

"Aye, I did," Walter said. "You have much skill for so young a man."

"Perhaps my guardians were not so wrong in their methods to train me."

Walter's eyes narrowed. "Good combat skills do not replace a normal life."

"You cannot be concerned for me, Sir Walter."

"All should be concerned for the young and innocent."

"Innocent. Now there is a word I have not heard used much to describe me."

For a moment Walter did not answer, only looked at Robert impassively. Did the older man truly care about him rather than just on principle? They had known each other too briefly for that to be so. Walter was the man who would help decide his fate with the League. And just because the knight regretted the League's method of his upbringing didn't mean that he would go easy on Robert.

Walter looked about, then spoke softly. "Did you enjoy your walk?"

"Everything went well," he murmured.

"Everything?" Walter repeated, eyeing him impassively. "I noticed that Mistress Sarah was absent as well." He looked pointedly at the bright ribbon around the bandage on Robert's upper arm.

Robert smiled, even as he kept his senses alert so they could not be overheard. "Aye, she was with me."

"And for what purpose?"

Robert met his gaze. "I told her *our* purpose as the king's men, and asked for her help in finding the murderer."

Walter went still, his gray eyes revealing nothing. "Why did you not mention your plan to me last night?"

At least he realized Robert had done it deliberately,

and not on a whim. "You have made it clear you suspect my methods. Enlisting Sarah's aid was a calculated risk on my part, but I think 'twas the correct move."

"Perhaps, but we cannot discuss it here," Walter said, when several knights began to play dice against the wall nearby.

"Tonight," Robert replied quietly.

"Is there anything else I should know?"

"Only that I have another idea for this afternoon."

"Perhaps I do not *wish* to know," Walter said with a sigh.

Chapter 6

Through dinner, Sarah could not stop watching Robert. She sat only briefly, feeling the need to move about the great hall, speaking with the servants, overseeing the kitchen staff.

But that was all an excuse. She didn't feel up to spending time at the head table with Robert. She wanted to look on him from afar, to think about everything he'd revealed to her.

Although the sun was shining through the thick glass windows, she felt cold to the depths of her bones, as if the stone of the castle had seeped inside her.

She kept looking at Francis, and tears would threaten her eyes at the knowledge that he should still have his father, that he should be the same happy boy. Now he sank into quiet moments, his gaze within, thinking of dark things no five-year-old should have to face. Did he feel orphaned? Alone, even in this large household?

But Robert had the ability to pull him out of such sad contemplation. She saw the large knight bend down over the quiet boy, who only picked at his food, and whatever he said made Francis's face brighten into laughter.

This same knight was here for a deeper purpose, of course, and although whatever truth he discovered would let all feel justice, it could not bring back a good man.

She gazed about the great hall, feeling a part of all its people, yet not. She had thought such a sensation long gone, but Robert's revelation brought it all back.

Someone here was a murderer.

She looked at the valet serving a platter of meat to the head table. He was barely out of boyhood, and had proven clumsy at his new position. Only months ago, he'd dropped a steaming mug of mulled wine on the late viscount's lap and been soundly scolded for it, which had humiliated him and his mother, who was eating nearby. Such a minor thing in Sarah's eyes, but could something like that lead to revenge? How to know what was in the human heart?

Then there was the gamekeeper, whose position kept him in charge of the lord's forest—and also forced him to punish those poor folk who poached from the land without permission. Could he have despised his lordship for the justice he'd been forced to mete out?

It all seemed so preposterous—yet the viscount was dead, and someone had murdered him.

Her sense of peace, of happy contentment, was gone.

Athelina, the chambermaid who'd first lured Robert into a dance the previous night, now approached him and put a hand on his shoulder as she spoke. He laughed up at her, those blue eyes bright with the interest he showed every woman. He was amusing and charming, and it all seemed so natural in him.

But his flirtation with Sarah had had an ulterior purpose. Rather than fun, he'd wanted her assistance. She should have expected nothing else.

"Mistress Sarah?"

She turned around at the sound of a male voice and found Sir Simon bowing his head to her. To her shock, he reached for her hand and kissed it. As he released her, he straightened, and she had to arch her neck to see his kind face. He was a sturdy-looking yet lean man, not truly handsome, but with the strength of prominent cheekbones and a strong, square jaw that gave him a masculine presence that women appreciated. She tried not to think of the other man in the hall who set women's hearts fluttering with just a lazy smile.

"A good afternoon to you, sir," she said to Sir Simon.

"And to you, mistress. 'Tis a fine day for a walk, and I can tell by your brighter freckles that you've been on one."

She laughed and blushed, probably making her freckles stand out more. "Aye, I took a moment to have some time for myself. I often like to explore the woodland for new places to take young Lord Drayton." She might as well use the story she'd tried on Robert.

"Perhaps you might do me the honor of accompanying me on a walk into the village on the morrow? I have not been in residence long, and would enjoy learning more about my surroundings."

Surprised, she could only say, "Of course, Sir Simon, as long as I can see Francis settled with his tutor in the morn."

"My thanks, mistress," he said, bowing as he left her to return to his table.

She stared after him thoughtfully until she noticed Robert staring at her. He wore a knowing smile that suddenly made her feel uncomfortable. Why should he care if she walked with a knight?

But of course, she'd offered to assist him however she could. What if he insisted he needed her at his side all day? Was that not where her loyalty to the late viscount demanded she remain?

Yet for the first time she'd met a kind man who showed an interest in her. She did not turn to mush inside when he looked at her—such silly emotion meant nothing. She'd long since learned to expect little of that in real life, only in fantasies. If she could have someone as a companion, someone who respected her and would face the long years at her side—someone she *trusted*—that was all that was important.

She found herself watching Robert again. The meal was over, and as people went about their afternoon duties, he and Sir Walter lingered in a discussion with the steward and the treasurer. Even the bailiff of one of the nearby manors was included. To her surprise, Sir Walter caught her gaze and held it a moment, giving only a cool nod before he turned back to his conversation. A chill washed through her.

Robert had said that Sir Walter answered to him, which seemed strange, given the disparity in their ages. What was their relationship like, and did Sir Walter approve of Robert using her assistance in their investigation?

The older man made her nervous with his calm, impassive expression, she decided. But then so did Robert, for exactly the opposite reason. It seemed nothing could please her this day. She turned her back on the men and smiled as she joined Francis.

The boy's shoulders drooped. "Father Osborne

says we're to study French today. Can I not go to the tiltyard?"

"You know your exercises will have to wait. You are a fine little lord, who needs to know about the world."

"I don't know why," Francis grumbled, dragging his feet through the rushes.

"Because you want to be as smart as your papa, do you not?"

Though it hurt the little boy, she didn't want to ignore the subject of his father. He needed to be able to discuss his feelings.

Francis gave a reluctant nod. "Papa would want me to be smart."

She ruffled his hair. "You're already smart, silly goose. Now you have to fill your brain up with things to be smart about!"

Together, they began to climb the stairs to the lord's solar, where the chaplain would be waiting for them. Once again, Sarah felt someone's piercing gaze as if it could touch her back. She wouldn't ignore Robert; she needed him to know she would not be cowed by whatever methods he planned to use to win her cooperation. She turned to give him a cool look, only to find Master Frobisher and the treasurer, Sir Daniel, both staring at her. She stumbled on the stairs in surprise, even as they quickly turned back toward Robert and Sir Walter.

"Mistress Sarah?" Francis said anxiously, catching her hand. "You are always telling me to be careful on the stairs!"

"I am so sorry," she said, patting his hand. She thought of how he would feel if he lost her, the last one who took care of him. " 'Twas clumsy of me, and I will never be so careless again."

She smiled at him with reassurance, although she felt anything but.

Robert saw the way Master Frobisher and Sir Daniel stared up at Sarah as she left the great hall. They turned back, shamefaced, shrugging their shoulders as if their stares had meant nothing. He had just told them about his mission from the king to discover Lord Drayton's murderer. Walter had remained silent when Robert made the announcement. Perhaps the Bladesman had even guessed his intentions from the beginning.

Robert had not named Sarah. But they had both looked at her. The League had named her the likeliest suspect—the only suspect. Did these two men think the same?

Objectively, either of them could be the guilty

party himself. The steward no longer had someone watching over his every move—and he ceded many of his duties to Sarah. What was he doing with his free time?

And the treasurer was in charge of the viscountcy's finances. His lordship could have been about to uncover misuse of his funds. A treasurer could kill for that.

But the League was convinced that Sarah was guilty. It would take a sizable amount of evidence for Robert to believe otherwise.

"Gentlemen, I tell you that your lord was murdered," Robert said coolly, "and your first reaction is to watch a nursemaid leave the hall?"

Master Frobisher cleared his throat, his round face earnest. "Forgive me, Sir Robert. I was actually looking at the young lord and feeling pity for him."

Sir Daniel's expression was harder to read behind his bushy gray beard, but he nodded vigorously, not meeting Robert's eyes.

Robert didn't believe them. Master Tallis, the red-faced, stout bailiff, stared between the two men in confusion but said nothing.

"Surely this is a mistake," Master Frobisher continued, his expression earnest. "We all saw how ill Lord Drayton was."

"And how carefully Mistress Sarah tended him,"

Sir Daniel added, glancing at the steward, "even though we all feared the black death."

The bailiff swallowed and looked about, as if the great hall had somehow become infected.

"'Twas poison," Walter said in his flat voice.

Sir Daniel inhaled sharply, Master Frobisher's mouth dropped open, and Master Tallis took a step back.

"The symptoms are clear indications for arsenic poisoning," Robert said, "as long as a person is informed of what to look for. Lord Drayton's illness came to the king's attention." *And the League's.* "The king's councilors are in agreement. 'Tis murder, gentlemen."

"What will happen now?" Master Frobisher asked in a weak voice.

"Sir Walter and I will investigate. We ask that you allow us to do our work privately. There is no need to panic the household. We do not believe this a random act, for no one else has sickened. Lord Drayton was targeted for a reason, and we will discover it, as well as the identity of his killer."

The two men Drayton had trusted now glanced at each other, then seemed to make a silent decision.

Master Frobisher took a deep breath. "We have noticed your interest in Mistress Sarah. We feel it is only fair that you understand that besides being the young lord's nursemaid, she was Lord Drayton's mistress."

"After his wife died?" Walter asked.

They both nodded, while Master Tallis simply looked confused.

"We *believe* so," Sir Daniel clarified. "He doted on her so much that he even moved her into his suite of chambers."

"That was to tend Lady Drayton," Master Frobisher quickly said, "and to be near the young lord."

Sir Daniel rolled his eyes. "We all know that she comforted his lordship after his wife's death. There was a respect between them that none of us could deny."

"And so now you allow her to oversee the household," Walter said.

"She is very skilled," Master Frobisher said, and then his skin reddened. "With the household," he added. "I know nothing else."

Robert nodded. "My thanks for the information. We will keep you informed of our investigation."

When the three men had gone, Walter gave him an impassive look. "Interesting that they felt the need to mention Mistress Sarah. There was already suspicion here. We'll discuss it tonight."

"I look forward to it." Robert watched the older knight walk away. Sir Daniel and the bailiff were whispering together near the great double doors, just as he'd known they would, he thought with satisfaction.

* * *

Sarah did her best to enjoy the hour she spent watching Francis exercising with the other boys of the castle. They practiced with small wooden swords near the tiltyard, pretending they were knights. Next the captain of the guard oversaw their wrestling training. The boys shouted and cheered each other on, and she was relieved to see Francis more actively participating than he'd done since his father's illness.

Or perhaps he was showing off for Robert, Sir Simon, and the other knights who occasionally paused in their training to shout encouragement. Sometimes Robert would look over at her and smile, as if he wanted to share in her pride over the boy. She nodded back to him, but without much enthusiasm. She was still feeling overwhelmed by all he'd revealed to her, by the terrible sadness of a good man's death.

She saw Margery walking toward her and she waved with relief, making room for her on the wooden bench.

Instead of her cheerful self, Margery looked pensive as she stared out across the courtyard at the men and boys honing their skills. Sarah waited patiently, knowing her friend would eventually say what was on her mind.

"Did you hear the news?" Margery said at last.

Sarah stiffened. "What news?"

"Sir Robert and Sir Walter are here investigatin' Lord Drayton's death. They're sayin' 'twas murder."

Sarah closed her eyes. How had the word spread so quickly?

"People are already whisperin'," Margery continued, her voice tired and flat. "Just look at them, Sarah."

Margery was right. Usually the castle servants walked confidently through the courtyard, going about their business, calling the occasional greeting, or stopping to speak to a friend. But now everyone seemed to be scurrying from group to group, from the dairy shed to the stables to the soldiers' barracks, heads bent together whispering, even as they glanced over their shoulders.

How had this happened?

And then she remembered the way Master Frobisher and Sir Daniel had looked at her after dinner, when she'd been leading Francis to the chaplain. They'd been in discussion with Robert and Sir Walter. Had Robert told them of his mission? Perhaps Master Frobisher had feared how she would take the news, worried about how she would tell Francis such a terrible thing.

And as for the news remaining a secret, Sir Daniel was discreet with the Drayton finances, but little else.

Margery was watching her thoughtfully. "Ye don't seem very surprised."

Sarah sighed, shaking her head. "I already knew. I found out this morn, when Sir Robert asked for my help in his investigation."

Margery whistled softly between her teeth. "Bold of him. Wonder why he picked you?"

"He says 'tis because I know everyone in the household."

"And ye think that's the case?"

Sarah frowned at her friend. "What do you mean? I do know everyone, and he does not."

"But . . . he's shown an interest in you, Sarah."

"But 'tis playacting, a way for us to be together without drawing too much suspicion on me as I help him. He doesn't want me in danger."

Margery looked unconvinced.

"You cannot tell anyone," Sarah said, looking about for fear of someone overhearing them.

"But why are ye doin' this, Sarah?" Margery asked softly, worry in her blue eyes.

Sarah looked away, trying to watch Francis as he rolled around in the dirt. But at last she looked down at her clenched hands. "You know why," she said in a low voice. "I suspected the truth, and I did nothing."

"Sarah, stop this! 'Twas nothin' you could do. Ye're a vulnerable woman, with no family to support you. His lordship was too ill by the time ye realized the truth. No one would have listened, and ye might have lost everythin', and perhaps been killed!"

"Instead Lord Drayton lost everything." Sarah closed her eyes, fighting tears.

"He was goin' to die anyway by then."

Sarah straightened her shoulders and lifted her head. "This is my chance, Margery."

The seamstress stared at her in confusion. "Your chance for what?"

"To make things right! If I help find the murderer, then at least I can look Francis in the eye. I can't bring back his father, but I can help Lord Drayton rest in peace."

Pressing her lips together, Margery nodded. "I understand," she murmured.

Still, there was worry and fear in her eyes when she looked at Sarah.

Sarah ignored it to say, "Will you help me?"

"What can I do that you cannot?"

"When I need you, will you stay with Francis? I am not sure yet how often Sir Robert will need my assistance."

"Of course I will stay with the little one. The women in the sewin' room can do without me."

"Only because you've trained them well," Sarah said, trying to smile.

Margery shrugged and looked down.

"Now you're blushing. I never thought to see such a thing. All it took was one little compliment."

They exchanged smiles, then looked back at the boys, who were covered in dirt and laughing at each other.

Sarah sighed and leaned forward, resting her forearms on her knees. "I wrote to Sir Anthony while Francis finished his studies after dinner. As guardian—and Lord Drayton's cousin—he needs to know about the investigation."

"'Twill be sad for him to hear that his cousin was murdered. Do ye think he'll come?"

"Aye, right away. He's a conscientious man."

They sat in silence for several minutes, until at last Margery took a deep breath and turned a grin on Sarah. "I saw Sir Simon talkin' to you."

"Oh. Aye." Sarah felt her face heat.

Margery rolled her eyes. "So what did he say?"

"He asked me to go walking to the village with him on the morrow."

"Finally! The man has been lingerin' near ye so long I thought he'd never work up the courage."

"'Work up the courage'? How can that be, Margery? We're talking about *me,* for goodness' sake."

Margery gave a disgusted snort. "Ye're a pretty woman, Sarah. Men think so, even if yer husband was too daft—God rest his soul," she added.

At the same time, they both noticed Robert walking toward them. He'd taken off his armor and wore the sleeveless leather jerkin over his breeches. The sun shone off his dark, wavy hair, and even off of his white teeth. Sarah wasn't too bedazzled to notice that she wasn't the only woman watching him stride across the courtyard.

He stopped in front of them, and they both had to lean back on the bench to see his face.

He grinned and pointed at the wilting ribbon still holding a torn handkerchief to his solid upper arm. "Am I permitted to remove this now without offending his young lordship?"

Margery covered her mouth, smirking, while Sarah swallowed and rose to her feet.

"I think Francis would understand," she said.

He held out his arm to her and grinned.

"Showing off your fine form?" she said without thinking, then gasped and covered her mouth.

He threw back his head and laughed, causing many heads to turn toward them. If he saw that people frowned with worry, he didn't show any concern. Perhaps he was glad to have his mission out in the open now.

With a hearty sigh, she pulled at the bow, now damp with his perspiration. The handkerchief was stuck to the wound.

"Wait a moment," she said, fetching a dipper of water from the bucket used to quench the thirst of exhausted boys. Carefully, she poured it onto the handkerchief and was able to pull it away without disturbing the scab.

"That's quite a talent," Robert said.

"I take off bandages at least every other day."

He grinned. "Do you cut yourself so often?"

Margery guffawed even as she rose to her feet. "We have not met, Sir Robert. I am Margery, mistress of the sewin' chamber."

He took her hand and bowed over it as if she were a lady born. "Mistress Margery of the sewing chamber, I am pleased to meet you."

Robert could make even Margery blush, Sarah thought.

"I have seen you and Mistress Sarah conversing," Robert continued. "'Tis good to have true friendship."

"I can see ye like to study people," Margery said, "but then I imagine ye need such skills."

He only quirked a dark eyebrow.

"The news of your investigation is now well known, sir." Margery studied him for a moment. "But perhaps ye knew that would happen."

Sarah inhaled with surprise.

"Aye, I guessed," Robert admitted, wearing a half smile.

"'Twas deliberate?" Sarah demanded.

He nodded, but he glanced briefly at Margery then back to her, as if to alert her that he would not go too far discussing his private mission in front of others. She thought about his purpose in revealing himself to everyone, and realized that perhaps in some ways it would make his work easier, for everyone would know up front what he was after.

Yet it might also make it easier for the true murderer to prepare himself—or even flee—although an unexplained absence would be very noticeable.

"Ye're a crafty man," Margery said.

He put a hand to his chest and bowed. "I'm very susceptible to flattery, mistress."

Both women rolled their eyes in unison.

Margery looked from Robert to Sarah. "Well, I need to return to me duties. Sarah, let me know when ye need my assistance." She nodded to the tall knight. "Good day to you, Sir Robert."

When she'd gone, Robert asked, "Assistance?"

"When I am helping you, she will watch Francis for me."

"'Tis smart to prepare for any circumstance."

"I don't know that I'm prepared," she said, crossing

her arms over her chest. "After all, you gave me cause to believe that your investigation would be conducted in secret. You asked me not to talk about it."

"Nay, *your* part is a secret. I made no claim about anything else."

"My mistake," she said with faint sarcasm.

"All you have to do is ask me, and I'll tell you what I can."

"Hmm."

He stood at her side, watching Francis take a deep, slurping drink when a dipper of water was passed around.

"Why did you comment on my friendship with Margery?" she abruptly asked.

He glanced down at her with amusement. "I was simply stating something I'd noticed."

"Why notice friendship?"

His smile grew faint as he continued to watch the little boys tease one another with a toss of water, then shriek with merriment. Francis stood on the fringes, not really participating, but smiling with enjoyment.

"I wasn't as fortunate as young Lord Drayton to have many friends."

Putting her hands on her hips, she peered at him. "You said you were from London. Surely there were thousands of young boys in such a city."

"There were." He shaded his eyes with his hand, then called, "Lord Drayton, shall we practice riding?"

When Francis ran toward him with enthusiasm, Robert nodded to Sarah and left her.

She stood still, contemplating what he'd revealed, and not understanding what it could mean. How could a charming, handsome man not have plenty of friends?

Chapter 7

At supper, Sarah watched how everything had changed. People she respected as friends and fellow servants now looked at each other with sadness and suspicion, and even some disbelief. Instead of laughter and chatter through the meal, people whispered softly to their neighbors.

Francis stared about him in confusion, no doubt sensing the undercurrent of uncertainty. What was she supposed to say to him? *Your father was murdered and we don't know the identity of the killer.* That would set his recovery back by weeks if not months.

So after she finished her own meal, she walked among the tables, smiling and asking her usual questions about one person's mild fever, or another's broken bone. Talking about their ailments distracted people, and finally, they began to question her about Robert. More than once she reassured people, claiming that he seemed to be a good man who only wanted the truth. Didn't they all want that? Some expressed fears that a guilty party would be named simply to have it over with, but Sarah didn't believe so, and was firm in stating that. Last, she asked that Francis's youth and vulnerability be considered, and that people refrain from discussing the tragedy in front of him or other children.

She moved from table to table repeating basically the same discussion until she was satisfied that she'd done her best to protect Francis and encourage the household.

Every so often she glanced at the head table to assure herself of the welfare of her charge. More than once she found Robert contemplating her, wearing a small smile.

The tables were eventually cleared of food. Games of chess, Tables, and dice began, while the occasional musician strummed a lute to someone else's accompaniment on the pipe. Sarah found herself alone with Robert near the hearth. No one else approached them, and she sighed, knowing this would be her lot for the time being. The people of Drayton seemed satisfied that she would keep their unwelcome guest occupied.

"So now they all know," Sarah said, allowing her resignation to show.

" 'Twas necessary."

He watched them all just as she did, hands linked

behind his back. This evening he wore an emerald green doublet over black hose, all his garments of fine quality. 'Twas obvious now to everyone that he came from the king's court, and there was respect in that.

"All shall be wary as they answer your questions," she said.

"Aye."

"Perhaps the murderer might lie."

He glanced down at her. "And the murderer wouldn't have lied about his deeds otherwise?"

"Oh, well, I guess he already is."

"And why do you assume 'tis a 'he'?"

A cold feeling of disbelief swept through her. "I . . . I had not thought otherwise."

"Never assume, Sarah," he said, his gaze once again sweeping the uneasy crowd. "Assumptions make for an incomplete investigation."

A faint frown passed over his usually pleasant expression, and was gone so quickly, she wondered if she'd truly seen it. She did not question him, for he would only reveal in bits and pieces what he wanted known.

She took a breath and boldly asked, "Is this not difficult for you, having people fear you?"

"I am pursuing the truth. If a person is innocent, he or she should have no reason to fear me."

"Yet people can be irrational in their fear."

"If you say so. This situation has never happened to me before."

She snapped her head up to stare at him. "But you said you've had other assignments from the king."

"They were all work I performed in secret, under other identities."

He smiled down at her, but she thought there were shadows in his eyes. He was used to keeping secrets. It must be a difficult way to live.

"I cannot imagine so exciting a life," she said.

"Sometimes 'tis merely tedious."

"And dangerous?"

He chuckled. "Sometimes."

"No wonder you train so hard on the tiltyard."

"So you have studied me?"

A hot blush swept over her face. "I have spent my life near men. I do not have to watch for long to know who merely goes through the motions."

"You mean like Sir Simon," he said, nodding in understanding.

She gasped. "I never—"

"I was only teasing," he interrupted, once again laughing at her. "Sir Simon is an excellent horseman and a skilled warrior. I might have to challenge him soon."

She narrowed her eyes.

He raised both hands. "As a sparring partner, of course."

Shaking her head, she looked away from him. She smiled at Margery, who'd glanced at her while speaking to one of the knights. Kind Margery was always so concerned for her welfare. The seamstress didn't realize that Sarah once had to do much to survive on her own. It wasn't something she often discussed, even with a dear friend.

"I watched you walk among your people," he said in a quieter voice.

She eyed him, waiting.

"What did you discuss?" he asked. "They seemed much calmer afterward, as if you were a gifted groom with a skittish horse."

She released her breath on a sigh. "They are concerned about being treated fairly by you."

He cocked his head, the smile never leaving his face as he waited.

"I reassured them. But my main concern was and always is Francis. I have decided not to tell him of your investigation for now. I asked that everyone not discuss it with their children, who are too vulnerable to a feeling of fear. Does this meet with your approval?"

"You are the little lord's nursemaid. I bow to your wisdom."

"Thank you. He seems to like your company, and I don't wish to tarnish that just yet."

"But you will when you feel 'tis necessary?"

He was watching her too closely now.

"Only if I must. But he doesn't need to know at so tender an age that someone has taken his father away from him on a cruel whim."

He gave a solemn nod. "I understand."

They stood silently for a short period of time until she found herself thinking too much about this stranger who had taken over her life. "What do you have planned for the morrow?" she asked, breaking the uneasy silence.

Uneasy silence on her part. Robert seemed content to watch people, as if even their simple pastimes interested him.

"I will still train early in the morn, to give you a chance to watch me."

She rolled her eyes. "Do not do so for my benefit," she said dryly.

He chuckled. "But later I would like a tour of the castle, especially the viscount's chambers."

She nodded. "What time shall I tell Master Frobisher?"

"I should like *you* to give me the tour."

"I see," she said, blinking in disbelief. And then she remembered her planned walk with Sir Simon.

At least she would have the early morn to accompany him.

"Will that be difficult for you?" he asked.

He was watching her again. She wanted to shout at him to stop it, but how could she?

She forced herself to relax. "Nay, no problem at all." She hesitated, then rushed through her next words. "I sent a missive to Sir Anthony Ramsey, Francis's guardian, letting him know about the investigation."

"That's fine."

"He was Lord Drayton's cousin and I believe he deserves—" She broke off. "You do not mind?"

"Nay, you did what was necessary. Were not the two men also good friends?"

She nodded, a lump forming in her throat. "They played chess any evening they were together. They even accompanied each other on journeys. Sir Anthony was devastated by his cousin's death, and when he hears it was murder—he will want justice served."

"I look forward to speaking with him."

"Sir Robert!" Francis came skidding through the rushes.

Robert grinned down at the boy. "What may I do for you, my lord?"

"I am learning how a gentleman plays chess. Do you know how?"

"Aye, I do. 'Tis one of my favorite pastimes."

Another one, she thought with a sigh.

Francis gripped his hand and pulled. "Come teach me!"

In their lodgings later that night, Walter and Robert sat down facing each other in the outer chamber. Walter folded his hands and waited silently.

Robert knew what he wanted to hear. "My decision to inform Mistress Sarah about our investigation will work well. Tomorrow she is giving me a tour of the castle, and I shall focus on the viscount's chambers, to see how she was able to poison him over weeks."

"'Tis unlikely she will somehow betray herself out of nervousness. She is a clever woman."

Robert nodded. "Yet with her at my side, I can judge her reactions as I interview the servants, residents and villagers. I'll be able to see everyone's reaction to her."

"Why do you care?"

"'Twill tell me much about her as a person, to better understand her motivations."

"We know her motivation."

"Rage at the viscount's decision not to marry her? We don't even know if they discussed marriage. I need to know more about her before fulfilling the League's mission."

"You mean before taking her life in punishment for murdering a nobleman."

He stiffened. "I am in command. We shall do things my way."

Walter nodded. "You made another decision today to inform the Drayton upper staff about our investigation."

"I anticipated that the entire household would then hear of it."

"Good of you to realize that," Walter said dryly.

"I would rather work in the open and hope for unforeseen assistance. Perhaps someone saw something, and they will come forward now that they know about the investigation."

"My thanks for the explanation, even though you did not need to do so."

Robert cocked his head in surprise. "But we are partners, Walter. I expect you to share with me as well."

"Then I will tell you that I discovered arsenic stored near the kitchens, for use against rats."

"Or viscounts," Robert said, sighing. "I cannot be surprised at finding it, of course." He looked down at his folded hands. "You know, I still remember the first day I met Drayton."

Walter remained silent.

"I had but twelve years, and he was a new member

of the Council of Elders. Though they were meeting in urgency for a reason I was not permitted to know, he deliberately came to meet my brothers and me."

"You were a curiosity among the Bladesmen."

"Aye, I knew it. My elder brother was proud to be so, to be a new generation. My younger brother was angry to feel on display, but I did not truly care one way or the other. I look back now and see that I did not show the proper respect when I met Drayton, a councilor. I was too impetuous with my remarks, I was told, but Drayton said I made him laugh. He said that a boy who could find laughter though being locked away from the world would mature into a man at ease with himself."

"Quite the compliment."

"He was a good man, and he did not deserve to die like this." He leveled his gaze on Walter. "The arsenic was easily accessed?"

The knight nodded. "By adults. 'Tis well above the floor, put away in a cupboard."

" 'Twas not used in anyone else's meal that we know of, so he surely did not eat it in the great hall, partaking from the same platters as others."

"Nay, I am told he enjoyed an occasional meal in his solar while he was working."

"So someone brought him a separate plate."

"I will look into that."

"On my tour with Sarah on the morrow, I will see the path from the kitchens to the viscount's chambers."

"The food could have been poisoned after it reached his solar."

"You mean by someone already with him. Aye, we will not discount that. I will question her about the viscount's private meals. Also, we should be hearing from Sir Anthony Ramsey soon, the boy's guardian. Sarah wrote to him today."

"You assumed she would, and she reacted as predicted. Very interesting tactic on her part."

Robert nodded. "She could be using Ramsey to deflect our attention."

"I would have thought, to protect herself and her position, she would wish to keep the master of the hall away as long as possible. But women like Sarah are good at manipulation, and she's taking her own steps in this investigation, rather than just reacting."

Before meeting her, Robert had assumed it would be easy to think of her as a murderer, a woman who deserved no mercy.

But she wasn't anything like he'd imagined. She had a true gift in the way she treated Francis. He'd met murderers before, but always they revealed themselves, even in small ways. He'd been trained to look for such signs. Sarah was skilled at projecting innocence.

Walter's reminder of Sarah's fate should she prove guilty was an uneasy burden on Robert's shoulders, the duty of the Bladesman in command. His dilemma followed him into his dreams that night, where he took Sarah deep into the forest and put a knife to her throat, and watched those expressive brown eyes widen in fright just before she screamed.

He came awake, rising up on his elbows, breathing unevenly. Embers in the hearth gave off a reddish glow in the dark bedchamber. He reminded himself of his duty, of his precarious future as a Bladesman. Then he sank back into the bedclothes and stared at the wooden beams of the ceiling. Sleep did not come again.

Chapter 8

In the morning, Sarah went to the kitchens to consult with Cook about the day's meals. The man was tall and terribly thin, as if he didn't even try his own concoctions. He always wore a scattered expression, his mind racing to the next meal while still preparing the current one.

When Sarah tried to discuss dinner, he finally came to a halt near the large block table and stared down at her, flinging his arms wide.

"I have everything in hand, Mistress Sarah," he said in an exasperated tone. "Can we not speak later?"

"Nay, I will be away much of this morn," she said patiently.

He frowned. "And where are you going?"

"Into the village." She tried for nonchalance. It was no one's business who she—

"With who?" asked Jane, one of the scullery maids, pausing as she carried a bucket of water.

It wasn't a secret, Sarah told herself. "Sir Simon Chapman."

Cook's eyes widened. "Whatever for?"

Sarah wanted to bristle, but she kept her voice mild. "Because he asked me to accompany him. He is new to the area."

"Oh, I see," Jane said, nodding as if her world had settled back into place. "Aye, ye know the place well, Mistress Sarah."

I know the place well? Sarah thought with disbelief. "I do not take your meaning."

Cook stirred a giant cauldron that was hung over the massive fire in the hearth. Wiping his damp forehead, he glanced over his shoulder at her. "Sir Simon is so new here that he does not understand your place at the young viscount's side. We thought he might be thinking of you as . . ."

He trailed off when he saw her staring at him coolly, hands on her hips. "Please finish your meaning," she said, wearing a perfunctory smile.

Jane and Cook exchanged a glance.

Jane said, " 'Tis simply that we all know how dedicated you are to his lordship, that a plain man could not . . ."

No one seemed to want to state it aloud. The other servants worked busily, their backs to her. Cook stared longingly at the vegetables being chopped at the table as if he wished he were doing anything else.

Sarah wasn't supposed to be interested in romance? Did they think she didn't want the same thing as other women, to be admired and respected—to feel like a *woman* instead of simply a nurse?

"Aye, I'm dedicated to Lord Drayton," she said at last, her tone cheerful. "But 'tis good after such trying times to have a moment away from it all."

"Oh, aye, these times be terrible," Jane said, nodding her head so quickly it was a wonder that her teeth didn't chatter. "What with Sir Robert and Sir Walter snoopin' about."

"They are doing the king's bidding, and you cannot blame them. After all, they would not be here if someone had not murdered a good man."

The kitchen became still as a tomb, and several people crossed themselves. Sarah regretted her harsh words, but she could not take them back. She nodded to Cook and swept from the kitchen, feeling unsettled and angry and exasperated all at the same time.

Sir Simon was waiting for her in the great hall, and when she saw him, to her relief she found it easy to smile. She would enjoy this outing. Life had to go on, even during a murder investigation.

*　*　*

Robert noticed that Simon Chapman did not make an appearance at the tiltyard. He would have thought little of it, until near the end of the session he saw the seamstress Margery walking with Francis toward the group of boys in training with the captain of the guard. He'd anticipated seeing Sarah this morn.

Where was she?

He was so distracted by that question that he almost let himself be knocked from Dragon's back as he jousted at the quintain. When he didn't hit it correctly, it spun about and knocked him across the shoulders. He held his seat, even as he straightened and pulled up on the reigns. Dragon danced briefly before settling down and allowing Robert to walk him away from the lists. He expected some good-natured jeering about his clumsiness, but the revelation of his identity was still too new. Knights and soldiers watched him with hesitation, as if they didn't dare upset him now. The openness of his mission had some good points, but also some drawbacks, as he was beginning to discover.

He could not blame the good people of Drayton Hall. He was the symbol of a murderer in their midst, a murderer who was one of their own. Without a person to accuse, they only had Robert at whom to direct their worry and fear.

At least he had Walter, who was obviously above the need to smirk at his poor performance at the quintain. But the Bladesman did wear a faint smile as he watched Robert ride by. Robert nodded with dignity and didn't stop to speak. He meant to take his time with Dragon before he went to look for Sarah and request his tour.

But then he saw her. She was just emerging through the gatehouse, arm in arm with Simon Chapman. Robert froze, barely feeling the horse beneath him react.

Though it was a cloudy day, her bright red hair seemed to light up the dreary courtyard like the sun. She smiled up at the knight, still talking and gesturing as if in the middle of a long conversation. Chapman bent his head toward her. Robert felt a dark, angry emotion churn his gut, and he couldn't even identify it, so foreign did it seem.

His gaze followed them across the courtyard until they disappeared through the gate to the lady's garden. It was a small plot of land next to the keep, surrounded by a half wall, where the lady of the household could escape into her own private garden.

Sarah and Chapman needed privacy?

Robert had never felt like this before. He barely noticed which groom took Dragon's reigns from him.

But the training that had been ingrained in him since childhood took over, and he pretended as if he were headed to the keep. After a last look around to see if he was noticed, he slipped into the lady's garden. The small trees and ferns hid him well, and although he felt ridiculous, it did not stop him from following the sound of their voices.

He'd been with many women, saw them with other men, and had never felt this overwhelming urge to tear a woman away from a man and challenge him.

Slowly, he moved through the garden until he saw the flash of Sarah's blue gown among the trees. And then she laughed, and the merry sound made him think of forest glades with water tumbling over rocks and birds singing.

Birds singing? he thought in disgust.

Sarah was a murderer, and his desire of her jeopardized not only his mission, but also his place within the League. He might need to harness these feelings, to use them to sway her to his side, but he could not allow them to touch the center of him.

He glimpsed her profile as she followed the gravel path meandering through the garden. Chapman was still touching her, their bodies brushing as they moved. She looked . . . happy.

Robert stepped out onto the path and walked with purpose until he took a turn and surprised the couple.

They came up short, Sarah's eyes wide, Chapman's full of confusion and then understanding.

Before the knight could speak, Robert nodded his head. "Forgive me, Mistress Sarah, but I believe we had an engagement this morn to tour the castle?"

"I had not forgotten," she said smoothly. "When I saw you at the tiltyard, I thought you still had to return to your lodgings to change your garments."

He smiled. "I am ready now." He glanced at Chapman. "I did not overly exert myself. I guess I need a more challenging sparring partner."

The man smiled back with confidence. "I would be happy to oblige, Sir Robert."

Sarah frowned, feeling the tension but not understanding its source. Both Robert and Simon were smiling, but their smiles did not reach their eyes. Here in this peaceful garden, where she'd always found comfort, two men were squaring off in a silent challenge.

Over her? Preposterous.

Surely there was something else going on, some problem at the tiltyard that only men cared about.

She turned to smile at Simon, and it took a moment before he took his eyes off Robert, she noticed. "You have my thanks for a lovely walk this morn, Simon."

He took her hand and bowed over it, a bit more elaborately than necessary, she thought.

"'Twas my pleasure, Sarah."

He spoke her name, and not her title, with more emphasis than was necessary. Men. They could be such crowing roosters.

Simon nodded at Robert as he departed. Robert watched him go, a bemused smile on his lips, before focusing once again on Sarah. That smile intensified, as if he'd won some sort of challenge. He waited.

If he expected her to discuss her morning with Simon, he would be waiting a long time.

"What part of Drayton Hall do you wish to explore first?" she asked.

His blue eyes narrowed, and she didn't understand what she saw there. She hovered in that silent, tense moment, feeling the pull of his forceful personality, wondering what he truly wanted from her.

And then he gave that charming smile he bestowed on all the women. She found herself strangely disappointed.

"I'd like to see everything, Sarah."

Unlike his smile, his tone of voice made her feel like she was the only one he wanted to speak to. She disregarded that immediately, knowing it was all part of his ability to charm. Had he been born with it, or honed it in witty repartee at the king's court?

"'Tis a large castle," she said dubiously. "But very well, we shall begin with the outbuildings here in the courtyard."

She went to move past him, but he didn't immediately follow.

"Can we not begin with this garden?" he asked.

She frowned at him. "'Twas simply the viscountess's peaceful retreat."

She watched him walk among the trees, down the path away from her, and she reluctantly followed. He passed a cozy bench tucked away amidst shrubbery, then smiled at the fountain in the center, where water bubbled from a stone boy's tipped bowl.

"'Tis such an interesting idea," he said. "The lady of the household can almost feel as if she's in a woodland glade, rather than in a fortress."

"Your mother did not have such a thing?" And then she remembered that he'd mentioned his mother's early death. She touched his arm. "Forgive me. Perhaps you do not wish to think of sad memories."

"That happened too long ago to be truly sad," he said ruefully. "The memory of my mother is only one of softness and a warm voice. I do not remember if she had a lady's garden." He frowned.

Had he not been in the same home after her death? she wondered, curious. "In London, perhaps there is not room for such things."

"Nay, a garden is even more necessary in the crowded city. But I did not grow up in my parents' home."

What did *that* mean? As if he'd said something he hadn't meant to, he turned away and began to walk briskly down a path toward the courtyard. She had to hurry to keep up, and reached his side as he went through the gate in the half wall. He swept his arm to encompass the bustling courtyard, and she obligingly took him to all the outbuildings, from the soldiers' barracks, to the carpenter shop, to the smithy, where the blacksmith and the armorer were consulting over the making of a plain chest plate. All stopped to answer Robert's questions about their work. She noticed that he was able to make people relax around him, even though they might fear the results of his investigation. At the dairy, he charmed the maids into offering him slices of fresh cheese or a dipper of milk, and at the bakehouse, he received a hot loaf of bread, which he offered to share with Sarah.

And always he brought her into each conversation, as he questioned people with interest about their duties. Most enjoyed speaking about themselves, and he seemed to take advantage of that.

She found herself more interested than she'd imagined she would be. He asked nothing about the viscount or his ugly death; he only got to know people. He put them at ease with his charm and handsome looks and polite interest.

Within the keep itself, he asked to begin his tour on

the ground floor, in the undercrofts with their columns and vaulted ceilings, which held up the castle. The food storage was there, all of which passed through the kitchens first, she told him. He was serious about this in particular, and then she remembered his accusation of poison. She shivered. Arsenic worked best hidden within food and drink.

In the kitchens, he explored the many chambers nearby, from the buttery with its linens and silver plate and spoons, to the pantry, reached by stairs circling down into the undercroft, where vegetables and barrels of salted meat were kept cool. In the butlery, he paid particular attention to the barrels of wine and ale.

For her ears alone, he remarked, " 'Twould be easy for anyone to fill a tankard here and not be seen."

She bit her lip and nodded. "We have never had the need to station guards throughout the castle."

"And your cook seems easily distracted."

"He is good at his craft," she said, feeling the need to defend the man.

"Then perhaps he needs someone to assist him with all other details, for my partner found arsenic in a cupboard, easily accessible."

She stared up at him in the dim chamber. "Does not every castle have arsenic to control the rats?"

"Aye, they do. But many limit its access, so that there is always a record of who used it."

"We do not do that," she admitted, her chest heavy with sadness.

"I imagine you will now."

She nodded.

"Please show me the most direct route to the viscount's chambers."

She hugged herself, imagining someone leaving the kitchens, carrying a plate of poison through shadowy corridors. This person watched a man die a slow and agonizing death. What kind of monster could do such a thing?

It wasn't a long trip, simply down a corridor, up the circular stairs, down another corridor to the front of the keep, where the viscount's chambers overlooked the courtyard.

"There are no hidden passages, or other corridors to travel between the two areas of the keep?"

She shook her head. "Of course there are longer ways to get here, going through other sections of the castle."

Outside the viscount's door, Robert said, "You said there are no regular guards, even here?"

"Lord Drayton thought himself so safe," she added wistfully. "The curtain walls had never been breached, even in past centuries when neighboring lords besieged each other."

He went inside, and although she followed him, she

remained near the door. He glanced at her as if curious, but did not insist she accompany his every step.

The room was decorated as befit a viscount, with wainscoted paneling on the walls instead of simple plaster. The inner chamber, where the lord slept, had wall hangings to keep in the warmth, and stained-glass windows letting in colored light. To the left, a door led into the solar, where the Lord Drayton had private meetings—*and private meals*, she thought, swallowing back a lump of sorrow.

Robert beckoned to her and she followed him through. A table and chairs dominated the center, with cupboards of fine plate lining one wall.

"Where do the doors lead?" he asked.

"One to a privy, the other out into the corridor."

"To bring his lordship a private meal, one could come through his bedchamber or the corridor."

She nodded.

To the left of the outer chamber, the door opened onto Francis's bedchamber, and she followed Robert in. Francis's four-poster bed was smaller than an adult's. The chamber had several coffers for his possessions, and on the table near the hearth he had displayed his rock collection.

She smiled as she fingered his newest find, remembering his excitement when he'd brought it to her.

But Robert was exploring the room, just as he'd

done in the master chambers, looking behind hanging wall cloths, opening the windows to peer out to the courtyard below.

"Where does the far door lead?" he asked.

"My chambers."

An unreadable expression crossed his face before he smiled and opened her door. She should bristle that he didn't even ask permission first, but how could she? Everyone was a suspect until he found the murderer. He could not treat her differently, even though she was helping him.

Robert felt as if he became even more alert when he crossed the threshold into Sarah's bedchamber. He reminded himself she was conveniently connected to his lordship's chambers. She'd been the man's mistress. She knew and understood a man's needs.

He would have thought her bedchamber would be more . . . welcoming to her lord, that there would be cushions and fine fabrics and even displayed gifts.

Instead, the room was at best functional. There were no mementoes scattered on cupboard shelves, not even a cushioned chair before the hearth. She had one coffer for her clothing, and pegs pounded into the plainly plastered walls to hold several gowns and a cloak. At least there was a carpet to keep her feet from the cold wooden floor.

She stood near the door, arms crossed over her chest, as if she were holding herself back. From what? He was invading her privacy of course. He wanted to move about the room and touch the things that were hers, but that would reveal more about him than her.

"Your bedchamber is conveniently near his young lordship," Robert said.

She nodded. "'Twas also convenient when the viscountess lay dying just beyond. I could reach her easily in the middle of the night, to offer comfort and the herbs that helped her to sleep."

And she could conveniently reach his lordship, whether to climb into his bed, or poison his food.

Why wasn't he consumed with hatred—or at least disgust?

"'Tis easy to see why the boy grew close to you," he said, "since he saw you with his mother so often."

"As Lady Drayton grew weaker, she asked for my help more. I relayed her orders to the household. She lingered for a year after I came to help ease her."

"You could not heal her?"

"She'd had a weak heart since childhood. The physicians even recommended that she never have a baby, but she ignored them out of love for her husband. Francis's birth was hard on her, I was told, and soon even the stress of climbing the stairs took her breath away. No healer can cure such an ailment. Gradually, her heart failed her and she passed away in her sleep. I was able to ease her pain, but that was all."

"And during this time, did not Francis have a nurse?"

"Aye, but she and her husband had to move from the county to help relatives near the Channel."

"Was this nurse gone well before his lordship took sick?"

"Aye, she was."

Her eyes widened, as if she realized his suspicions had to include everyone. So far, he didn't think she realized how close to her own life his questions skirted—or why. The longer he could keep her innocent of suspicion, the more freely she would speak to him.

"I understand that Lord Drayton ate private meals in his solar when he was working."

She nodded, coming a step farther into the chamber. "He was a busy man, with many manors and property to oversee."

"Who brought him his meals?"

He saw her swallow before answering. "Usually he sent for a kitchen maid, but it was never the same one each time. Even I brought him an occasional plate," she added, lifting her chin.

Of course, that was something she couldn't hide—

many would have known she brought food to his lordship.

"There were many people who handled his meals," she continued, "but only one in charge of the kitchen, where the food was made. Surely you do not think Cook would want to kill Lord Drayton?"

"It seems unlikely, although I do not rule it out. But motive is important in such a crime. Why would Cook want to kill him?"

"His position here was quite secure. Ask anyone— Lord Drayton was vocal with his appreciation of what was served each night."

"Then was someone with him regularly when he ate, someone who could slip arsenic into his meal or tankard?"

"He was ill over many weeks," she said softly. "More and more of his business was conducted in his chambers. Gradually people came to meet with him there almost exclusively."

"And when he was too ill to perform his duties?"

"He still had visitors who came to comfort him— until the physician began to suspect the black death."

Everything Sarah said could be proven by many members of the household, so she would not be foolish enough to lie.

He found himself distracted again as she walked across her bedchamber. She went to a small table where her brush and combs and a hand mirror were laid out neatly side by side. Unable to stop himself, he followed her. A variety of ribbons were spread out, so that she could see which one matched the day's gown. Without conscious volition, he ran his finger down the fine material of the ribbons. He heard her intake of breath, but didn't let himself look at her.

Also occupying the table were several bound books, parchment and quill, and a wax tablet. One book was of poetry, another a history of England, and the last about common plants.

Did she have these on hand for Francis? But then, she wasn't his tutor. She wanted more from life than simply to be taken care of.

But of course, she'd allowed herself to be taken care of before.

He was too close to her bed, with its heavy curtains tied back to the posts. Many cushions were piled above the bedclothes to give her comfort in the night.

He glanced over to her at last. She did not seem embarrassed at his boldness, only more and more curious, as a frown gathered on her forehead.

"What are you doing?" she asked in a clear, cool voice.

Chapter 9

Sarah told herself to be offended by Robert's behavior, but instead she found being alone with him in her bedchamber far too exciting. When he'd touched her hair ribbons with his large fingers, she'd shivered as if he'd stroked her skin.

And now he was lingering near her bed, and if only for her own peace of mind, she'd had to ask his purpose.

"Your bedchamber is another way that someone could have accessed the viscount's lodgings." His smile was far from innocent, even though his explanation was.

She rolled her eyes. "There are doors into each room of the master chambers."

"Yet I had to see for myself."

"So my ribbons interest you?" *My bedclothes?* she stopped herself from saying. And then she felt her face betray her with a hot blush.

"Everything about you interests me," he admitted.

She held her breath.

"And I fear that you interest others in the household as well."

"What do you mean?" she demanded.

"Do you worry that my attention to you will harm your standing?"

She blinked in confusion. "You already said they will think you flirt with me. I accept that."

"And you do not think some might be suspicious about *why* you're allowing my forward behavior?"

"Suspicious? I am a young, unmarried woman."

"Yet I will have to do much more to show my interest," he said.

And then he was walking toward her, his broad smile replaced by one more subtle, more wicked. He took her hand, and she inhaled, startled.

"Soon I will take your hand in the great hall," he said, studying her hand as if fascinated.

She wanted to scoff at his effect on her, but she couldn't. Her small hand seemed swallowed by his. His skin was rough with calluses, tanned by the sun, with dark hairs along the back, so very masculine against her fingers.

"Will you forget this is a pretense between us," he murmured, then lifted her hand to his mouth, "and blush when I do this?"

He pressed a gentle kiss to her fingers. She wanted to snatch her hand away—and she wanted to turn it over and let his mouth touch her palm.

"Already you blush." Laughter shined in his vivid blue eyes.

"How can you blame me?" she whispered. "We are alone here."

"But I only kiss your hand. You have been married, you have been a man's mistress. Surely you cannot care about so simple a thing as a kiss on your hand."

She gaped at him, forgetting his "practice" flirtation. "What did you say?"

He frowned. "Caring about a kiss on your hand?"

"Nay, before that! Did you say I have been a man's mistress?"

"Aye. 'Tis common knowledge here."

"But—" She pulled her hand away and backed up a step. "I have only shared one man's bed, and I was bound to him by the vows of marriage. Of what foolish 'common knowledge' do you speak?"

The flirtatious twinkle faded from his eyes, and now he watched her closely. "You know it is my duty to talk to various members of the castle. When I was trying to understand the hierarchy of the servants, I asked why the young lord's nursemaid was also in charge of the household."

" 'Twas because I helped Lady Drayton in such a capacity."

He cocked his head and quietly said, "All believe you succeeded Lady Drayton in her husband's bed after her death."

"What?"

She covered her mouth with both hands, for fear her cry was heard in the corridor. She had made no secret of her purpose with Robert today, but then she'd been ignorant of how others saw her.

She felt hot with fury and disbelief.

"They saw the respect Lord Drayton showed to you," Robert continued, "granting you power in his household, so everyone else offered the same. Do you deny their claims?"

"Of course I do! Lord Drayton was as a father to me. I could never—I would never—" Her words trailed away as a sick feeling of confusion sank deep inside her.

"Sit down," Robert said. "You suddenly look pale enough to swoon."

She pushed his hands away, backing up until she could clutch the back of a wooden chair. "I do not swoon. I just . . . need to think. I feel . . . like I do not even know myself, or what my life has been here."

He continued to watch her as if he could read her mind. But then he could study her face where she usually revealed all with each foolish expression.

"You know what your life has been," he said firmly.

"Do I? Everyone down there, all of my friends—" She broke off, thinking briefly of Margery. "They all believe I gave myself to a nobleman in exchange for comfort and security."

"You do not know how they viewed it. By the respect they show you, 'tis obvious to me they believe you comforted Drayton. Sir Anthony allowed you to remain Francis's nursemaid, a definite mark of respect."

"But—" She couldn't form words as her thoughts jumbled together. "Is that all Simon wants of me?" she whispered sadly. "He thought me a man's mistress, thought I would—"

"Stop this. Any man would want you for wife. 'Tis not your fault that your bloodlines were not pure enough to be a viscountess."

"I never even thought such a thing!" she cried. "Why would I, when I was already a failure as a wife?"

His eyes narrowed.

She didn't give him a chance to question her. "God above, now I understand why Cook and the other kitchen servants were surprised by my outing with Simon. I thought they didn't think of me as a normal woman who wanted romance. Instead they must simply have wondered why he bothered courting me, when he could easily have me for a price." She heard the growing bitterness in her voice.

"Stop this," Robert said firmly, stepping forward to grip her shoulders. "No one thinks you a prostitute."

"And now they're leaving you to me," she continued, her voice rising shrilly, "because they think I'll distract you from your mission, protect them, even if 'tis with my body." To her mortification, she choked on a sob.

He gave her a little shake. "You are exaggerating everything, Sarah. You have been in control of this household for at least a year. Why wouldn't they all assume you would deal with me? They are grateful for your assistance to me, just as they've been grateful for your care of Francis and your care of them. You don't seem to realize that even though they all are mistaken in one belief, it did not affect their respect for your compassion and hard work."

Her hard work on her back. But she didn't say those terrible words aloud. He was trying to comfort her, even though he didn't understand how her world had been shaken. She suddenly felt as adrift as during her marriage, belonging nowhere. But that didn't mean she deserved to be abused once again.

She took a deep breath and stepped away from

him. "You think I am overreacting," she said, trying
to sound calm.

"I do not presume to understand what you're feeling. But I believe you should not think the worst. Perhaps you can begin to correct the misunderstanding,
slowly, one person at a time."

She nodded, but she felt distracted, trying to grasp
all the implications. "So people must think I'm choos-
ing between you and Simon as my lover."

He folded his arms over his chest and leaned a
shoulder against the bedpost. "You're drawing conclusions too quickly. Do you not think many women
would be with a viscount if he asked them—or perhaps even feel pressured to accept? Why would you
think they blame you for such a thing? He was lord of
all here, and they might believe you had no choice."

"He was a good man," she said in a soft voice. "He
would never treat a woman so."

"Regardless, you seem to be able to understand
people, to guide and oversee them as you do. Does
anyone here resent you, or look down upon you?"

"Not that they've shown me," she said, hearing her
quiet bitterness.

"But you could look into someone's eyes and see
something hidden."

She sighed. "Aye. I've had to develop that skill."

Although she, obviously, could not see into the heart of a murderer.

Again, she felt his focus intensify.

"Why?" he asked.

"Because I was a naive fool when I married, and I had to learn the hard way what people thought of me."

Robert found it difficult to hold back his curiosity. He wanted—needed—to know everything about her.

Her insistence that she wasn't Drayton's mistress complicated and changed everything. If she truly wasn't the man's mistress, that brought up other motives for her to have committed murder. Perhaps she *wanted* to be Drayton's mistress—or even his wife—and he wouldn't have her. Or this denial could be a deliberate attempt to make it seem as if she had no motive to kill the man.

When he'd told her that all believed her Drayton's mistress, her redheaded complexion showed her stark blush, then the way she'd paled in sorrow. Could she truly fake all of that? He felt confused and wary.

Casually, he said, "Are not all young women naive when they marry?"

She turned away from him toward the window, rubbing her arms as if she couldn't get warm. "Aye, I imagine so. Brides trust their fathers, as I trusted mine. I was so foolishly carefree in my youth. My parents doted on me, since I had no siblings who survived infancy. I had few chores, for we did not farm for a living. If I forgot my chores while lingering too long in the village, I was seldom scolded. I lived for the moment, gave no thought to the future."

"You were a child, Sarah."

She shot him a look of disbelief over her shoulder. "I was a young woman who should have known better. I studied the healing arts, reading, and my sums, but little else. When my mother died, I had twenty years. I began to grow up then, because my healing could not help her. I studied harder. Anxious over my unmarried state, my father devoted himself to finding me a good husband. And he thought he did."

Those last words were spoken bitterly. She faced him from across the chamber, her chin lifted.

"I knew he wanted what was best for me, but I did not see that he was as poorly prepared as I."

Robert frowned. "What do you mean? Francis said your father was a knight."

"But he could not read. He could only make his mark. My marriage contract was weighted in favor of the groom and his family, and they misrepresented it to my father. I brought a monetary settlement, but no land, nothing that could be returned to me on my husband's death. I learned that my father only leased our manor from his liege lord." She laughed without amusement. "Did I mention how foolish I was? I thought I would have a comfortable life with Andrew, the son of a local landowner."

"Did you love him?" Robert asked, knowing it was none of his business.

She tiredly shook her head. "I did not know him well enough to love him. When I was little, I thought I wanted to marry for love, but I did not mind its absence. Andrew was handsome and considerate, and I thought love would grow from that."

"And it didn't?"

"Nay. And I didn't know enough then to look into someone's eyes for the truth—or at least for something hidden. He became a different man after the wedding. I thought if I gave him a good home and a happy life, we would grow closer. But nothing I did made him happy."

She looked down, her cheeks paling. He wondered if she hinted at the more intimate part of a marriage— or something else. The rumor was that she'd killed him, and she made no secret of the fact that she and her husband were unhappy together.

She took a deep breath and straightened as if to bolster her courage. "I tried to be a good wife to him, regardless. And I gathered much more knowledge during the marriage than what I'd brought to our union. I learned how to manage a large household, and discovered I was good at it."

"The people of Drayton have surely benefited from this, Sarah."

She nodded as if she were trying to convince herself. "At least I learned not to be so foolishly carefree. Life is serious, and is meant to be taken so."

His mouth quirked in a smile. "Then you must think me foolish. I do not think that life is always serious." He'd learned early that treating his circumstances as if they molded his life for the worse only made it so.

"But how am I to know what your true feelings are? You are here to investigate a murder, and could be portraying yourself however you think would work best."

She was correct, of course, he thought with reluctant admiration. "I enjoy flirting with women, so it helps me to use that in this situation. But I am not a sober, serious man. Can you not see that in my eyes?"

He held her with his gaze, and she studied him. The force of her regard was powerful. She thought of herself as an equal, able to judge him. It was far too attractive.

"But you do sober, serious work, Robert."

"Sometimes. But my work does not have to define me."

She looked doubtful, but did not argue with him. Nor did she continue with her story.

He wasn't ready to let it go. "So you were not able to improve your marriage before your husband died?"

"Nay, 'twas not to be," she said, shaking her head.

She looked sad and resigned, and he would have stopped questioning her for now if he were only a man. But he was a Bladesman.

"How did he die?"

"He fell from his horse and hit his head on a rock, right in front of me, only a year after my father's death." She met his eyes, her smile grim. "And then I found out how little I truly had."

He waited in silence. He could hardly say, *Not only do people think you're a man's mistress; there are rumors that you murdered your husband.*

When she didn't speak, he said, "You mentioned that your father hadn't understood the contract?"

"My husband's family took everything—legally."

"They forced you to leave?" *Because they believe you killed their son.*

"Only after they were certain I carried no child, of course. There was much they blamed me for, and not giving them a grandchild was almost a sin."

A stark sadness glimmered in her eyes. Women usually wanted children, and she'd had none, after how many years of marriage? It was too personal to ask for details without making her suspicious, but he would have to find out everything eventually.

"How did you come to Drayton Hall?" he asked.

Her eyes narrowed. "You are full of questions for me today."

"'Tis what I'm good at, talking to people," he said, spreading his hands wide. "And you fascinate me, Sarah. I find I want to know everything about you."

"There's no one here to watch your flirtation, Robert," she said dryly. "You can stop performing."

He looked deeply into her eyes. "I am not performing."

She held his gaze a long moment, then turned and walked to the door. "We've been alone here too long. I can't have people believe I've already chosen my next paramour."

"Sarah—"

"Nay, you cannot stop how I feel. I will overcome this, and find some way to make people believe the truth."

She left the room ahead of him, and he found himself looking back at her ribbons, remembering how he'd felt when he'd flirted with her, kissed her hand. It was all for the greater good, but he was too caught up in his act, drowning in forbidden desire for her.

At the midday meal, Sarah moved smoothly between the kitchen and the great hall, answering questions and guiding the dance that was the serving of the meal. She told herself that nothing had changed—at least not in the eyes of everyone who lived and worked at Drayton Hall. But inside her, everything was different, as if she weren't the same person who'd woken up that morning.

They all thought she was a harlot, a woman who would sleep with a man for security. Or was Robert right? Did they believe she had no choice?

But that would make her a victim, and she'd always been determined never to be that again.

She wanted to shout the truth at the top of her lungs—she wanted to slink away and cry. She'd worked so hard to help Drayton Hall and its people, but everything had been based on a misconception.

Whenever Robert caught her eye, he smiled at her, as if nothing were wrong. She didn't trust that easy smile—she didn't trust him. And then she saw him talking to Simon at the head table, and her suspicions blossomed. Were they talking about her?

Yet . . . Robert was talking to everyone. He hadn't narrowed his investigation to any one person as far as she could tell. But he'd spent the most time with her.

A sick feeling twisted her stomach. Was he so focused on her because she was a major suspect?

She didn't even realize she'd come to a standstill near the kitchen corridor until someone accidentally bumped her from behind.

"Excuse me, mistress!" said the mortified footman, bowing his head.

She forced a smile. "I was thinking rather than watching where I was going, William. Please excuse me."

She moved out of the way and watched the other servers, even though she wasn't paying attention. Robert had said everyone was a suspect, and hadn't ruled out women, either.

But they all thought she'd been Drayton's mistress— wouldn't that make her closer to his lordship, and even more likely to have a reason to kill him?

She found herself growing light-headed from breathing too quickly, and forced her jumbled thoughts to slow down.

Whatever Robert thought when he arrived, now he knew she hadn't been Drayton's mistress. Surely that would lessen her importance as a suspect in his eyes.

But what if he didn't believe her? If she were a murderer, she would certainly have no qualms about lying to protect herself.

She put a hand on the cold stone wall and struggled to appear calm. Robert and Simon were still conversing, Robert wearing his usual smile, Simon so earnest and serious. What were they talking about?

She abruptly remembered the Drayton upper staff staring at her when they'd first heard about the murder investigation. Nausea swirled inside her, followed by a heated panic.

She'd felt so safe here, so protected. And now it had all gone up in smoke. This was the only home she had, the only place where people cared about her.

Was she going to lose everything, even though she was innocent?

Chapter 10

When Sarah finally sat down for dinner on the other side of Francis, Robert couldn't stop staring at her. She looked too pale, too calm. Their conversation in her bedchamber had changed everything.

If it was true that she'd never been Drayton's mistress, then she was still absorbing the fact that all of her friends believed that of her, but she'd never known.

How had no one ever discussed it? Wasn't it rather obvious that it would affect *something* in her life?

Walter gave a single look between Sarah and him, and only arched an eyebrow. But that look said it all: *What has happened?*

"Sir Simon," Sarah said, "I noticed that you and Sir Robert have become friendly this afternoon."

Robert leaned forward and Chapman did the same. Their gazes met.

"Friendly, Mistress Sarah?" Chapman echoed in

that somber voice. "We are not enemies; therefore we can speak politely to each other. I would not yet call us friends."

"Acquaintances then," she said impatiently. "Every time I came out of the kitchens, you were still talking, wearing serious expressions. Is everything . . . well?"

"Aye, mistress," Chapman said, frowning. "We are going hunting this afternoon with many of the household, and we were comparing techniques and hunting stories."

"Oh."

She seemed to deflate, Robert thought, hiding the unwilling amusement she provoked in him. Had she assumed they were talking about her?

Then she turned to him. "Sir Robert, I am surprised to hear you are doing something for entertainment, when all know you are here for a serious, important reason."

Now she was questioning his methods in front of her people, he thought, unable to stop his smile. She'd surprised him with this tactic, and he always enjoyed being surprised. But he reminded himself that Francis was present, looking from one to the other with resigned confusion as he chewed his bread. He didn't want the boy to learn the reason for his investigation.

"Part of my mission is getting to know and understand the people of Drayton Hall, mistress. What better way than to spend the afternoon with the male half of the household?" He grinned. "And of course, I will give equal time to the Drayton women."

He heard the chuckles from all around him. Even Sir Simon seemed to press his lips together to hide a smile. Sarah glowed with another lovely blush, and didn't have an answer as she returned her attention to her meal.

Sarah was very thankful when the meal was over. She escaped the table as quickly as she could, feeling frustrated and foolish and so confused. For a while she oversaw the servants as they began to clear the tables, but they were well trained and did not need her constant supervision.

The men had gathered near the hearth, including Simon and Robert, making their plans.

Oh, she'd made a fool of herself. And she'd discovered nothing that could help her. Then she saw Sir Walter standing apart from the others, and without thinking too much, she walked purposefully to join him.

He was an intimidating man, she thought, as his pale gray eyes settled on her. He wasn't incredibly tall, but the width of his chest and shoulders made him seem so much bigger and more powerful. She licked her suddenly dry lips and gave him a faint smile.

He nodded. "Mistress Sarah, how may I help you?"

"You are not going hunting with the others, sir?"

"Nay, I am not. I have other duties to attend to."

He was not the friendly partner in this investigation. She wondered how his methods differed from Robert's. But she would not dare ask. He, too, must think her an important suspect in the viscount's death. She suppressed a shiver, realizing her danger. She forced herself to breathe, to remember that she had learned much in her life, that she was no longer a vulnerable, naive girl.

"Mistress Sarah?" Walter said as he studied her.

She gave him a brief smile. "Forgive me. I was thinking about my own duties yet to be accomplished this day, and that was not fair to you."

"You are a busy woman," he said.

She wanted to wince. What could he mean by that? But if she read a second meaning into everything these two men said, she would eventually run mad.

"I like keeping busy, especially now. When I have too much time to think I'm . . . too sad." Oh, that was a mistake. It sounded as if she were trying to press her innocence upon him.

"These are sad times for Drayton Hall," he said impassively.

"Are you truly concerned about us? Or are we merely another assignment to you?" She held her breath, shocked at her boldness—or stupidity. Perhaps he didn't like to be challenged, unlike Robert, who'd seemed to enjoy her dinner table discussion.

Sir Walter continued to study her before saying, "I treat each assignment from the king with the importance it deserves, mistress. Bringing a murderer to justice and giving a family peace is not something I take lightly."

"Of course not," she murmured, feeling flushed and foolish. "And we will be grateful when you have discovered the truth."

"Some will not be so grateful," he said dryly.

"Nay, but that person or persons will deserve whatever punishment they've earned."

"So you think there could be more than one person involved, mistress?"

She blinked at him in surprise. "I—I do not know. When you said 'some' will not be grateful, it made me realize that perhaps a murderer might need help. After all, arsenic had to be regularly administered to Lord Drayton's food and then brought to him. It might seem suspicious for the same person to serve him each day, and I know that did not happen."

The grave expression in his eyes seemed to lighten. "'Tis a good thought. But you know something about healing, mistress. Would the arsenic need to be given every day?"

She wanted to protest that she'd proven far too un-skilled. "I know little of poison, Sir Walter. But his lordship became so sick that it would seem to me that missing a dose every other day or so near the end would not have reversed his illness."

"Hmm," was his only answer.

Was that what he wanted to hear from her? Or had she made everything worse?

"Forgive me for keeping you from your duties, sir," she said, bowing her head as she began to move away.

"You may speak with me at any time, mistress. Do not forget that."

She nodded and hurried away, wondering if he wanted her to confess.

The mounted knights and officers of the Drayton household rode out from the castle in a group of twenty or so. Robert kept to the rear, where he could see everyone before him. He didn't know what he hoped to accomplish, although he'd said otherwise to Sarah. There would be little time for discussion.

But it had been well over a year since he'd gone on a hunt. Once his brother had revealed himself as the rightful earl of Keswick, Robert had lived with him in London as Adam fulfilled his duties at King

Henry's court. The last hunt he'd been on had been with Bladesmen, all excellent hunters.

There was always a purpose when Bladesmen were together, almost a contest, as if one had to constantly prove oneself. Robert had not seen the importance of such things, so he'd always been able to study the other men's behavior, amusing himself, rather than take part in such vain showmanship.

Yet this Drayton hunt seemed a way for the men to relax and forget the tension in the household, now that the murder had been revealed. On horseback, they thundered through the trees until they reached a clearing, dismounting to await the signal from the huntsman, who was off in the forest stalking roebuck with the hounds and their handlers.

Much as Master Frobisher and Sir Daniel, the steward and treasurer, were there, Robert did not feel the time was right for another discussion with them. They and several other knights of the household all seemed too nervous around him. He put that down to superstition and fear; they couldn't all have been involved in the murder of their lord.

He maneuvered himself near Simon Chapman. Together they picked over the fruit and cheese heaped on platters that had been laid out on trestle tables for the hunting party.

Chapman glanced briefly at him as he munched on a piece of dried apple, then glanced again as he took a drink of ale from his horn. His look was speculative, with just a tinge of hostility. Was the man feeling proprietary toward Sarah?

Robert smiled. "So you are almost as new to the household as I am."

Chapman frowned, as if trying to see a hidden meaning behind Robert's words. "My liege lord, Sir Anthony Ramsey, has been connected to this household his entire life."

"But before he became guardian to the new young lord, he remained at his own home, and you must have as well."

"Aye," Chapman said, nodding.

"But you visited often?"

Another nod. But the knight didn't offer anything voluntarily.

"'Tis nearby?"

"Less than half a day's journey."

"Then we should see Sir Anthony soon."

"You have written to request his presence?"

"Mistress Sarah wrote to tell him the truth of Drayton's death."

"Then aye, he will come. He and his lordship were close, and this will strengthen his grief."

Robert nodded, popping several berries into his

mouth. "Why did you remain behind after he became the young lord's guardian?"

Chapman gave him a look as if it should be perfectly obvious. "Sir Anthony requested that several of his knights remain here to watch over the new viscount. He feels his duty deeply."

"But Drayton has its own contingent of knights and soldiers."

"Nevertheless, the young lord is Sir Anthony's responsibility."

As was all the wealth that came with the viscountcy, Robert thought. The elder lord's death had given Sir Anthony control over a sizable estate. Very convenient for Sir Anthony.

"You've been here several weeks then, since Drayton's death?" he continued. "I imagine it has been rather uneventful."

"Nay, Sarah makes sure my time is pleasantly spent."

Robert grinned, but Chapman did not even smile back.

"So your duty became so routine that you began to look for other entertainment," he mused. "The young lord's nursemaid must have proved a challenge."

Chapman's face darkened. "I do not take your meaning."

"She is in charge of the household, is she not? Becoming friendly with her will give you another way to keep track of your lord's ward."

"I would never use a woman to make my duty simpler," he said. His voice didn't sound desperate or outraged, only certain of the truth. "Or perhaps *you* believe that using a woman in such a way is justified."

An impressive strike, Robert thought, holding back an admiring nod. He wondered if Chapman thought Sarah had been used by the late Lord Drayton. Or since he was so recent an arrival, perhaps he didn't even know she'd been considered the man's mistress. "A woman has never had to accuse me of using her," he said, smiling. "Mistress Sarah wants justice for her lord's memory. Surely you want justice in this situation, too."

"I do," he said gravely, "and so will Sir Anthony."

There was a stirring behind them, and they both turned to see the huntsman emerging through the trees to approach Master Frobisher. They spoke and gestured to each other.

"He's found a quarry worth pursuing, do you think?" Robert asked.

Master Frobisher suddenly blew a short series of notes on his hunting horn, alerting the dogs and their handlers who waited out in the forest to begin the chase.

Robert said, "It seems the hunt is on."

Chapman headed for his horse, leaving him to loosen his bow from his saddle as he mounted Dragon. He wondered what Chapman would report to Sir Anthony when the man arrived. Sir Anthony should know that he, too, would be considered a suspect, along with everyone else.

Was Robert believing his own stories now?

Sarah told herself it was another beautiful afternoon, with the sun shining through the mullioned windows to highlight Francis's curls. His head was bent over a small lute as a local minstrel gave him his music lesson.

Where was the rain? How could so many days be lovely when a cloud of grief and suspicion hung over Drayton Hall?

She looked at the sewing resting in her lap, realizing she'd hardly paid attention to it. Several embroidered stitches had to be plucked out so she could start again. She was making a new shirt for Francis. Since he'd begun to eat again, already he seemed to be growing.

Thanks to Robert, she supposed. In just a few days, he'd already had an influence on the boy.

Of course, he'd had an influence on her, too. He'd told her the truth of her life, when no one else had.

"Mistress Sarah!" Francis suddenly called.

She jumped in surprise, since she was practically next to him. "Aye, Francis?"

"Did you hear—I know a song!"

"Your effort has made all the difference. Congratulations."

"Will you sing it while I play?"

The minstrel was an older, balding man with a face weathered by much time spent traveling out of doors. He gave her a gap-toothed grin and arched an eyebrow as if daring her.

She sighed even as she smiled. "Of course I'll sing."

Francis strummed the lute, and in time with him she slowly sang the song about a lowly girl at court and the king who fell in love with her. It all ended well for *that* girl, she thought, then berated herself for her pessimism.

Someone clapped enthusiastically when they were done, and she turned to find Margery approaching them. The woman smiled at Francis, who grinned back before moving on to the next part of his lesson.

When Margery would have sat down, Sarah jumped up and said, "We don't wish to interrupt your lesson, Francis."

She took her friend's arm and guided her closer

to the hearth, away from the sunny windows. With a sigh, she sank onto a cushioned chair.

"'Twas a lovely song," Margery said, sitting down beside her. Her black hair peeked out in wispy strands from beneath her cap. "'Tis a shame ye spoiled it by forcin' yourself to sound bright and happy."

Sarah rubbed her face with both hands, then dropped them into her lap. "Francis does not need to know what is truly happening in his home."

"Aye, 'tis true, of course. But . . . ye look worse since I last saw you, and I know ye spent time alone with Sir Robert." She peered closely at Sarah's face. "Did somethin' bad happen?"

Sarah shrugged. "Apparently it happened a long time ago and I never knew about it."

"Ye best be explainin' that one."

She faced Margery to study her expression. "Everyone thinks I was Lord Drayton's mistress."

The seamstress relaxed. "Oh, aye, there is that."

Sarah stiffened. "You knew! And you believed it?"

"Well, nay, I never did, but when ye talk about somethin', even to deny it, it makes the gossip worse. So I kept silent."

"But you could have told *me*!"

Margery put her hand on Sarah's arm. "Dearie, I knew ye'd only be hurt. And no one thought the worse of you for it. In fact, some thought that since his lordship trusted you, they should, too."

"But—'twas all a lie!"

"How did ye find out?" she asked, her eyes brimming with sympathy.

Sarah sank back into the chair and murmured, "Robert told me."

"Well, he found out quick, now didn't he?"

"I know why he told me, too. I'm a suspect in his eyes, Margery. He didn't say so, but I know it."

"You?" Margery chuckled. "Ye must be teasin' me!"

But Sarah didn't laugh, and gradually her friend's smile faded.

"But Sarah, we're all suspects, are we not? You the same as me."

"But don't you see, Robert thought I was Lord Drayton's mistress, which meant I would be closest to him of all at the castle. Closeness implies that I'd have even more reason to kill him, should we have had problems."

"By that logic, Francis is the guilty party," Margery scoffed. "But ye told him ye weren't a woman like that, did ye not?"

"Oh, I told him, but why should he believe me?"

"Then *I'll* tell him!"

"Why should he believe *you?*" she asked patiently.

"You're my friend. And you do realize, that even if he believes my story, I've just presented him with even more motives in the murder. Since everyone *thought* I was his mistress, perhaps I wanted to be, and killed him when he wouldn't have me."

Margery stared at her openmouthed. Sarah only raised her eyebrows.

At last the seamstress said, "Ye're too educated for yer own good, Sarah."

That finally made Sarah smile. "I ought to be. I worked hard enough at it."

"I can't solve yer problems, dearie. I can only say that ye know ye're innocent. The truth will out itself eventually, since that Sir Robert seems a smart fellow. I been watchin' him. He can't believe ye're guilty."

"Why would you think that?" she asked doubtfully.

But Margery was already onto the next thought. "Now that other fellow, Sir Walter, him I don't know about. Perhaps there's never been a person born *he* can trust."

Though Sarah smiled, she did not forget what they'd been discussing. "You cannot believe that the flirtatious looks Robert is giving me are because he thinks I'm innocent."

"Well—"

"He told me himself that flirtation is part of his

method." And then in her mind she was back in her bedchamber, alone with him. No one there but the two of them, and he'd looked at her like . . . She shivered.

Margery took her hand and squeezed. "Take heart, dearie. Ye're an innocent woman—and ye haven't even been wrongfully accused. Someone else did this foul deed, and Sir Robert will ferret him out."

"You place a lot of trust in a stranger," Sarah warned. "But aye, you're right. I cannot act like I'm waiting for the worst to happen. I'll live up to my offer to help him find this murderer."

"That's my girl! And ye'll not turn away a man's interest, wherever you find it?"

Sarah frowned.

"Because ye need cheerin' up as much as the next girl."

At least that made her laugh.

Chapter 11

When the men arrived home from their hunt, just before supper, the great hall was filled with their deep voices and laughter. Sarah watched Francis's excitement as he took it all in, and she was glad for him. The castle had been too quiet since his father's death. He moved from man to man, listening to their conversations. Somehow he still ended up at Robert's side.

Robert was talking and smiling, but he looked down at the boy and put a hand on his shoulder with affection. Sarah felt a jolt of sweet sadness. She prayed that Francis wouldn't somehow be hurt in the end, that his new hero would prove worthy of such a title.

Then Simon came to her, smelling of the fresh outdoors, taking both her hands as he leaned down to kiss her cheek. She found herself blushing, not certain if she was pleased or embarrassed at such a display.

But Simon seemed so happy to see her that she could not be upset with him.

When all had sat down to supper, one of the knights in the garrison, seated at a lower table, called out, "Master Frobisher, did you see the way Sir Robert took down his deer?"

Sarah watched Robert's easy smile. She'd known that several deer had been brought to Cook, but she hadn't known the identities of the marksmen.

Master Frobisher shook his head. "Did the lad perform some great feat of skill?"

There were guffaws all around, and Sarah marveled at the new ease among the men regarding Robert. He seemed to have a gift for knowing how to make people like him.

"'Twas indeed quite skillful," Simon said.

Sarah almost gaped at him.

Robert laughed. "You all do give me too much credit. I simply wanted to eat."

Sir Daniel waved a hand. "Nonsense. I saw you. Once the deer was sighted, you galloped without a hand on the reins, your bow and arrow taut and ready."

"That is not unusual," Robert said as if they were all exaggerating.

The young knight picked up the story. "And then when he'd spotted our quarry and couldn't line up the sight, he leaned to the side as if he were going to tumble from the saddle. 'Twas like magic, the way he held on with his legs and let his arrow go."

"Shot dead in the heart," Sir Daniel said, shaking his head as if in disbelief. "I have never seen anything like it."

The hall continued to buzz with admiration, and although Robert smiled, he did not add to it, only continued to eat. Sarah could not help noticing that he did not look at his partner. Sir Walter's expression was as impassive as always. Did he disapprove? she wondered. And why should he?

At last the enthusiasm died down as the attention of the famished hunters returned to their meals. Robert was speaking to Sir Daniel on his far side. Sarah could not hear much of their discussion, but at last, Robert looked at her over Francis's curly head.

"Mistress Sarah, Sir Daniel and I need some privacy to speak. Will you accompany us?"

There was something he wasn't saying.

She had promised to help, but she hardly needed a reminder. Her curiosity was enough to allow her to nod.

As benches and chairs were pushed back to allow the servants to clear everything away, she was surprised when Sir Daniel took her arm and laughed as if she'd just said something funny.

Wearing a false smile, she allowed him to lead her across the hall toward a corridor deeper into the castle. Robert followed behind, leaning close as if speaking. Both men burst out laughing again.

She remained silent after their little performance, and they followed her example. She wasn't certain where they were going, but she was surprised when they left the main keep, walking the corridor that ran beneath the guest lodgings. Robert lifted a candle from a table, lit it from a torch on the wall, then led them up the stairs to his own quarters.

Sir Daniel shut the door behind them and slumped against it with weariness. "Thank you, mistress," he said, heaving a sigh.

"I did nothing but follow along," she said dryly. "May I ask why I was necessary? I'm certain the two of you could have laughed at nothing without me."

Robert crossed his arms over his chest and half sat against the edge of the table. "Sir Daniel seemed to feel that being seen talking to me might implicate him as a suspect."

Sarah calmly looked at the treasurer. "We are all suspects, are we not?"

"But I perform a vital duty for the Drayton estates," Sir Daniel insisted, thrusting his bearded chin forward defiantly. "Money is always a powerful incentive for murder."

"I cannot deny that," Robert mused.

Sir Daniel's eyes widened. "But I vow that I've given no cause for mistrust!"

"Glad I am to hear it."

"I am simply reluctant to show you the private ledgers without Sir Anthony's approval. But . . ." the treasurer's voice faded away, then he seemed to make up his mind. "I would obey the king's man. I simply need proof of your mission."

Sarah inhaled sharply. It was not her place to know what proof Robert had shown the steward—if he'd even been asked to produce any at all. When Robert smiled, Sir Daniel's tension seemed to ease.

"You are a cautious man," Robert said. "I do not fault that, especially for someone in your position of authority. I shall return in a moment."

He continued up the circular stairs to the second floor. Sir Daniel didn't seem to know where to look, but at last he met Sarah's gaze.

"Do you think me a fool, mistress?"

"Nay, I do not. And I also do not believe that Sir Robert will hold your caution against you. If you are innocent, you have nothing to fear."

Robert came down the stairs, unrolling a parchment, and handed it to Sir Daniel. Sarah glimpsed the king's seal, although she could not read the decree. Then Robert opened his hand, and in his palm rested a gold ring, precious stones outlining an *H* for Henry.

Sir Daniel released his breath and nodded. "My thanks for your trust in me, sir."

"Now will you return the same courtesy to me and answer my questions?"

The treasurer nodded.

"I need to know if there were any irregularities in the ledgers in the months before the viscount's death—unexplained entries not in your own hand, or missing money."

"Nothing like that, Sir Robert! Lord Drayton was meticulous with his expenses, and expected everyone else to be, whether it was his cook or a bailiff from one of his properties."

"I'd like to see for myself."

Sir Daniel nodded and once again led the way, this time back to the lord's solar. From a coffer, he removed a heavy bound book and spread it across the table. For long minutes, both men poured over it. Robert examined several pages of entries, so quickly she did not think a man could possibly absorb it all. But she sensed that he knew exactly what he was looking at, and how everything should be ordered.

What kind of man was he? At four and twenty, he had the trust of the king, had completed other assignments for him, rode a horse as if he were one with the animal, and now understood the finances of a large estate?

Robert finally straightened, and Sir Daniel looked up at him. Although the treasurer seemed uneasy, he did not look panicked or guilty, Sarah thought.

"Excellent records, Sir Daniel," Robert said.

"Then you know of which you speak," Sir Daniel said wryly. "You have my thanks."

"It has not been two months since Sir Anthony Ramsey became Francis's guardian. Did he meet with you then?"

"Aye, he did. He looked everything over, just as you did. I thought him quite competent."

"Why?" Robert asked.

Sir Daniel shot an embarrassed look at Sarah, as if he now regretted his choice of words. "Because he changed nothing, Sir Robert. He trusted me to continue as I've been doing, with the understanding that I send him regular reports and answer to Master Frobisher."

Robert smiled. "Then you've answered all my questions."

Sir Daniel quickly rose, then hesitated. "I know you have probably not heard this before . . . people are always fearful, but . . . thank you for what you're doing to right a terrible crime."

Robert's smile faded. "You are welcome."

Sir Daniel nodded, then hurried out of the solar, shutting the door behind him.

Sarah stared at Robert. He arched an eyebrow, as if waiting for her to speak.

She couldn't help smiling at the patience he displayed toward her. "Why did you bring me with you on something so private as investigating Sir Daniel's possible motive for a murder?"

"His unease and panic were obvious. I assumed that your presence alone could reassure him. I was right. And remember"—he added before she could speak—"you did agree to assist me whenever I need you."

"Aye, I did," she said, summoning her bravery to walk toward him.

His eyebrows lifted, but he didn't move, as if he'd block her way. Instead she stopped and looked at the ledger still spread out on the table.

"Sir Daniel was always well trusted by Lord Drayton," she mused, running a finger down the meticulous columns. The sun was going down beyond the windows, but she could still see well enough.

"I had heard that, but I had to be certain."

"He is a man beyond middle age, and he has been here his entire life, with never a complaint against him."

"I have heard that the Drayton estates are some of the most profitable in the land," Robert said slowly. "'Twould be easy to take some for himself."

"He has always been well paid, and Sir Anthony continued the tradition—or so I was told."

She still stood too close to him, feeling bold, telling herself that she had to be. If she didn't stand up for herself, if she looked at all hesitant, he would think her guilty.

"'Tis interesting to hear that Sir Anthony changed nothing of the financial arrangements once he became guardian," Robert said.

She continued to look up at him calmly. "Why should he? This is all Francis's now. And he and Lord Drayton consulted on everything. I imagine nothing in our finances was a surprise to him."

Robert only nodded. For a moment, his eyes seemed unfocused, as if he saw something else, thought of something else. Was he putting more of the pieces together in that mind of his? Where did she fit into the puzzle of this crime?

The shadows in the room had lengthened, and it had grown darker, more intimate without candlelight.

Then suddenly those eyes sharpened on her, where she still stood too close. Something in them flared to life, invoking a matching response of heat inside her.

She took a deep breath, not understanding what she was feeling, but wanting to. They remained silent, still, too close, as his gaze centered on her mouth.

God Above, she thought, he wanted to kiss her.

She didn't know where that thought came from; no man had ever looked at her like this, with a longing hunger, as if only her kiss could satisfy him.

It was preposterous.

It was seductive.

She told herself he had looked at many women this way, but somehow his past didn't seem to matter. They were alone; there was no one else for whom he needed to pretend a flirtation. This sudden tension had gone beyond flirtation.

And then another idea struck her—did he have a weakness for her? Was this . . . emotion . . . that sparked between them a vulnerability in Sir Robert Burcot?

Vulnerability? Why was she thinking such things? He thought she could be a murderer!

But she didn't move away, and neither did he. He didn't reach to touch her. Instead she watched his mouth, and those eyes that looked suddenly darker, smokier. He wasn't smiling; he was more serious and intent than she'd ever seen him.

And that captivated her, left her feeling hesitant, uncertain, trembling. She could feel the warmth of him, heard the sound of his quick breathing, which so matched her own. Did his heart sound like it would beat from his chest, as hers did?

"I should go," he whispered, his voice low and husky.

Before he could leave her, she stood on her tiptoes and kissed him. It was like nothing she'd ever experienced, not in any dream. Though at first he hesitated, tense, she drew a response from him as their lips lingered and teased. They still touched nowhere else, and she ached to lean against him, found herself arching, wished he would hold her—

Then he lifted his head, breaking the kiss. She simply stared wide-eyed at him, her fingers twisted together to keep from pulling him back. Warmth had swept from the crown of her forehead clear to her toes, intensifying deep in her belly. Oh, this was desire, something she'd wanted desperately from her husband early in their marriage, but never had.

She lifted her hand toward his face and he did nothing as her fingers touched his cheek. A single tremor moved through him, she realized with shock, unable to imagine what that meant.

"We shouldn't be doing this," he rasped.

"We should stop." Her voice didn't sound her own. With her eyes closed, she swayed in this realm of heady passion, this need, this ache.

How could these sensations be true? They had only just met—and he was at Drayton Hall for such a dark, ugly reason.

Then he stepped away from her, breaking the spell.

Embarrassed by her own boldness, she reached to close the ledger, relieved her hands weren't trembling. She struggled to speak in a normal tone. "Are you done with this, Robert?"

He nodded, but for a verbose man, he said nothing.

Even walking away from him to return the ledger was a difficult thing to do. When she bent over the coffer, she thought he made a sound, but when she looked over her shoulder, she only saw him in profile, his hand flat against the table, his body rigid.

"Did you say something?" she asked too breathlessly.

He shook his head.

Again, no words.

"We should go," she said.

Together they left the lord's solar, not speaking. They walked down the corridor, moving in and out of the torchlight. They passed a maidservant, who bobbed a quick, hesitant curtsy to Robert even as she scurried away.

For a moment Sarah wanted to tease him, but

things were different now between them. The ground had shifted, and she had to think about what it meant in their relationship—and what it could mean for her future.

What must he be thinking of her brazen behavior?

Chapter 12

Robert needed another tankard of ale, but he knew his limits. He had to keep a clear head in the great hall, as the evening wound down after supper. Walter was watching him too closely, and it took everything in him to appear his usual cheerful self.

What had happened when he'd been alone in that darkening chamber with Sarah Audley?

He knew what lust was—he'd felt it in his youth before even being allowed to see women regularly. He'd felt it when he'd escaped the League at the age of fifteen, and tasted the kisses of an eager dairymaid.

But this—this had been something altogether different.

He faced the fire and clenched the now empty tankard in his hand. The heat enveloped him, seared him, and he wished it would sear away every memory of those stolen moments, but they were now emblazoned in his mind.

He'd always thought lust and desire the same thing, but now he knew better. He *desired* Sarah with a need that went beyond the simple gratification of the flesh. Oh, but that was a part of it, of course, an urgent, pounding part of it. When he'd seen Chapman dare to put his lips to her cheek, he'd felt almost irrational with outrage, as if Sarah were his. He closed his eyes. Her mouth had been sweet and innocent, not the kiss of an experienced, married woman, but he already knew her marriage had not been normal.

But that brief, tentative taste had whetted his appetite for more. He wanted to lick a path down her throat, between her breasts, taste the scented flesh beneath the under curve. His mind was tormenting him with images of what could have been, what might yet be—

But only if he gave up everything he thought he wanted in life, if he gave up the League. For wasn't this their problem with him, the reason they had Walter watching his every move? They thought him a womanizer, an undisciplined libertine. He could at last admit that he felt betrayed by their mistrust. They'd distorted his childhood, yet he still believed in them, wanted to help bring justice to those who deserved it the most.

He'd known they were wrong about him, knew that

he'd just been enjoying himself in London, like any young man freed from the shackles of his past.

But this—this overwhelming sensation, this need for Sarah, made him realize that he truly didn't know himself at all. He'd wanted to crush her against him, forget everything they both were, and assuage the need that burned hot inside him. He didn't want to think of her motives, or whether her hesitant attempt at seduction meant she was truly guilty. None of that could matter as he completed his assignment.

Was the League right? Would he be unable to control himself in every situation?

Nay, he would not believe that! He was well trained, and he was dedicated to justice and helping the innocent, the causes of the League that he so believed in.

He'd simply never met anyone like her before. He would soon be able to accept how he felt and wrestle it into submission. Nothing would change. He clenched his free hand into a fist, gritting his teeth.

"Sir Robert, are you not standing too close to the fire?"

Robert whirled around to see Francis staring at him with uncertainty, a pear-shaped lute held awkwardly by both arms against his chest.

He smiled and stepped back. "Aye, foolish of me to be daydreaming so, my lord. Good of you to remind me."

Francis's expression eased as he held up his lute. "Look what I am learning."

Robert took the lute into his hands. "A fine instrument. The ladies at court enjoy it when a gentleman sings to them."

"Do you sing to ladies?"

He smiled, then looked up as he realized they were the focus of more than one pair of eager ears. But not Sarah, who stood sipping a goblet of wine while she spoke to Chapman.

That dark sensation surfaced again inside him, and this time he recognized it as jealousy. Though he fought it, in a sense he realized he could not totally let it go, for he needed to keep up his flirtation with Sarah before the household. If he paid too much attention to her without flirting, they might all begin to suspect her as much as the League did. He could not have someone else attempting to punish her—taking things too far. Her punishment was his duty.

"I enjoy singing, Francis," Robert said, "to whomever wants to listen."

"Then sing for me!"

With a chuckle, he didn't resist. He held the lute tucked under his arm and began to strum it idly, thinking of the perfect song. He began with an adventure story that a young boy would appreciate. Francis stared enraptured at him, laughing at the hero's foibles, occasionally staring at Robert's fingers. One by one, others approached the hearth and began to nod their heads in time with the music. He lifted his voice, let it capture the growing crowd, even as he knew he was trying to lure Sarah's attention. But she was still deep in conversation with Chapman.

When the song ended, Francis cried, "Another one, please!"

The maidservants applauded, and Robert bowed to them as if they were ladies at court. He began another song about a man's earnest love of a woman, and walked among them, always moving closer and closer to his goal.

Out of the corner of her eye, Sarah watched Robert meander toward her. It was becoming more difficult to concentrate on Simon's discussion of the horses he'd trained over the years. She normally enjoyed the topic, but from the beginning, Robert's voice had tugged at her, taunted her, teased her with its pure baritone. And she'd felt guilty at her reaction, for she'd seen Simon's impatient glances at Robert.

She knew Robert had sung for Francis, and the funny lyrics had been perfect for the boy. But the next song was not for a boy, and luckily, the lyrics' true meaning of physical love was subtle. But all the women present understood and appreciated it, for Robert walked among them, smiling in that wicked way of his. The women watched him with adoration, the men with relief, for when he was wooing women, he wasn't thinking about his murder investigation. But she was getting to know Robert better, and she didn't think his mission ever left him. He had a reason for singing, besides enlivening the evening for the women.

And *she* was his reason. He may not have meant to kiss her, but he was still going to flirt. He was slowly but surely heading right for her. A frisson of excitement and nervousness chased down her spine as she remembered the subtle power of their intimate connection. The sound of his voice was almost as powerful, smoothly sliding through her mind, almost as physical as his touch. Her body swayed without volition to the melody.

"Sarah?" Simon said.

She realized with a start that this was the second time he'd called her name. "Forgive me, Simon. What did you ask?"

Dismay crossed his features so swiftly she almost didn't see it.

"We were speaking of selecting a pony for young Lord Drayton."

"Oh, aye, 'tis a fine idea."

"We already agreed upon that," he said dryly. He glanced at Robert, who was now close enough to be obvious in his intentions.

Sarah should feel embarrassed, sympathetic toward Simon, but somehow she couldn't. Never in her life had two men tried to win her, even for all the wrong reasons.

Simon spoke between clenched teeth. "Sir Robert enjoys being the center of attention."

"To be fair, Francis did ask him to sing."

He said nothing, for now Robert was openly singing the song before her. She didn't have to hide her pleasure in his attention, for she was supposed to play along with his flirtation.

Yet even as she smiled and blushed, she felt a rising sense of confliction, wondering if he knew her response was real.

The crowd behind him parted around one of the chambermaids, who'd begun to dance alone to the music. It was Athelina, who'd responded to Robert from the moment he'd arrived. As if sensing the disturbance behind him, he at last turned around. Athelina lifted her arms in sensual abandonment, and the men murmured low, rumbling approval.

The crowd began to clap in time to Robert's lute, and the girl increased her pace, laughing. Robert looked from her to Sarah. Sarah thought he should have the decency to at least appear regretful that his wooing had been interrupted, but he only laughed, shrugging, and continued entertaining everyone in the hall.

Sarah watched the talented Athelina, almost wishing she herself could still care so little what everyone thought. Once Sarah had been like that, secure in her parents' love, at ease with her place in the world.

Athelina did not know how swiftly life could change.

Robert had long since finished singing when Walter gave him the "'tis time we speak" look. Many had already found their chambers for the night, and the lowliest of the servants wrapped themselves in blankets and lay on the rush-strewn floor near the hearth.

Sarah had earlier taken Francis up to bed, but she had not come back down, much as Robert wished for it. But perhaps it was a good thing, he thought, as he followed Walter back to their lodgings.

In the outer chamber, Walter sat down at the table, hands folded in front of him as usual, and waited for Robert to take his seat.

Robert smiled as he did so. "And what did you do today, Walter?"

"Are you asking for my report, sir?"

There was a faint trace of humor in the man's eyes that made him chuckle. "I am."

"I spent most of the day talking to people, learning who have lived here their whole lives, and who are the newcomers."

"Are there many of those?"

Walter shook his head. "Surprisingly few. People have been loyal to the Drayton family and remained for generations. Seldom have new servants been necessary. A few stable hands were hired about five years ago, several new farm tenants three years ago, but no one with a reason to kill their lord."

Robert arched an eyebrow. "And then there's the last newcomer, Sarah."

"Aye. She's been here two years now. Apparently she was only skin and bones when she arrived."

Robert frowned.

"Everyone knew of her husband's death," Walter continued, "but no one mentioned rumors of murder."

"Did you?" he asked stiffly.

"Nay, I did not." Walter eyed him. "Did you think I would inflame them all against her?"

"Of course you would not jeopardize our investigation."

The Bladesman nodded, but Robert sensed he'd made a mistake, revealing too much sympathy for Sarah.

"Had she been ill?" Robert asked.

"None mentioned it. They all thought she'd fallen on hard times after her husband's death."

"She revealed a bit to me about her life before she came here."

"Then your methods are winning her over?"

If Walter was being sarcastic, he was hiding it well. And how could Robert talk about his methods? They might be working *for* him in some ways, but *against* him in others. So he only nodded, then spoke about Sarah's childhood, her father's disastrous hand in the marriage contract, and her unhappy marriage.

"Many reasons to murder her husband," Walter said thoughtfully.

"Why? She lost everything when he died."

"But if she was as ignorant of the marriage contract as her father, then she didn't know what the outcome would be. She might have thought she'd be rich and in command of her own destiny."

"She said her husband fell from his horse when they were together."

"And it sounds like there were no witnesses, if people only believed her guilty of murder but could not swear to it. I have already sent a man to her late husband's family. We will receive details soon. I also left a report about our progress for the League."

"Did you have much to write?" Robert asked with faint sarcasm.

"Enough. We are proceeding slowly, but the pace is necessary. You toured the castle with Sarah today. What did you learn?"

Robert explained their conclusions, but found himself hesitant to talk about her denial that she was Drayton's mistress. It might sound like he was defending her, as if he'd let his supposed instincts as a womanizer influence him.

"I spoke a bit more about Sir Anthony with Simon Chapman, for Francis's guardian has another strong motive for murder."

"The man is a knight, well respected at court."

"Murderers can't be well respected?" Robert asked, a smile tugging one corner of his mouth. "Then I went over the account books with Sir Daniel."

"And Sarah, too."

"Aye, I kept her with me for her reactions, and the treasurer's reaction to her. There was nothing suspicious from either one of them, and the ledgers were flawless."

"Then 'twould seem that the treasurer has no motive to harm his lord."

"True," Robert admitted.

And returning to the topic of Sir Anthony, he told Walter that the guardian had made no changes in running the estate since he'd taken over.

"That means nothing, of course," Robert added. "If

Sir Anthony killed Lord Drayton, he would be foolish to alter things so quickly. He has Francis's whole
childhood to do as he wishes. And if Francis somehow dies before he comes of age, all the better for his
guardian."

Walter only nodded.

Robert found himself wanting to insist that Sir
Anthony had just as much of a motive as Sarah, but
he did not need to press the point. He felt conflicted,
angry, as his brain and his loins seemed to fight over
Sarah.

Walter took a breath. "Sarah came to speak with
me as you were leaving on the hunt."

Robert tensed, which surprised him. He had never
been one to worry about things not in his control.

"We spoke of nothing important, but I sensed something . . . different . . . about her. Have you spoken to
her about being a suspect?"

"Nay, not specifically," Robert said. "But she knows
everyone at Drayton Hall is a suspect until we've ruled
them out. Yet, we had a discussion that might have
made her realize the precariousness of her situation. I
spoke to her about being Drayton's mistress, and she
denied such a relationship."

He waited for Walter to express some kind of surprise or curiosity, but there was nothing. Did the man
not even care that the League might be wrong?

"She seemed genuinely stunned to me," Robert continued, "if her scarlet blush meant anything. And shocked, too, that her friends would believe such a thing of her."

"In this matter, I believe she's telling the truth."

Robert stiffened. "But that is against everything the League told us."

"I spoke with Drayton's personal valet."

"I haven't even met him yet."

"He is a very private man, above participating in gossip of any kind, even to deny a rumor. But he reluctantly admitted to me that Drayton never took Sarah Audley to his bed. The viscount did not have a mistress at all."

Robert sat back in his chair, feeling stunned and trying not to show it. "And you believe him?"

"I do."

"But that changes everything the League wanted us to do."

"Does it? Perhaps Sarah wanted to be his mistress, even planted the rumors herself to induce Drayton to succumb. Her chambers were connected to his. In some ways she probably felt like his wife, especially since she was caring for his child. Did she want more, and when he wouldn't give it to her, she killed him?"

He just couldn't imagine the Sarah he knew as that cold and calculating. But those were his personal feelings, and not something that mattered in their investigation.

Yet—was he truly beginning to think she might be innocent?

He had to speak up now, regardless of what Walter thought his motivations were. "I need more proof if I'm to be certain she's the murderer."

The Bladesman said nothing.

"We came here with specific instructions because the League had deduced that Sarah Audley was our target. We were only to gather the final proof, and carry out her punishment, if there wasn't enough evidence to bring her openly to justice." He looked into his partner's eyes. "But Walter, the League's determination of her guilt was based on incorrect assumptions. She was not Drayton's mistress. We came in here with preconceived notions, when we should have been impartial."

"You have looked from the beginning at the others in the household."

Was that a compliment? "It isn't enough. I want to broaden the list of suspects. Anyone could have used that arsenic. I haven't fully investigated the steward yet, and who knows? Perhaps someone was Drayton's secret mistress, letting Sarah take the blame, and we just haven't found her yet. And I have a special interest in Sir Anthony Ramsey. With his cousin's death, he came into control over a very large group of estates."

"But only temporarily."

"Aye, but a boy's life is fragile, and Ramsey's control could become permanent. Money is a powerful motive," he said, remembering the treasurer's words.

"You are in command," Walter said.

"Yet I'm going against what the League wished of us."

"'Tis your choice, and you will have to abide by the results." He stood up. "Robert, be careful not to call attention to your skills."

"My singing was that impressive?" He held up both hands, smiling. "I know, you mean during the hunt. I will be more careful. You only learned League skills as an adult, where I've had them bred into me since childhood. Just remember, the only hunts I've ever been on have been with Bladesmen, a most competitive group when all together."

"I know," Walter answered.

He turned and left without even a good night. Robert thought that didn't bode well. Walter seemed to be rigidly adhering to the assignment from the League, and obviously wasn't impressed that Robert was altering it. Did Bladesmen never show initiative? But he'd been taught to do so, for a Bladesman never knew what he might face on his own.

Butting heads with Walter made Robert wonder if

the League would have even chosen him if he hadn't spent his childhood being trained by them. Perhaps as an adult he hadn't proven worthy.

He felt a sharp pain that was almost physical, but wasn't. Grief?

Nay . . . loneliness.

He'd never felt it before. He'd always had his brothers. But Adam was married, with an earldom to rule, and Paul was simply . . . gone. Paul, who was almost another side of himself. Their friendly competitiveness with each other had carried him through endless lessons, forcing him to do his best.

Robert ran a hand through his hair, feeling exhausted. Now everything rested on him, including a partner who didn't believe in his methods and conclusions. He was truly alone.

But whatever the outcome to his own career with the League, he had to treat Sarah with fairness. If she was innocent, he would prove it and find the real killer, working against the League if he had to.

Chapter 13

Sarah didn't sleep well. Too many nightmares about murder and imprisonment—then too many dreams about Robert's sweet kiss, and what might have happened between them.

After mass, as they all broke their fast in the great hall, Robert watched her, smiling. He only nodded at the maidservant Athelina, who displayed her disappointment far too obviously by flouncing from the hall.

Sarah escorted Francis to his studies with the tutor, and helped raise the boy's excitement by promising that he could begin thinking about having his own pony.

Francis clapped his hands together. "Really, mistress? At last, my own pony?"

"You have shown yourself ready," she said, smiling.

She was startled when he threw open the door to the chaplain's quarters.

"Father Osborne, guess what!"

The priest looked up from the books spread at his table, his balding head gleaming in the sun that shone through the windows. He winced at Francis's exuberance, and Sarah gave him an apologetic shrug, even as she backed out and shut the door behind her. The poor priest would have to be the one to calm the boy down.

"Good morning."

She jumped and gasped, then heard Robert chuckling behind her. She slumped back against the stone wall, hand to her chest, even as he loomed above her, his face full of smiles.

"Robert!" she cried, though she had enough of her wits not to speak too loudly. She looked both ways down the corridor, but saw no one observing them. "My heart beats so loudly I fear it will burst."

Without thinking of the consequences, she took his hand and put it over her heart. "See what you did?"

His charming smile faded and her eyes widened as she realized his palm rested on the upper curve of her breast. Her startled nerves transformed into a jumble of confusion and yearning. His hand was warm even through her clothing, so large that if he slid it lower, he could cup her entire breast.

Then he removed his hand and spoke as if she hadn't just forced him to touch her.

"I have something to tell you. Where can we speak in private?"

She almost suggested her own bedchamber. She was shocked at her own bold thoughts where Robert was concerned. What was wrong with her? Was her mind playing tricks, making her think his pretend flirtation was real?

"I know not," she murmured helplessly. "These chambers are for other servants of the Drayton estate."

"And none are empty?"

"Oh, well, since Master Frobisher is also the bailiff of this castle, not just the steward, there is one chamber not in use—"

"Take me there."

She hurried away, feeling him follow her closely. She was nervous and could barely lift the latch on the door, but at last they were inside. The room smelled stale and unused, with a few simple furnishings. Robert closed the door behind him and just looked at her, his white teeth shining in the gloom. She opened a set of shutters nearby so that she could see him better.

"Is something amiss?" she asked.

"Lord Drayton's valet confirmed that you weren't Drayton's mistress."

Thoughtlessly she clutched his hands, ignoring his

startled expression. She stared at him with such hope and gladness that she felt as if only his touch held her tethered to the ground. Did this now help remove her from his list of suspects? She had to hear the truth from his lips, not just assume what he—and Sir Walter—thought about her.

"So you could not take my word on this?" she asked, trying to distance herself just a bit. "You had to question another?"

"Sir Walter spoke to Drayton's valet."

"And you would have believed me without such proof."

When he said nothing, she let go of his hands. But she couldn't blame him. He was here at the king's behest.

"This was something Walter needed to hear," Robert continued.

"Because I am a suspect in my lord's murder."

"Everyone is, Sarah. You know that."

"But Robert, if you both thought I was Drayton's mistress, then that must have made me even more suspicious in your eyes. Tell me the truth."

"I care not for suspicions that have no proof."

"Then you believe me?"

He said nothing, but his jaw clenched and he closed his eyes. A struggle was obviously going on inside him, between duty and—and what?

"Robert, do you *believe* in me?" She whispered the words now, cupping his face with both trembling hands, her chest tight with an ache she couldn't describe, couldn't begin to understand. But just touching him soothed her.

And then it was as if something in him released in a giant rush of movement. He turned and pressed her up against the wall, his expression harsh and urgent. His mouth covered hers, and the sweet kiss of yesterday was gone, replaced by one of fierce hunger. She parted her mouth because his demanded it, felt the sweep of his tongue, the roughness of his hands holding her still. Never before had a man kissed her as if he would die if he couldn't have her, and it was this kind of desperation she sensed in Robert. His body held hers immobile, but instead of feeling frightening, it made her light-headed with arousal. He explored her mouth with greediness, even as his hands moved restlessly from her shoulders to her sides to her hips. He cupped her buttocks, pulling her closer. Helplessly she parted her thighs, felt the pressure of his leg so intimately against her. She moaned at the sensual contact, the heat, the movement. With his mouth he captured every sound. Her hands slid up his arms and across those shoulders, so broad and bunched with muscle. She returned his kiss with equal passion, stroking his tongue with her own, leaning up into him, wanting more, needing more.

The sheer overwhelming temptation of it all was what finally penetrated her foggy brain. She broke the kiss, gasping for air, for sanity.

"This is wrong," she whispered.

She felt his chest expand with his own need to breathe.

He growled the words, "This doesn't feel wr—" Then he broke off, his expression almost angry, but she sensed that he wasn't angry with her.

She couldn't move, and he didn't release her. His body he pressed deeper between her thighs, until his erection against her most sensitive flesh made her shudder. She licked her dry lips, gasping for air, even as he watched her mouth.

"If anyone sees this," she whispered, "it will only make me look more guilty."

"They won't see it, because it won't happen again."

How could he say that, when the desire that simmered between them seemed uncontrollable? Her reputation, her very life, was at stake.

"Sarah, I'm not—I can't be the man you—" He gritted his teeth on a groan.

She knew so little about him, had thought he was a man who enjoyed himself, even though he had a serious mission. But now, looking into his eyes, she thought she saw more, a man under assault by forces she didn't know about. What had shaped him—what had harmed him?

She tossed her head, needing to challenge him. "Then I guess I'll have to dream about Simon."

His frown was forbidding. Even his nostrils flared. Then he took her mouth in a rough, wet kiss. "Has he even tried to kiss you like a lover?"

"He is a gentleman."

He slid his hands up her sides, until they just touched the outer curves of her breasts. "I am no gentleman."

They stared at each other. Though Sarah wanted to revel in this heated moment, there was a part of her that could not forget her danger. He hadn't said he believed in her innocence, and surely, Sir Walter was not convinced. Robert might be her only chance to save herself, but he was fighting what they felt. She needed him to be sympathetic to her.

"Perhaps I prefer a gentleman," she said breathlessly, aware of his fingers so close to her breasts. "Simon is a persistent man, and I cannot just . . . spurn his advances. We're eating a meal today away from the castle, out of doors."

He gave her a rakish smile. "Why, thank you for inviting me to join you."

She was relieved at his persistence. She felt a wave of regret and sadness, knowing she might be using

Robert and his feelings for her, but also knowing she had no choice.

For a moment, he leaned down as if to kiss her again. She waited, barely breathing. He closed his eyes and stepped away. It was as if she had forgotten how to hold herself up. She remained slumped for a moment against the wall, staring up at him, and was relieved when he put his hand on the back of a chair to steady himself. She wasn't the only one overwhelmed.

"Do we leave just before dinner?" he asked.

She could only nod.

"I'll be waiting."

And then he was gone, and she was left to remind herself of all the reasons why she'd been happy with Simon's courtship. Foolishly, she'd once thought because he'd been careful and restrained as he pursued her, that he was safe, that he wasn't pretending to desire her, as her husband had done. She'd been trying to be so cautious—

But now she didn't even remember caution when Robert was near. He put her in danger, physically, mentally, emotionally—and she couldn't stop herself from wanting him.

Even though he might still think her a murderer.

Robert felt dazed as he departed the chamber, as if he'd left part of himself behind. He'd gone to relieve some of Sarah's anxiety, and instead, he'd put her against a wall to have his way with her.

Where had *that* come from?

He walked the corridors, nodding when he passed the occasional servant, but it was all by habit. His mind was too busy trying to understand how he'd let himself succumb so quickly, so completely, to his passion for Sarah.

Again, he felt like he was a child's toy, spinning out of control, not knowing which way he would land the next time. How soon would it be before someone else in the household saw his surrender—before Walter saw it? This was his last chance to prove himself to the League, and he was destroying it. He had to remember what was most important to him.

He found himself outside by habit, knew he should be in the tiltyard this morn. Hard work would help clear his mind, help him focus on strengthening his body for any battles to come.

And then he saw Simon Chapman, the man who opposed him for Sarah's interest, donning his gauntlets in preparation. Robert had known he should let Sarah and Chapman have their time together. It would be better for all if Sarah turned away from Robert. But the dark demon of jealousy yet raged inside Robert, and had won a battle.

As Robert approached, Chapman glanced up, his

helm tucked beneath his arm. "Sir Robert," he said in that formal, even voice of his.

"Sir Simon," he answered pleasantly. "A perfect day for a meal in the countryside."

Chapman arched a brow, his expression turning cool. "You heard about my outing with Mistress Sarah."

"She told me about it. She felt so bad that I, as a guest, had nothing special to do that she invited me along."

He waited for Chapman to scoff, to become angry, to show *something*. But the man had a belief in himself that only allowed him to nod.

"By all means, Sir Robert, do join us," he said. "How kind of Mistress Sarah to take pity on you."

Robert laughed, reluctantly admiring the man.

But Chapman was a member of the Ramsey garrison, a knight who'd served under Francis's guardian. It could not hurt for Robert to learn more of the knight who controlled Francis's inheritance, his very life.

As Robert donned his own chest and back plates, Chapman waited with his sword tip in the ground, both gauntleted hands resting on the hilt.

Chapman said, "Mistress Sarah is a gentle woman, but you do not expect *me* to take pity on you."

The morning had just become more interesting. "Of course not, Sir Simon. I assume you do not yet have a sparring partner."

"As a matter of fact, I do not. Are you volunteering, Sir Robert?"

"I will always volunteer my services to help those in need."

Chapman gave a faint smile. "Then consider me in need of a demonstration of your skill."

Robert bowed, even as he turned to examine a collection of swords. There were some who would only use their own, but he always preferred to test his worth with any weapon at hand, for as a Bladesman, one never knew what weapon might be his only resort in battle.

When he felt someone watching him, he looked up, expecting to see Chapman, but it was Walter who regarded him coolly. He hefted his chosen sword in an informal salute to his partner, who only nodded in return.

As usual, much of the tiltyard paused to see how the men representing the king fared in practice. Robert had grown used to the curiosity these past few days. Chapman glanced about briefly at the unabashed attention, then donned his helm.

Robert had studied the technique of every man practicing each day, committing strengths and weaknesses to memory in case he had to face a man in battle rather than training. Although Chapman had proven himself quick in reflex, his swordsmanship was average at best, and not very original. Robert would have to make the fight seem even, without overwhelming and embarrassing his opponent.

But Chapman seemed inspired after learning about Robert's intrusion on his time with Sarah. Robert actually enjoyed himself, testing the knight's defenses, parrying aside several unexpected sword thrusts. Chapman's final slash had Robert rolling on the ground to avoid the sword, then coming up to knock it from the knight's hand.

Chapman stood still a moment, breathing hard, his hand surely stinging from the blow though he tried not to show it.

"Well done, Sir Robert."

He grinned. "I return the compliment, sir."

"The way you disarmed me—I barely saw the twist of your wrist. Quite a skill."

Robert only bowed. Around them, he heard the clash of swords as other men continued their practice now that the display was over.

"How are you with a dagger?" Chapman asked, with no attempt at casualness.

He chuckled. "Fighting with one, or throwing it?"

"Throwing it."

"Fair, I would say," he lied. "Shall we test my ability?"

* · * *

Sarah felt almost pretty after changing into a red gown. She'd convinced herself to look forward to her afternoon courtship. Having two suitors should be enjoyable—

If only she were playing fair with them both.

But she wasn't. She was treating Simon lightly, unable to be careful about hurting his feelings when her own life was in danger. And now she might hurt him worse, as she used him to make Robert jealous. This was not her finest moment, but she was desperate.

And then there was Robert, whom she wanted to kiss until she was senseless—yet she could not trust him in the least. He'd lied to her, even though he had reason, and she sensed there were other things he was not telling her. How could she be certain if he wanted to prove her innocence—or her guilt? Were they simply using each other, for different reasons? Yet none of that seemed to matter when she was in his arms. All she wanted to do then was . . . feel.

There was a quick knock on her door, and she wondered if someone had grown too impatient. But before she could even call out, the door opened and Margery ducked inside.

The seamstress grinned. "Guess what."

"I cannot imagine," she said, hands on her hips.

Though her first instinct lately was to assume the worst, Margery's demeanor discouraged that.

"Sir Simon and Sir Robert challenged each other today on the tiltyard."

"Challenged?" Sarah repeated incredulously. "Seriously challenged?"

"Challenged as a means of trainin'."

Robert had been trained in London, skilled perhaps far more than Simon. And he knew it. What kind of tension would permeate what was supposed to be a pleasant afternoon—or did she *want* that tension simmering between them? But she couldn't allow Robert to know that. She would have to pretend outrage for his benefit.

Margery considered her with obvious curiosity. "By yer expression, ye're not pleased."

"I am not. Where is Sir Robert at this moment?"

"Changin' his garments. I understand that you, he, and Sir Simon are supposed to meet—"

"My plans are already known?" she cried in disbelief.

Margery spread her hands wide in a helpless shrug. "Not exactly, but Sir Simon was makin' it no secret that you and he—"

Sarah groaned and swept past her friend. "Will you still be able to eat with Francis at dinner?" she called over her shoulder.

"Of course! And I will be receivin' details when ye return?"

"If I leave anyone alive."

She heard Margery's laughter even as she marched down the corridor. Rather than cross the open court-yard, she followed the passage beneath the guest lodgings, then stomped up the circular stairs to Robert and Walter's chambers. She banged on the door, then threw it open, expecting to ascend an-other floor to his bedchamber, but came up short in stunned disbelief.

Robert was sitting in a bathing tub before the bare hearth in the outer chamber.

Naked.

They stared at each other in surprise. She should have given him her back immediately, or at least turned her gaze away while she debated how best to handle such a situation—especially after he gave her a slow, knowing smile.

But she couldn't look away. She simply stared at him with wide, appreciative eyes. She knew a man's body, of course, but her husband had been the son of a landowner, more concerned with business dealings than the tiltyard. He paid for whatever military pro-tection he'd deemed necessary.

But Robert's wide shoulders and muscular chest spoke of a very different life. Scars nicked his flesh here and there, but they did not detract from his handsomeness.

He didn't even cover himself, she thought, forcing her sagging mouth to close. Instead, he spread his arms on the rim on the tub, which looked too small to contain him.

She found herself wondering how else his physique differed from her late husband's.

"Does someone else need the bathing tub?" he asked, one eyebrow lifted in a deliberate taunt.

"Why are you not in your bedchamber?" Instead of commanding, she sounded far too breathless.

"The two footmen were so scrawny, I didn't have the heart to ask them to carry this up another floor, let alone make so many trips with the water buckets." He grinned and sent a splash toward her that didn't quite reach. "But I commend their diligence, for the water is hot."

"To soothe your aches?" she asked between gritted teeth, reminding herself that she had to pretend to be angry.

"My aches?"

"Or was the only pain to your pride, after your deliberate battle with my suitor?"

She stalked toward him, and to her satisfaction, that damnable smile of his began to fade.

Chapter 14

Robert had been surprised when Sarah barged into his lodgings. Walter could return at any moment, and that would not bode well for his future. But she looked adorably furious. He'd expected her to turn away at his nudity, perhaps cover her eyes, but she'd unabashedly stared at him with interest.

And his traitorous loins had responded with a salute.

Now she was moving toward him, and he wondered how close she would dare to come.

"You think I 'battled' Sir Simon?" he asked.

"You talked your way into accompanying us, and then you had the gall to challenge him?"

He sat up a little straighter in the tub. The water sloshed dangerously, and he was satisfied to see her momentarily taken aback. Did she worry he'd stand up to confront her?

"I did not challenge him," he said lazily.

"Then why did you end up sparring with him? And did you harm him?"

"I am glad you knew that I would be the one in position to do harm."

She rolled her eyes. "You were raised in London, and have been chosen by the king for your talents."

Chosen by men the king trusted, he thought.

"So tell me what your purpose was!"

"I had no purpose at all. He asked if I would spar with him, and I agreed." He rubbed a small cloth in the soft soap and began to slowly wash his chest. To his satisfaction, her gaze dropped to his hands, before returning to his face. And then she looked down again.

He smiled.

She scowled.

"Of course," he continued, using the soapy cloth down his stomach, "I had just informed him that I would be accompanying the both of you on your little walk."

She groaned and briefly closed her eyes. "You simply could not resist."

"Nay, I could not," he answered, trying to appear abashed. "He did mention his belief that you were only taking pity on me. Are you, Sarah?" He grinned.

"You were the one who wanted my help, Robert. I have been giving *you* the opportunity to pretend flirta-

tion toward me before all of Drayton Hall. *You* were the one who forced me to allow you to accompany me—"

"Forced?"

"Aye, forced!"

She advanced another step, and he realized how rewarding it was to provoke her. "You could have refused," he pointed out, smiling.

"Refused?"

Something in her expression changed, intriguing him. What had she meant to say before thinking better of it?

"I am too polite," she said, lifting her chin smugly.

"So 'tis politeness you feel when we kiss?" he asked, letting the timbre of his voice drop. He shouldn't pursue this, he should tell her to leave—

Her eyes widened, and that smugness fled. "You know how you make me feel," she whispered, suddenly serious. "You think you have me flustered with this—this masculine display. But I was a married woman, not a virgin you can so easily tease."

Now she was *challenging* him? How unexpected from a woman he considered so in command of her emotions. She was staring into his face, but she was close enough now that if she looked down, she would see more—although he wasn't certain how much, considering the soapy haze in the water.

"I do not think of you as a virgin," he answered, reluctantly amused.

She was circling the tub now, her gaze inscrutable. "You obviously don't think of me as an innocent, with the way you last kissed me."

"Compared to the way *you* kissed *me* the first time?"

Her cheeks almost reddened enough to match her hair.

He tilted his head back, letting his eyes drift down her body, enjoying himself, though he knew this was too dangerous. To his surprise, she moved behind him and he tensed, wondering if she would touch him, and what he would do in return. His arousal became an ache that was difficult to deny.

God, how she affected him. He wanted to pull her into the tub with him, to let her wet hair fall all about him, to pluck each wet garment from her skin and see what was hidden beneath.

He didn't turn his head, reveling in the excitement of the unknown and the forbidden.

She whispered behind him, "You mustn't forget to wash your hair."

And then she dumped a bucket of steaming water over his head. He half came out of the tub in surprise, and she gave a squeak as she fled the chamber.

He sank back in the tub and laughed helplessly.

* * *

Sarah rode her horse between her two suitors and told herself she would enjoy the day. The sky had grown cloudy, and a faint breeze now stirred, but it was lovely to leave the castle and some of her cares behind. For a moment, she felt a stirring of guilt, but she squashed it.

They followed the road toward the village, speaking little. The silence should be pleasant, but she was finding it increasingly difficult not to look at Robert and remember him nude in the bathing tub. She hadn't been able to see much beneath the water, but she was dismayed by how much she'd wished otherwise. She felt embarrassed and overheated even as she thought he'd been aroused. It had taken so little—she hadn't touched him or bared her own flesh.

"This way, Sarah," Simon said, pointing down a path that took them into the woodland.

"Ah, a man who knows where he's going," Robert said cheerfully.

"A woman expects such treatment," the other man responded.

Strangely, their verbal sparring began to cheer her.

The path narrowed, forcing Simon to take the lead and Robert to ride behind her, limiting further discussion until they reached a clearing, where the trees thinned and running water could be heard. Simon stopped, and she was able to ride up next to him. She sighed her delight. Light speckled the glade through the treetops; a stream rushed in a small waterfall down an embankment, tumbling over rocks, and then threading its way through a patch of blue forget-me-nots.

"How lovely," she cried, smiling up at Simon, reaching to gently touch his arm.

His answering smile had begun slowly, but now he looked down at her hand and brightened.

"Indeed," Robert called as he came up beside them. "What a romantic you are, Sir Simon."

Simon glanced at him impassively, then proceeded to dismount. He was just a bit quicker than Robert in reaching to help her down, and she rewarded him with a pleased smile. They each reached to take her horse. Robert gestured for Simon to do the honor. While both men saw to the horses' comfort, she walked toward the stream and sat on a boulder, listening to the twittering of the birds and the buzzing of insects.

She inhaled the faint scent of the forget-me-nots and the cool moistness of the water and tried to relax. But she couldn't. The darkness of suspicion hovered over her, and all she had between it and her was her hope that she could convince Robert of her innocence.

The men came toward her at last, and she turned to face them. They were both good-looking men, and any woman would be thrilled to have them with her. They eyed each other competitively as they approached.

She leaned back on her hands to look up at them. "Should I be worried that you two chose today to spar with each other on the tiltyard?"

"I like to test myself as often as possible," Robert said. "Sir Simon presented a good challenge."

Simon harrumphed. "He is being far too modest. His skills are superior to mine." His voice said he was not offended in the least—where military training was concerned.

Robert glanced at him ruefully. "I hope I did not make you regret sparring me."

"Of course not. You never make anyone think ill of you in any way, Sir Robert," Simon said, openly facing his rival. " 'Tis a natural ability that must aid you well on such assignments. Yet it can be . . . annoying."

Robert laughed. "Good of you to admit it."

Simon continued to study him. "You do not seem to let the tension of your investigation bother you."

"I cannot afford such a weakness," he said, propping his booted foot on a boulder near Sarah. "The success of my mission depends on my ability to be objective. If I let everything bother me, I would not prove useful to the king."

For a moment, she thought she sensed a tension

within Robert's words, belying his easy demeanor.

"And how is your mission progressing?" Simon boldly asked.

Robert grinned. "'Tis progressing as well as can be expected."

"Are you close to knowing the identity of the murderer?"

She waited tensely.

"Closer than when we arrived," Robert said, giving a faint shrug.

Simon shook his head. "That is not much of an answer."

"I cannot discuss it, of course."

"Simon realizes how difficult it is to live like this," Sarah said.

Both men looked at her.

She spread her hands wide. "We all go about our business knowing that at any moment, we could be talking to a murderer, a person who cruelly took a man's life, who made a boy an orphan. 'Tis . . . disconcerting."

"Wouldn't you rather discuss something else?" Robert asked. "I, too, looked forward to this afternoon as a means of escape."

"So you're not evaluating either of us?" Simon asked.

He chuckled. "I've long since evaluated both of you."

"Should we be offended, Simon?" Sarah asked in a dry tone.

"Nay, because all are suspect," Simon responded.

"But perhaps I want to be simply evaluated as a woman." She held her breath, shocked by the words that had tumbled unthinkingly from her lips. But she needed Robert's attention on her.

Robert's smile slowly widened into a wicked grin. Simon's eyebrows rose.

"How terrible of us to ignore you," Robert said, coming to sit beside her on the boulder.

She was forced to inch sideways, yet she could still feel his hip pressed along hers.

Simon frowned. "I shall fetch our meal."

When Simon was out of earshot, Sarah elbowed Robert. "How terrible of you to tease him."

He pressed a little closer to her. "I am enjoying myself."

It seemed her attempt to make him jealous was working. But they could say no more as Simon returned with a leather satchel and knelt down in the grass far enough away from the mist of the stream. He removed several parcels wrapped in cloth, then two corked bottles. He had linens, plates, goblets—two of each.

"I did not have enough notice that you were joining

us," he said to Robert, his smile full of regret that was so obviously insincere.

"That is all right," Robert replied. "Sarah will share with me."

She sighed.

When at last they were all sitting on the blanket, Sarah with her legs tucked beneath her, she smiled with appreciation at Simon as he placed chunks of cheese and bread on her plate, as well as freshly picked berries. She chose cider while the two men opted for the red wine. Simon filled up his goblet, then offered Robert the bottle, who raised it in thanks before taking a swallow. He leaned back on one elbow, his body long and lazy.

To fill the silence, Sarah asked, "Do you have family, Simon?"

He nodded. "A sister, Isabel." His normally peaceful expression turned faintly melancholy.

"Are you close?" she asked softly.

"Once. But we are not together often, and we do not agree on much."

"Is she married?"

"Nay, and that is what we do not agree on," he said dryly.

Robert looked interested. "From your words, I assume your parents are dead. Does that not make you her guardian, which gives you a say in her marriage?

Not that I have any sisters . . ." he added, raising both hands.

"Isabel believes she knows best," Simon said. "If I put forward a good man's name for her consideration, 'tis a guarantee she will not be interested in him."

He said the words lightly, but Sarah sensed a deep pain he tried to bury. To be at its best, marriage needed to be a willing partnership. Her husband hadn't wanted the position, not in the truest sense of the word. But it was an ache that was part of her past, and she was surprised that it did not hurt quite so much.

"Perhaps she is simply confused about what she wants," Robert offered. "I, for one, truly do not know what marriage entails."

Simon swung his head around to stare at Robert. "And what does that mean?"

Sarah, too, waited with avid curiosity to hear the response.

"My parents died when I was very young. I did not see another marriage up close until I was nearly grown."

"How can that be?" Simon demanded.

"For protection, my brothers and I were raised in a monastery."

Sarah gaped at him. "You—in a monastery? With priests?"

"And no women," Robert said with an exaggerated sigh.

"You seem to have figured out what to do with them," Simon said flatly.

Robert laughed aloud. "Aye, I waited a long time for the chance to be near women. I even escaped once."

"Did the monks treat you so badly?" she asked in a hesitant voice. She tried to imagine a life in the cold world of men, without a mother's comfort. In her mind she could see dark-haired little boys, brothers who only had each other, alone in the unforgiving night. Who had taught Robert about women—and not in a sexual way? He was making light of it all, but surely he had to have felt very different and confused when he first emerged into the outside world.

"Nay, I was treated well," Robert said. "I simply wanted to see a girl. Any girl. I had but fifteen years, and girls dominated my thoughts."

"Why am I not surprised," Simon muttered.

"You were fifteen once," Robert shot back. "Do you not remember it?"

Simon shook his head with exasperation, but Sarah could sense he was suppressing a smile.

"And what happened on your daring adventure?" she asked, intrigued.

Robert stretched out onto his back, hands clasped beneath his head as he grinned. "I met a dairymaid."

She leaned forward eagerly.

"But alas, I only was granted several kisses before my brother arrived to cart me away. But they were kisses that had to live in my solitary dreams for the next several years."

"Are we supposed to feel sorry for you?" Simon asked.

"Nay, I have long since made up for my abnormal youth." He smiled at Sarah.

"Why did you and your brothers need protection as children?" Simon pressed.

Robert returned his gaze to the trees. "Our parents were dead. 'Twas deemed a prudent decision."

Not a very good explanation, for it only whetted her appetite for more. Had the king chosen him because he was far too familiar with the consequences of murder? Surely that was jumping to conclusions. She could tell he wouldn't confide anything further to Simon. But perhaps, someday, to her . . .

"It goes without saying," Robert continued, "that since I was not in the presence of married couples, I was also not near children. I was rather amazed when young Lord Drayton took to me so easily."

"You accept him and treat him as a friend," she said. "Children sense such things."

Simon's lips thinned as he pressed them together.

"Oh, but Simon, I do not mean to imply that you

are supposed to befriend a five-year-old boy," she hastened to say.

"'Twould not be my place," Simon said. "I am a mere knight in his guardian's household, and he is a viscount."

"And I am only a stranger who represents something new," Robert said. "'Tis Sarah whom Francis loves."

She gave him a faint smile, toying with a berry in her hand until the juice ran down her fingers. She put it to her lips and saw that Robert watched her too closely, his smile fading. In just that moment, she felt a pulse deep in her belly, as if it answered him.

After Simon packed most of the left-over food and plates in the satchel, he went to the horses.

Sarah turned back to Robert, who was watching her intently, his smile gone. "I may know nothing about marriage," he finally murmured in a low voice, "but I enjoy the softer world of women, who are like presents from God to savor as one unwraps their secrets." He frowned and looked away, as if he regretted speaking.

Sarah's entire body flushed with heat and she found herself moving restlessly, that pulse deep inside her ever stronger. She'd wanted to make him jealous, but she herself had learned a lesson in how easily he affected her.

As Simon returned to them, she heard a low rumble in the distance. They all looked up, none having noticed that the sky had gone gray.

"I think 'tis about to rain." Simon lifted a hand as if to test for droplets. "And I just finished tightening the saddle girths."

"What a shame to end our afternoon," Robert said, rising swiftly to his feet.

Both men reached a hand down to her, then looked at each other. Simon was patient and intractable, as if he only had to wait out Robert's infatuation—or his departure.

She took each of their hands and allowed them to pull her upright. As they rode back through the trees, droplets of water began to fall softly on her.

Robert was doing everything she wanted him to do, as if she willed it. Yet she worried about using his desire for her, should her situation grow worse. What kind of woman did that make her?

The rain began to fall harder.

Whatever kind of woman she was, she would at least be alive and free—and strong because she had to be. She wouldn't trust Robert, of course, because she felt as if he had another purpose, one she didn't understand. He'd lied to her already; who knew when he would do so again?

Chapter 15

As Sarah, Robert, and Simon entered the great hall after the midday meal, she felt the gazes of many people linger on them with open curiosity. The two men stood at her back, one serious, the other cheerful and teasing—but with a serious mission that belied the façade he showed the world.

They were soaked through to the skin, of course, and she knew her hair had partially fallen to her shoulders, standing out in humid curls. She shivered a bit, though she felt more damp than cold.

"I regret I did not think to bring a cloak," Simon said.

"'Tis the height of summer," she answered, smiling back at him over her shoulder.

"And if you thought of everything," Robert quipped, "we would think you far too perfect."

"Mistress Sarah!"

Francis came running toward her, his white face full of relief.

"My lord?" she said curiously.

He flung his arms wide, and although she tried to stop him due to her wet garments, he managed to throw himself against her legs.

"You're back!"

She looked up and found Margery's gaze. The other woman could only shrug, her expression confused.

"Of course I'm back, Francis," she said, gently separating him from her. "But you can see how wet I am. I do not need you catching a fever."

"Are *you* going to catch a fever?" he asked, freckles standing out in his pale face.

Oh, she'd spoken thoughtlessly to a boy whose father had so recently died. "Of course not!" she said, chucking him under the chin as she always did. "I am just so protective of you. But though we were caught in the rain, 'tis so warm we won't even take a chill."

Francis looked past her to Robert and Simon, and for a moment, she thought he looked almost jealous that someone besides himself had had her attention. He worried his lip between his teeth. This was as new to him as it was to her.

Simon nodded down to him. "My lord, thank you for allowing me to spend the afternoon with your nurse."

To her surprise, Robert squatted down on his haunches.

"I offer you my gratitude as well, my lord," he said. "Sometimes men forget that boys need their nurses. We hope you understand."

"Why did *you* need her?" Francis asked, kicking his toe repeatedly in the rushes.

Simon and Robert exchanged another look. Sarah could almost imagine the thought Simon directed at Robert: *You're so glib; you answer.*

"We like her company," Robert said, "just as you do."

"Does she make you laugh?"

He smiled. "Sometimes she does."

"I think *you* make her laugh," Francis said. "She says I don't laugh enough anymore, but she doesn't much either."

Her throat seemed to swell closed for a moment, and she had trouble swallowing back her tears.

"Is it my turn with her now?" Francis asked.

"Of course, my lord," Robert said, rising to his feet. "And what plans do you have today?"

"We're going to the dairy shed."

"Oh?" Sarah stared down at him in surprise.

"Master Frobisher says there's something wrong, and only a woman can fix it." He frowned. "Or only you can fix it. I can't remember which."

"Then let me change and talk to Master Frobisher. Will you await me here?"

He nodded, looking back up at Robert and Simon again. Simon bowed and walked away, but she noticed that Robert hesitated.

"Have you learned any new songs on the lute today?" he asked.

"But are you not cold and wet like Mistress Sarah?" Francis asked.

"What is a little dampness to us men?"

Grinning, Francis took his hand and tugged him toward the hearth. Sarah knew she was wearing a silly, pleased smile.

Only a half hour on the clock had passed before she returned. She'd managed to find the steward in his office, where she learned that two of the dairymaids had been arguing, and it was affecting everyone's work.

When Sarah returned for Francis, she half expected Robert to ask to accompany them, now that she knew his fondness for dairymaids, but he excused himself with a bow and left for his lodgings.

Outside, Sarah walked across the courtyard, holding her cloak overhead against the rain so that Francis would do the same. He skipped at her side, his cloak flapping above him. It seemed like all was right in the world now that he had her. She only wished that this could last. But he was a growing boy, and soon he'd be offended that he needed a nurse.

Most of the cattle were kept on the pastureland outside the castle, but several dozen cows were housed in a shed within the curtain walls for the convenience of the residents. Dairymaids did the milking, as well as prepared cheeses and churned butter. When Sarah and Francis walked into the dairy, already she heard the squabbling.

"He's comin' to see me, not you!" cried one female voice.

Young, by the sound of her. Sarah sighed. Why did the cause of arguments always have to be a man?

"Did *he* say that?" taunted another voice.

Francis looked up at her in confusion.

"Go on into the shed, Francis," she said. "Be careful as you pet the cows."

He gave her a happy smile and sped off through a timbered door frame. Sarah entered the dairy itself, where there were several large tables and stools, along with butter churns, cheese molds, and shelves of aging cheese.

Five women looked up, but only three appeared happy to see her. Two of the younger women glared at each other and sulked.

Sarah had barely begun to hear their respective stories, and already she was tired of the jealousy. She

instructed the two maidservants that neither was to
have a man courting her while she was on duty, and if
they couldn't agree to that, then perhaps they should
work at one of the distant farms, where they would
see fewer people. They quickly insisted their argu-
ment wouldn't happen again.

She was glad to leave them and wander out to the
shed, where she could see the long line of cows con-
tentedly munching hay, their tails swishing away the
summer flies.

Abruptly, she heard Francis cry out. She couldn't
see him anywhere, because he wasn't as tall as the
cows. Her heart turned over as she sped down the row,
looking between each cow.

"Francis?" she cried.

Then she heard a sob. She found him at the far end
on his hands and knees near the wall, almost beneath
the large body of a placid cow.

He looked up at her with a tear-stained face,
panting.

"What happened?" She dropped to her knees
beside him and tried to pull him up into her arms.

She saw his grimace of pain. An answering pain
clenched her heart.

"Where are you hurt?"

He pointed to his head and chest, and then his tears
fell faster. She hugged him to her gently, and at last his

shuddering began to ease. The dairymaids had followed her shout, and now crowded behind her, wide-eyed and whispering. Sarah gestured with her head to urge them away.

"Tell me, Francis, what happened?"

He sat back in the straw, looking up at the cow nearby, which seemed to tower above them. "I was . . . petting her," he said, between breathy hiccups, "when she . . . let out a loud moo . . . and bumped right into me!"

"Bumped right into you?"

"She . . . pushed me right against . . . the wall. I—I couldn't breathe."

A shiver of fear curdled her stomach. She should have been with him, should have known he was too young to go wandering between such large animals.

"Breathe for me now, Francis. Does it hurt to do so?"

He complied, wincing when he inhaled deeply.

"It only hurts a little," he muttered.

She had him lie down in the straw, so that she could feel his rib cage and arms. Nothing seemed broken, but that did not mean he wasn't well and truly bruised.

"How is your head?" she asked, when at last she brought him back into her lap.

"It aches. I slammed it against the wall." His sobbing had died down enough for him to glare at the animal ignoring them. "Stupid cow."

"Did you startle her?" she asked, stroking his brown curls away from his damp forehead.

"Nay! I was only petting her and talking to her. I thought she liked me," he added, frowning.

"I'm sure she does, Francis. Something startled her. Mayhap 'twas a cat."

He perked up. "I've been looking for the cat that lives in the stables."

Sarah smiled. "Hiding from you, is he?"

"I never saw him."

"Perhaps he was too quick for you. Shall we go see if he ran to the stables, or would you rather lie down in your bedchamber?"

"The stables!"

That answer eased her tension, but not completely. She wiped his face with her apron, then held his hand as they left the shed. She wondered if her distraction over the investigation and Robert had played a part in Francis getting injured. What was wrong with her, that all of her decisions lately seemed flawed?

When a horn sounded just before supper, Robert felt an eager satisfaction. An important visitor must have been spotted outside the walls. He was glad for the distraction, for although he was talking with members of the household in the great hall as he always did, his mind kept returning to the afternoon out of doors, and the way the dappled sunlight had shined in Sarah's red curls—and the way her mouth had glistened with berry juice. She had been playful and teasing, so different once she was away from her duties. He'd wanted to lick the juice from her fingers, to—

He controlled a groan. It had been far too long since he'd bedded a woman. Why else would he be in this constant state of near arousal?

Then he saw Sarah coming in to the great hall through the double doors. The relaxed amusement of the early afternoon was gone from her expression; now she looked like a woman with a purpose.

"Master Frobisher!" she called, and when the steward hurried toward her, she told him, "There are travelers in the distance, a train of them with carts for luggage. I believe 'tis Sir Anthony and his wife."

Sir Anthony Ramsey, Robert thought with satisfaction, Francis's guardian, the man with a compelling motive to kill Drayton. Robert was looking forward to the subtle questioning, the back-and-forth of inducing a man to reveal more than he'd intended. In Robert's view, Ramsey had a much stronger motive for murder than Sarah did.

Was that what his investigation was coming to—his desperation to find someone other than Sarah to blame? But nay, he was, one by one, crossing people off his list of suspects. Logically, Ramsey was next in line.

From the hearth, Robert watched as the party entered the keep. Ramsey was in the lead, dressed in practical traveling garments that in no way displayed that he was a knight with wealth. He had light brown hair that fell straight, almost to his shoulders. He was younger than Robert had imagined, with perhaps thirty years, tall and lean, with an athletic walk that suggested he knew the tiltyard well.

His wife, Caroline, Lady Ramsey, gave a cherubic smile when she saw Francis. She was blond and femininely plump, dressed with a simple elegance that hinted at wealth, yet was still practical enough for a journey. Robert had heard from the steward that the Ramseys had no children as of yet, although they'd been married for at least five years.

Both the Ramseys greeted several servants by name, which was impressive. But then again, Ramsey had been as close to Drayton as a younger brother. Then he approached Francis and went down on one knee to hug him. They were cousins, after all, and Francis was smiling happily. Whatever Ramsey said next caused Francis's smile to slowly die, and the little boy only nodded. A reference to his dead father, perhaps? Surely the man wouldn't mention the murder investigation to a five-year-old.

Sarah stood beside Francis, listening solemnly to Ramsey, then put a hand on the boy's shoulder. Francis looked up at her, biting his lip even as he nodded and went off to play with several children.

Robert approached Sarah and Ramsey. She glanced at him casually, then with more awareness. Ramsey followed her gaze.

Robert bowed when he reached them. "Sir Anthony, I am Sir Robert Burcot." He'd long since gotten used to calling himself by any last name and thinking nothing of it. After all, his real name had been, necessarily, a secret his whole life.

"Sir Robert, lately of the king," Ramsey said, his expression solemn. "Sarah wrote to inform us of your investigation."

His wife came to stand at his side, her pleasant smile fading.

"'Tis a sad day to learn that one's cousin died because of someone's foul deeds," Ramsey continued. "May I speak with you about the investigation after supper?"

"Of course, sir," Robert said. "I will await you."

"How is young Francis?" Ramsey turned to Sarah, his gaze softening as he spoke of his ward.

"Better, Sir Anthony," she responded. "The first few weeks were difficult, but he's begun to return to his old talkativeness."

"Such an intelligent boy for one so young!" Lady Ramsey said.

"And thanks to Sir Robert," Sarah continued, "he's become better at riding, so I've told him he will be able to choose his own pony."

"Sir Robert?" Ramsey asked, glancing at him in surprise. "You spare time from your duties to the king for a young lad?"

Robert allowed himself a shrug. "I cannot question people all day long, sir."

Ramsey watched him a moment longer, a smile lingering on his mouth. "My thanks for your attention to him, since I could not be here."

But now I am, seemed to be the unspoken thought.

Ramsey glanced back at Sarah. "Glad I am to hear about the pony. Might I attend you when he chooses one?"

"Of course, Sir Anthony," she said, smiling.

Robert recognized her hesitation, her curiosity. Was it unusual for Ramsey to pay attention to the boy? The man turned to speak to his own servants, giving orders as to where their baggage was to be taken.

"Lady Ramsey," Sarah said, "allow me to send for

Emma, the lady's maid whose services you approved of the last time you visited."

Lady Ramsey smiled. "How thoughtful of you, Mistress Sarah. She can accompany us to our chambers."

"Sarah," Ramsey said, "a missive came to us, meant for you. Baker, where did you put it?"

Robert watched Sarah's frown as she stared at the sealed parchment the servant handed to her. Without reading it, she tucked it within the girdle belted at her waist. He found himself wondering how often she received correspondence.

He did not know everything he should about Sarah Audley. Was it professional curiosity on his part, or the beginnings of an obsession?

Sarah returned to her bedchamber to change her gown, which must surely smell of cows after Francis's adventure in the dairy shed. She was still shaky at how easily such a little boy could have been hurt. Of course, there were so many simple ways for that to happen, from a fall down the stairs—to a cow trampling him. She could not protect him from everything; she simply *wished* she could.

As she began to remove her girdle, the missive fluttered to the floor. Bending to pick it up, she broke the seal and glanced at the signature first. It was from

Mistress Maud, the healer who'd taught her art to Sarah as she was growing up.

Sarah sank down on the edge of her bed, feeling her heart lighten. The old woman's cheerful missives came infrequently, but they always reminded her of the happy times spent at Maud's table, grinding dried herbs as the healer spoke of the intricacies of her craft. Maud had helped her recover from her mother's death, taught her what to do to encourage her father to eat so that he could become part of the living again.

Even though her father had since died, she smiled as she began to read the missive, but the smile soon faded. Maud wanted Sarah to know that two strangers had come asking about her, as well as Andrew Audley's death. Maud revealed nothing to these men, and she assured Sarah that no one in the village even knew of the rumors. For this was Sarah's home, not the seat of her husband's family, where surely the strangers had already thought to investigate. And they'd probably heard the worst, for the Audleys believed the worst.

These men had to be part of the king's investigation. Who else would care enough to look into her past? And Robert, who said Walter answered to him, must know all about it.

She covered her face, feeling so tired. She was trapped, unable to go to anyone else for help, because she truly was a suspect. Though the people of Drayton had become her friends, they'd only known her for two years. They would rather see her take the blame for a murder than one of their own. It would make sense to them.

All she had was Robert. She had to keep seducing him to her side, convincing him of her innocence.

Seducing, she thought, dropping her hands into her lap. It was a word she hadn't meant to use.

But had it really come to that?

Chapter 16

Robert ate supper at the head table and tried to remain quiet as he listened to the Ramseys. Both of them made much of Francis, asking him questions about his studies and the sort of pony he hoped to choose. They seemed to be kindhearted people, but Robert felt that Ramsey himself was a shrewd, intelligent man who would know exactly how to keep from being perceived as suspicious.

After the meal, when the trestle tables were being taken down, and minstrels were warming up at the far end of the hall, Ramsey approached Robert.

"Do you have time to speak, Sir Robert?"

"Of course I do, sir. I assumed you would have many questions."

"I understand you have a partner here? Might we speak with him as well?"

Robert motioned for Walter, who hadn't gone far. Robert made the introductions, then called for tankards of ale for the three of them. They went to stand away from the others, near an immense, colorful tapestry depicting a hunt from several hundred years ago.

Ramsey eyed them both. "So tell me how this all began."

Robert told the tale of Drayton's symptoms being linked to arsenic poisoning, the king's concern, and the assignment he had granted them both.

"And I assume you have done such service for the king in the past," Ramsey said.

"Aye," Walter said, while Robert nodded.

Robert wondered about Walter's past, and how many years he'd worked for the League. 'Twas a shame he could never hear the man's stories.

"And you were successful?" Ramsey pressed.

Walter nodded. "I am confident that Sir Robert and I will succeed in discovering the truth."

Ramsey looked between them with curiosity. "And what have you discovered so far?"

"We cannot compromise our investigation by speaking of it, sir," Robert smoothly said.

"This is my cousin we're discussing, Sir Robert. I would not reveal your information to anyone."

"I am sorry, but I cannot relent," he said.

Ramsey looked surprised, frustrated, but not exactly angry. "I accept your terms, although I cannot say I agree with them. Can you explain your methods to me?"

"I do not mean to make this sound simple, but we ask questions," Robert said. "People tell us things. We discover what happened in the past, and then we piece the details together. I would like you to participate, sir. Can you spare the time to speak with me tomorrow?"

Ramsey's lips quirked in a half smile. "I guess I expected you to question me."

"We question everyone," Walter said in his impassive way.

"Of course I will make myself available for as long as you need me. Drayton was my cousin, and the crime perpetrated against him touches my entire family."

"You have my thanks, Sir Anthony," Robert said formally.

"If you will excuse me," Ramsey said, bowing as he took his leave.

Robert watched him head toward Sarah, then said to Walter, "He didn't obtain the information he wanted from us. I imagine he's going to see what she can tell him."

"I do not blame him. He is the young lord's guardian, and is responsible for Drayton Hall and all of its people."

"I can think of another reason for his behavior," Robert said dryly.

Walter only arched an eyebrow, as if Robert's theories weren't worth discussing.

Sarah had tried not to watch the three men in deep discussion in a corner of the hall, but she could not help herself. She was playing chess with Francis, and when he was thinking out his move with adorable concentration, she had time to let her thoughts wander to the conversation she wished she could hear. Lady Ramsey had been a minor distraction, asking about the new loom in the weaving chamber and many other domestic things that seemed superfluous compared to the undertone of murder that lingered in the castle. But if Lady Ramsey wanted to lighten the mood, she was all for it.

At last Sir Anthony left Robert and Walter, heading straight for her. Sarah stiffened and made a foolish move with her queen that had Francis howling in triumph.

"I win!" he cried.

Sir Anthony had reached them by this time, and he smiled indulgently at the boy. "Francis, will you try to teach Lady Ramsey the game? She says I confuse her too much."

The woman gave her husband a fond nod before

saying to Francis, "I am truly terrible at chess. Perhaps you can help me."

"Mistress Sarah is not trying very hard anyway," Francis said. "You can talk to Sir Anthony, mistress."

She grinned at his perceptiveness. "Thank you, my lord." Turning her attention to Sir Anthony, she said, "You have need of me, sir?"

He lowered his voice. "What is your opinion of the king's men?"

"They seem fair, and do not make quick judgments— or if they do, they do not betray their thoughts."

"They tell me they question everyone, probably so that I will not mind their questions on the morrow," he said ruefully.

"They do question everyone, sir, so please be not offended."

"I'm not," he said with a sigh. "I am simply still in shock, from the moment I received your missive. To think that Drayton was deliberately killed in so cowardly a fashion."

She nodded with sympathy.

"And we all thought it was the black death," he said, then glanced at her. "Including you."

"Aye, Sir Anthony, I can make no excuse for myself. I have never been confronted with arsenic poisoning, and in my limited knowledge, the symptoms were not clear to me."

"I do not blame you."

But she blamed herself.

"How is the mood of the household?" he continued.

"Wary, of course. Suspicious, yet I have not seen people treating each other badly. 'Tis as if all have silently agreed to await an announcement."

"As if they don't believe this investigation could touch them."

She glanced up at him in surprise. "True, sir."

For a time, Sir Anthony watched Francis trying to teach Lady Ramsey how to play chess. Sarah remained nearby, knowing it would soon be time for the little boy to retire for the night. But for a while, he could have the triumph that the kind Lady Ramsey was offering him.

Robert had gone to sit with Master Frobisher, and soon the two of them were deep in conversation, as well as deep in their cups. Sarah took Francis to bed and then returned, only to find the two men still together.

Master Frobisher, never one to hold his ale, became more boisterous, and at last Robert helped the man to stand and took his arm around his shoulders.

Sarah took several steps toward them to offer assistance, but then Walter moved in front of her. She hadn't even known he was nearby, stumbling to a halt before she collided with him.

"Mistress Sarah, Sir Robert has the situation under control."

She stared up at him in surprise. Walter had always maintained a quiet, solid presence, but now, for the first time, she thought he seemed a little . . . threatening.

Did he think she wanted to interfere for her own dark purpose?

She felt a little angry and a little frightened, but she backed down. "Of course, Sir Walter. I did not think otherwise."

The steward's bedchamber was already lit with several candles by the time Robert dragged Frobisher across the threshold. The farther they'd walked, the less Frobisher seemed to be able to support himself.

The steward sank into a chair near the bed with a heavy sigh. "My thanks for your assistance, Sir Robert."

"Any time," he answered, taking a stool opposite him. "I imagine you would not want to appear inebriated in front of Sir Anthony."

Frobisher's shoulders slumped. "That would not do. Must . . . keep up my dignity."

Robert had spent the evening questioning the steward about other members of the household. He was a genial, good-tempered man who enjoyed his position and the authority that went with it. Robert had not heard one reason the last several days why Frobisher could have wanted Drayton dead.

"Your dignity is intact," Robert said, smiling.

"I don't normally do this," Frobisher said, his words slightly slurred as he pierced Robert with his gaze.

"I didn't think you did."

"'Tis just that . . . everything is different now that his lordship is dead."

Robert nodded, hoping his silence encouraged him to keep talking.

"Not that his young lordship is difficult, but I don't answer to him yet."

"You answer to Sir Anthony. And is that terrible?"

"Nay, he has not intruded on the management of the estate in any way." He put his hands between his knees and hiccupped forlornly. "But he has his own steward. What if he decides he doesn't need me?"

"But how could his steward even find the time to add all of the Drayton properties to his own duties? 'Twould seem far easier to keep you on, considering you are being paid out of Drayton coffers, not Ramsey's."

Frobisher seemed to perk up. "I had not thought of that."

"He has not complained; therefore he must appreciate the work you're doing."

"Oh, Sir Robert, glad I am to have talked to you

this night." Then his smile faded. "But I spoke too much before."

Robert felt his every sense heighten.

"I was childish."

"In what way?" Robert asked.

He looked down at his feet, rubbing patterns in the carpet. "It has been difficult for me, the way the household took to Mistress Sarah. She works diligently and cheerfully, and she does not deserve"—he lowered his voice—"my jealousy."

"There is no reason to be jealous. I can see how respected you are."

"My thanks, but it does not excuse that my jealousy might have made you and Sir Walter think . . . worse of her. For there is no reason, I assure you!" he added with conviction.

Robert smiled and rose to his feet. "Thank you for clarifying your feelings, Master Frobisher. I do not think worse of Mistress Sarah."

"I can tell." The steward slowly tilted sideways until he landed part way on his bed. "Need a little . . . help here."

Robert lifted the man's legs off the floor until he could roll completely onto the bed. The steward made no other sound except a snore, and Robert left his bedchamber, satisfied with what he'd learned.

* * *

When the castle had quieted, Robert moved sound-lessly down the corridor outside the viscount's suite, then slipped into Sarah's chambers. A candle still burned at her bedside table. She lay propped on cush-ions, asleep, the newly arrived missive in her lap. But his curiosity over that meant little at the moment. Her wild mane of curls was down around her shoulders, a brush nearby as if she hadn't finished taking care of it. Her nightdress was long sleeved and high necked as befitted a nursemaid, but it was fine enough that it hugged her curves and let him imagine the duskiness of her nipples through the cloth.

He stood over her for a long moment, drinking in the sight of her, the freckles across her pert nose, her softly parted lips. And then she opened her eyes.

He tensed, ready to cover her mouth if she tried to scream, but she only widened her eyes.

"Robert? Is something wrong?" She sat up, and the missive fell to the floor, but she ignored it.

"Nay." He cleared his throat, for his voice sounded raspy in his own ears. "I simply brought something to show you." He pulled a large roll of parchments from the satchel over his shoulder.

Then she seemed momentarily nonplussed, looking around as if she didn't know what to do. The candle's faint glow highlighted her profile, her frown—her em-barrassment. He should turn away, allow her to draw on her dressing gown. But he didn't. He stood rooted to the spot, waiting for her to tell him what to do.

And in his best dreams, he had never thought she would do as she now did, sliding her legs to the side, pushing the bedclothes away, and rising to her feet. It was torture, wanting to touch, and knowing he couldn't.

"You'll want to spread those out on the table," she said calmly.

So at ease, she took the candle to the larger table, then lit several others there. He followed her, feeling foolish and dazed, watching the way her nightdress clung and moved with her, sinuously gliding along her legs. Surely he had seen far more revealing garments on a woman.

But this was Sarah, who made him feel things he'd never felt before.

"What is it?" she asked, nodding toward the roll in his hand.

Her curls slid forward around her shoulders, and he watched, dry mouthed, as she raised her hands to push her hair back. Her breasts lifted with the movement.

His desire was unimportant, he told himself, forcing his gaze back to the parchment in his hand.

He cleared his throat. "This is Lord Drayton's will."

Her eyes widened. "But the chaplain told me we

will read it on the morrow now that Sir Anthony is here. Why did you bring it here?"

"Father Osborne agreed to allow me to borrow it," he said.

"But why, Robert?"

"I am wondering if this will show that you had little to gain financially from Drayton's death."

"And you preferred to know before everyone else? You thought *I* should know before everyone else?"

He said nothing. How could he explain himself?

She sighed. "He was good to me, Robert. What if he continued to be good to me in death?"

"Let us find out."

They both sat down in chairs side by side, and Robert unrolled the first parchment. He scanned it, looking for Sarah's name, but of course the first and largest bequests were to Francis. Sir Anthony Ramsey was to receive several personal mementoes and a small manor, but it was hardly worth killing for. But then again, Drayton's death made him the guardian of Francis and his viscountcy.

At last, they both saw Sarah's name at the same time, and together they leaned forward, shoulder to shoulder.

"This mentions that you will receive a small brooch of pearls that was beloved by Lady Drayton."

Sarah's eyes shone with moistness in the candlelight. "Aye, I know which he means. How good of him to give me something that was hers. Surely this does not seem that bad, Robert?"

"He is not finished, Sarah. This mentions a piece of property in Warwickshire, complete with a manor, Oldbarow Hall, near the village of Oldbarow in the Forest of Arden."

He thought her face paled.

"Mentions it?" she murmured.

"More than mentions it. Drayton gave it to you upon his death." He stared at her somberly. "Do you not understand what this means?"

Many people would kill for such security, he thought, especially a woman who had nothing of her own. He knew how this would look.

She met his gaze helplessly. "But this is not some random gift. Do you not understand, Robert? This was my home, the manor I grew up in. Dear Lord Drayton knew what it meant to me."

"Then explain it to me, Sarah."

She nodded, running her fingers nervously over the words on the parchment. "I told you that I could inherit nothing from my father, because he'd only leased the land from Lord Morton. After my husband's death, when I returned to Oldbarow, I helped my teacher, Maud, with the ills of the villagers. I came to Lord Morton's attention in this way, and he recommended my skills to Lord Drayton, who was visiting him. This was how I came to be with Lady Drayton. Her husband knew all about my father, knew I had nothing to support myself but my healing. He was being kind, do you not see, Robert?"

"But others will remember how you arrived here, undernourished, and will think you are leaving here a woman of property."

"But—I cannot help what they think. Lord Drayton surely knew that Francis would only need a nurse for a few more years. He wanted to thank me for my assistance with his wife, with his son."

"Many people assist in such things, and do not benefit from it in so large a way. And he left you jewelry, Sarah."

"From his wife! Oh, Robert, will everyone truly think I knew about this, and would kill for it?"

And then she turned and flung herself into his arms.

He was surprised by her spontaneity, that she wanted the comfort of the man investigating her. Then, far too quickly, he was overwhelmed by the soft feeling of her unbound breasts against his chest. She was between his thighs, her belly pressed against his erection—surely she could tell how she affected him?

He slid his hands across her back, feeling nothing

but warm flesh beneath her thin nightdress. He should push her away, warn her that this behavior could harm them both—but instead he buried his face in the curls that so fascinated him, drank in her sweet lavender scent that shut down his brain.

She wasn't trembling, he didn't think she was crying; she only clung to him as if he were all she had.

Or all she wanted.

Chapter 17

He was so warm, Sarah thought, closing her eyes, letting herself feel rather than frantically think of all the things she had no control over.

His body was hard and strong, sheltering, making her feel like he might stand between her and all the bad things in life and would win.

It had taken everything in her not to cover herself when he'd first arrived, but she'd understood what she had to do to keep him with her. Though she was frightened of the future, she was also wary of the desire shimmering between them and where it might lead. Now that she'd set their relationship in motion, she didn't know how easy it would be to stop such a man, a man who seemed to want to touch her in any way he could.

This was all a fantasy, she told herself. It wasn't real, could never last. Was that the way to think about it, the way to live with herself?

She didn't want to move as his broad chest comforted her, held her. When he slid his arms about her, she felt so safe, even if it was only temporary. She was fragile against him, womanly, a rare feeling for her.

If she didn't know his heart, she knew his body and what it craved. She was pressed between his open thighs as he sat in his chair, felt the length and thickness of his erection.

And wanted to rub herself against it.

She was shocked by such a wanton urge, but she could no longer change the direction of her thoughts.

She pressed her hands against his chest until she could look up into his face. The playfulness was gone; those eyes that usually twinkled now smoldered.

She reached up and gently, tentatively, cupped his cheeks, felt the day's growth of beard, and the warmth of him. "Thank you," she whispered.

His gaze focused on her mouth. "For what?"

"For showing this to me, warning me. I will not forget it."

He searched her eyes with his, saying nothing more. He seemed to be watching her, waiting—waiting for what she would do next. He was not a man to force himself upon her, to use his obvious strength. That eased her trepidation. How had such a man learned gentleness, when he'd had so little in life?

"You know I was married," she said, "yet I find myself unprepared. I want to kiss you."

She let her fingers trace his lips. He gritted his teeth and closed his eyes, but didn't push her away. Then she pressed her mouth to his, and the kiss was so right she sank against him, arms about his neck, wanting the feel of him hard against her aching breasts.

Their kiss grew deeper, needier, open-mouthed with hunger. She tugged on his bottom lip with her teeth. Hands deep in his hair, she held him to her through endless kisses.

She let her head drop back, let him explore her neck with his hot mouth, lick paths that teased her, made her squirm. She couldn't get close enough to him, couldn't stop moving, pressing herself between his thighs. At last his hands drifted down over her backside, molding the curves, then sliding lower to her thighs. He parted them, lifting her until she straddled him, her knees bent on either side of his hips. Her nightdress rode dangerously high, but she didn't care. She clutched him hard with her thighs, pressing against him, feeding the fire that burned hotly inside her. Desire and passion and need all became one as she clung to him.

His hands slid back over the curve of her hip and then up. His fingers brushed the sides of her breasts and she shuddered, rocking against him. Then he looked into her eyes, and she knew his need, for she felt it, too.

She took his hands and cupped them to her breasts, moaning. He needed no further urging. He took her mouth in another swift kiss, then palmed her breasts, kneading, caressing, teasing through her nightdress. He slid his face back down her neck, and his teeth tugged at the string about her throat. She felt the loosening of the garment, the erotic feel of it sliding down her shoulders, then the draft of air on her nude skin.

He was breathing hard, staring at her breasts. She leaned back in his embrace, baring herself to him in the candlelight, reveling in the sensation of being so desired, something she'd never felt before. And then he bent down, his mouth just above her trembling breast. His eyes met hers. Then he licked her nipple, a long, hot caress. It was as if her body was no longer her own, shuddering in pleasure, arching against him trying to find more.

He drew her nipple deep into his mouth, and she muffled a groan, shocked by the ripples of bliss that poured through her. His palms found her bare thighs, her nightdress pooling over his hands as he slid them ever higher. His thumbs made gentle circles up her inner thighs, making her quiver with excitement and longing and trepidation. She'd never felt this way before, never imagined it could be like this between a man and a woman.

Then he lifted his head to watch her as his fingers deepened, tracing the wet folds of her body. She gasped, mouthing his name helplessly. He tongued her nipples, stroking below with his fingers until he circled the little button of flesh that sent her ever higher. She tightened with awareness, centered on his mouth and hands and the amazing things he was doing to her. Then her whole being seemed to plummet into waves of shuddering pleasure. She clung to him through endless moments, until the passion waned and a languid feeling of quiet satisfaction took hold of her.

She opened her heavy-lidded eyes to find him watching her solemnly.

"Have you never known a woman's pleasure?" he asked.

She shook her head, not trusting herself to speak.

Was she now supposed to offer herself to him, give him the same pleasure, as if that would somehow pay for his protection?

She couldn't do it.

"This has gone too far," she said, feeling helpless because she knew *she* was the one who took it there.

She slid from his lap to her feet, gathering her nightdress back up over her shoulders. She swayed with weakness, and he caught her hips in his big hands. They stared at each other.

"I'm so sorry," she whispered.

"Do not be." His voice was firm and calm. "You've told me of your past. I know that your husband did not gift you with the pleasure that was your due. He must have hurt you, and I grieve for the marriage you suffered through."

She closed her eyes, not wanting to see compassion, not after the way she was treating him. Perhaps more of the truth would ease her conscience. "I didn't tell you all," she whispered.

Through his hands on her waist, she felt him stiffen, but he didn't move to stand, only looked up at her. "You can tell me anything, Sarah."

She looked away, still humiliated though several years had passed. "I could not give him a child, and his anger was all-consuming."

His fingers tightened on her. "Go on."

"He would hit me, not often, but enough."

He inhaled sharply. "Sarah—"

"There was nothing I could do. I learned quickly that defending myself made it worse. Pleasure was not something I ever learned to expect from him. To find it now . . . I never imagined it."

He stood up at last and took her into his arms, holding her fiercely yet tenderly. "Rest now, Sarah, rest easy."

He guided her to the bed, waiting until she was within before tucking the warm blankets about her. He rolled up the will and returned it to his satchel. After blowing out the candles by the table, he hesitated at the last one at her bedside.

She wanted to see gentleness and understanding, but she couldn't read his expression. Then he blew the candle out and left her bedchamber. She rolled over, put her face into her pillow, and cried. *Rest easy,* he'd said. Did that mean she should have no worries, that he believed in her? Fear and loneliness kept her restless mind from sleeping.

Robert's chamber felt cold and barren after the warmth of being with Sarah. In his bed, he lay awake, frustrated and unfulfilled, knowing he could satisfy himself, but it would be so lonely.

This . . . relationship . . . between them had sprung up so quickly, flared so hotly that it overwhelmed him, brought out thoughts and feelings he wasn't used to.

Especially jealousy. Was Simon sharing such moments with her?

Robert fisted the bedsheets, then forced each finger to relax.

Nay, she was a woman who'd been hurt by men. She'd confided the worst to him, and he knew she would not share such a thing easily. She did not trust herself to such intimacy. And he saw how she was with Simon, and it was not the same.

Yet he still couldn't sleep. She was affecting him too much, and he wished he had someone to talk to about it. In the past, he'd always had his brother, Adam. He'd teased Adam when Florrie had come into his life, saw the way his brother changed because of her.

Was that same thing happening to Robert? Could he be falling in love with Sarah? After all, no woman had ever taken him so close to lovemaking and then made him stop. And he'd totally understood, had sympathized, even as his body ached with need of her.

He was at war with himself and his duty. He wanted her, he wanted all of her, given to him willingly. Tonight he would have taken her, regardless of what he thought the League meant to him. He was helpless in the face of his desire for her.

But she hadn't told him about the missive, and he'd kept himself from asking, hoping she would willingly share it with him.

Did he want her trust more than he wanted his own future success?

* * *

Sarah felt eyes on her throughout mass the next morning. It had to be Robert. Her memories alone were enough to make her feel overheated and wicked.

But it was Simon, she realized, when she glanced over her shoulder. Guilt swept through her, even as she gave him a pleasant nod.

Things had gone too far with Robert. She could no longer allow Simon to think, to hope, that she might want more with him.

She'd spent her life wishing that a man would want to cherish her—and now she had *two* men offering themselves! She bowed her head as she prayed for strength.

Much as she enjoyed Simon's company, she did not feel the same way about him as she did for Robert, who made her giddy and hopeful, aroused and unsure. His smile made her heart melt, his laughter made her wish she could be the one to make him happy, forever.

Forever? she thought to herself in surprise, even as she rushed out of the chapel ahead of everyone else. How could something be forever, when she was trying to force him to take her side against his partner?

As she broke her fast, she was afraid to speak to Robert, for fear her blushes would give their intimate relationship away to everyone present. And it wasn't fair to Simon to see her that way. She concentrated on Francis, let him ramble on and on about the kind of pony he wanted, promising that after his studies, he could choose one at last.

When she saw Simon leaving the great hall, she asked Margery to take Francis to his tutor, then impulsively rushed after Simon, avoiding Robert's impassive gaze. She would explain everything to Robert when she next had the chance.

She caught up with Simon in the courtyard, and ached at the sight of his pleased smile.

"A good morn to you, Simon," she said. "May I speak with you before you go to train?"

He seemed surprised, but he nodded his head. She led him toward the lady's garden, then found a secluded bench and gestured for him to sit beside her. He said nothing, simply waited, and she could no longer delay.

"Simon, I want to thank you so much for the interest you've shown in me."

"But I'm not to show my interest any longer." His voice was flat, with a faint tinge of anger.

Her gaze shot to his in surprise. "Oh, Simon, 'tis just that—"

"You do not have to explain." His entire body was stiff. "From the moment Robert Burcot arrived, I have seen the way of things, even though I did my best to make you want—" He broke off, then finished with, "He is a seducer of women, and he's worked his wiles on you."

She began to feel offended. "You make it sound as if I am not behaving rationally. I assure you 'tis not true. I have thought this through very carefully."

"Not carefully enough. When it's time for him to go, he'll leave you behind. He is the sort of man who does that to women. He is about the conquest."

She swallowed, feeling tense and queasy as Simon's words played to her insecurities. Then she remembered that Simon didn't know the truth, that Sarah was the one planning to conquer, regardless of what happened beyond that.

"Simon, I am so sorry," she murmured.

"When he leaves, do not return to me."

"I won't." Her shoulders sagged. "I had hoped we could remain friends."

He stood up. "I—I will think on that."

He strode away, ducking beneath the branches of a tree, leaving her alone. She sat still for a while, feeling sad and confused. At last she resigned herself to accepting that she'd hurt Simon, but that it couldn't be helped. Even if she'd felt more for him, she could not have allowed him to court her. He could very well be tarnished by the investigation of her.

And then she thought of Robert, and knew that she could never have felt the same way about Simon.

She left the lady's garden and wandered toward the tiltyard. It was Robert she wanted to see, even though she'd avoided him in the early hours of the morn. He was easy to spot, and she realized that he was sparring with someone she didn't recognize at first.

But it was Sir Anthony. The two men crossed swords, gauging each other in the way of men that seemed so incomprehensible to her. She watched for several minutes, hugging herself, not even breathing as they moved gracefully in a deadly dance. It was soon obvious that although Sir Anthony had half a dozen years of experience on Robert, he could not match his skill. Could he see that Robert was holding back, as Sarah could?

At last they separated, removing their helms, smiling at each other, saying something she was too far away to hear. When Sir Anthony turned away to find another partner, Robert noticed her. For a moment it was as if they were alone, their gazes locked, their bodies tense, their need so obvious to each other.

At last he turned away, breaking the spell he'd woven about her. It took her a moment even to remember that she'd promised to show Lady Ramsey the new loom in the weaving chamber. She hurried back into the keep.

* * *

Robert spent several hours working himself to exhaustion so that he wouldn't have to think. He sparred with every man who challenged him, jousted atop Dragon until even the horse breathed heavily with the exertion. He didn't want to think about Sarah running after Simon, and what might have happened next.

Jealousy ate at him, and he didn't like what it did to him. Where was the man who'd been able to enjoy women for the brief time allotted him? Why wasn't that enough with Sarah?

If this was love, he didn't like the feeling.

The only thing that mollified him was Simon's black mood on the tiltyard.

"Sir Robert!"

He looked up in surprise when he heard Francis's voice. The boy came running into the stables, where Robert was absentmindedly currying Dragon.

"I'm going to pick out a pony," Francis said, reaching to grab his hand. "Will you come help?"

Robert looked up to see Sarah and Ramsey in the doorway. Sarah looked hesitant as she stared at him, though her eyes betrayed a longing she tried to hide from Ramsey. The unhappiness inside Robert eased just a bit, although he still had to force his usual grin.

"I would enjoy looking at ponies with you, my

lord." He tossed the currycomb to one of the stable boys. "Care for Dragon, please."

Francis continued to pull on his hand. Out in the sunny courtyard, Robert noticed the sweat-streaked dirt on his bare arms.

To Sarah, he said, "Forgive me for not being presentable, mistress."

"You have worked hard this morn, Sir Robert."

He well knew she'd been watching.

"I will forgive you this once," she finished, the faint flirtation back in her voice.

Even in front of Ramsey. Interesting.

They all followed Francis to the side of the stables, where three ponies trotted and played together in the paddock.

Robert and Ramsey answered Francis's questions, discussing the ponies as seriously as if each might become a warhorse. Robert had to concentrate so that he wouldn't keep glancing at Sarah, her hair shining in the sunlight, as she rested her forearms on the paddock rails and laughed at the antics of the ponies.

At last, Francis chose a chestnut mare with a white marking above her eyes and a playful manner. He thought the mark looked like lightning, so that was what he chose to call her. He wanted to ride, of course, and the three adults applauded his skills as he showed off Lightning in the courtyard.

Robert saw Sarah's curious expression when Margery approached them.

The seamstress bobbed a quick curtsy to Ramsey. "Father Osborne is ready, milord. I'll watch Francis for you."

Ramsey glanced at Sarah and quietly explained, "'Tis time for the reading of Drayton's will. The estate lawyer is in London, so Father Osborne will do the honors. He says that you should come, too, Sarah."

She nodded, keeping her eyes on the ground. "Aye, sir." Then she glanced at her friend. "Margery, thank you for staying with Francis. Please take care with him."

Margery nodded, her eyes full of questions she didn't ask. "Please take care with him" was a strange thing to say to a woman who regularly helped watch over the boy, Robert mused.

In the lord's solar, the mood was strangely more tense than somber. Father Osborne had the will spread out before him. The steward, the treasurer, and Walter were waiting, along with Lady Ramsey, who smiled at her husband as he took his seat beside her.

"Did Francis choose a good mount?" she asked.

Ramsey nodded. "I am sure he will show it to you this afternoon."

Father Osborne cleared his throat, and several quiet conversations halted. Since Robert had already seen the will, he watched the others' expressions. Master Frobisher and Sir Daniel both seemed touched by the bequests left to them and other senior members of the household. Ramsey shook his head, a sad smile on his face, when he heard about the property left to him. Lady Ramsey dabbed her wet eyes.

"And to Mistress Sarah Audley," the priest intoned dryly, "his lordship granted a brooch, a favorite of Lady Drayton, to whom she gave so much comfort."

Father Osborne handed a wooden box to Sarah, who rubbed her fingers across the delicate carving and kept her face low.

"Please show it to us, mistress," Lady Ramsey said softly.

Her husband nodded. "Aye, Lady Drayton would have wanted you to wear it proudly."

Sarah quickly wiped beneath her eyes with her fingers, and then opened the box with trembling hands. Robert didn't think displaying the brooch was a good idea, but he remained silent.

Lady Ramsey rose to her feet and walked to Sarah. "You are overcome, my dear. Allow me to help." She pinned the brooch near the neckline of Sarah's simple gown, then patted her shoulder. "She mentioned many times to me how glad she was that Francis had you."

More tears slid down Sarah's cheeks, and while she

murmured her thanks, she fumbled for the handkerchief up her sleeve.

Father Osborne cleared his throat again. "Lord Drayton had another bequest for Mistress Sarah, a small manor, Oldbarow Hall, in Warwickshire."

Sarah made an appropriate gasp. Robert saw the swift glances that passed between the steward and treasurer, then Ramsey's look of interest. The mood in the chamber shifted from sadness to unease.

Sarah bit her lip, then looked at Ramsey. "That is the property of my childhood, Sir Anthony. My father only leased it from Lord Morton, and I thought it lost to me forever. I cannot believe Lord Drayton's kindness . . ." Her voice faded off and she quietly used her handkerchief, eyes downcast.

"You are well provided for, Sarah," Ramsey said, patting her back. "Your service must have impressed his lordship."

The eyes of both the steward and treasurer went wide, and they hastily looked away. Robert knew what they were thinking, that Sarah's service had been performed in Drayton's bed. Did Ramsey know this rumor? It was difficult to tell.

Robert glanced at Walter, whose gaze back at him was piercing.

When the reading was finished, and everyone began to leave, Walter drew him aside in the corridor.

"You already knew the contents," he said quietly.

Robert looked about, but saw no one listening. "I did. But I only discovered it late last night."

"And you told Mistress Sarah."

"I wanted to see her true reaction."

"What was it?"

"Shock, fear. She knows how suspicious this looks."

"But not to you."

"She wasn't Drayton's mistress, Walter. 'Tis not her fault that he was kind to her."

"But you saw the reactions of all the others."

"I did," Robert said solemnly.

"'Twill be more dangerous for her now, once word spreads."

"I will watch over her."

Walter crossed his arms over his chest, his stance stiff with disapproval. "And perform your other duties as well?"

"I have never failed in my duties, Walter, and you know that."

They stared at each other for a long moment.

Walter finally nodded. "Ramsey did not receive much of consequence."

"Except the boy's guardianship, which will last thirteen more years. That is a long time to have sole control of a large estate—with no one looking over his shoulder."

"Drayton trusted him."

"And mayhap it was misplaced."

"Very well, Sir Robert. We will see what happens next."

He was confident in himself, confident in his strategy. But once again, it was obvious Walter did not agree with him. This was another strike against him that Walter would certainly relay to the League, but Robert did not care, when Sarah's life was at stake.

Chapter 18

During dinner, Sarah heard the whispers. No one openly treated her with anything but respect, yet . . . she heard the whispers.

Now everyone was putting together the belief that she was Drayton's mistress, along with the impressive inheritance she'd just received, the ability to support herself for life. She'd be the lady of a manor now.

Even though some might despise her, for the first time since her childhood, she had security. Now she could only pray that Robert was truly on her side.

When she left the kitchens after discussing the evening meal with Cook, she found Simon waiting for her in the great hall.

He didn't ask for privacy, but he spoke in a low, cool voice. "Mistress Sarah, I have heard about the contents of Lord Drayton's will."

"I am not surprised," she said, regretting the trace of bitterness in her tone.

"Did you reject me because you knew you were going to inherit the manor?"

Her eyes flew wide. "Nay! My decision regarding the two of us had nothing to do with this inheritance." Although she *had* known of it before she'd spoken to Simon that morn . . .

He studied her, wearing a sad, resigned expression. "I would understand, of course. You would be a lady of property, and I only a lowly knight."

"Nay, Simon, that would never occur to me at all."

He sighed. "'Tis a shame I know not what to believe of you anymore."

As he walked away, she stiffened, holding her head high, fighting back tears. Was this how it would always be now, her friends and fellow servants unable to trust a word she spoke?

"Mistress Sarah!" shouted Francis.

She blinked hard and put a smile on her face to see him running toward her ahead of Margery. The seamstress was watching Sarah with concern, and she couldn't help wondering what her friend had seen—or perhaps what she'd heard.

"I'm going to wrestle today!" Francis said, practically jumping up and down before her. "I'm good at that."

"I know you are," she said, smiling even as she ran

her hand across his brown curls. "Go on ahead and we'll be right behind you."

He headed for the double doors, and Sarah fell into place at Margery's side as they followed him.

"Ye've had a rough morn," Margery said, briefly touching her arm.

The kindness made those foolish tears threaten again, but Sarah held them back. "Aye, I have. And I think the day will not get better."

They stepped outside into the courtyard, where they could see Francis catching up to a half dozen boys of various ages.

"The brooch is lovely," Margery said softly.

Sarah sighed as she looked down at it. "I almost wish to hide it away. It seems to shout, 'Drayton's mistress.'"

"Nay, it does not," Margery said, though she was obviously trying not to smile.

"Did he have a mistress, do you think?" Sarah asked contemplatively. "He was a man of middle age, hardly ancient."

Margery watched the boys, shading her eyes. "I know not, Sarah."

"Because a mistress really does have a motive, and combining that with a handsome inheritance, I look very guilty."

"'Tis a piece of land, not all the jewels of the kingdom."

"Hmm."

"I refuse to be sad about this, Sarah. Ye have a place of yer own to settle on when Francis no longer needs you. Perhaps ye'll need a seamstress . . ."

Sarah smiled and bumped Margery's shoulder with her own. "Perhaps."

Late that afternoon, Robert and Sir Anthony Ramsey retired to the lord's solar for privacy. Ramsey asked his wife to join them, and Robert wasn't surprised. They spent much of the day together, as if they couldn't bear to be separated. It seemed a pleasant way to live, he thought.

They began their discussion with Ramsey ruminating on his relationship with his cousin, that they saw each other at least once a month, that their wives were close. Lady Ramsey nodded her agreement, her eyes moist. Ramsey also confirmed that he was in residence at Drayton Hall in the weeks leading up to Drayton's death. But so were many people, Robert knew.

"Drayton never mentioned any problems with the staff or neighboring lords," Ramsey continued. "He was so well respected. 'Tis hard to believe anyone could have a reason for killing him."

"I've heard that often these past days," Robert said dryly. He paused, then asked, "Did Drayton have a mistress?"

"Not to my knowledge," Ramsey answered promptly.

"Once I heard a rumor about Mistress Sarah and his lordship," Lady Ramsey offered.

Ramsey frowned. "'Twas not our concern, my love."

"Yet I asked you to speak to Drayton about it, considering she is the boy's nursemaid."

"And did you, Sir Anthony?" Robert asked.

"Aye. Drayton was bothered by the news, for he said he had something else in mind for Sarah."

Robert did not betray his alertness. "And what was that?"

Ramsey spread his hands wide. "He told me he was going to ask Sarah to marry him."

Though his mind raced at these new implications, Robert only nodded.

"I can remember sitting with my cousin while we watched Sarah playing with Francis in the distance. Drayton was wearing a fond smile. He abruptly said that he was going to ask her to marry him, that she would make a good mother for Francis."

"Mistress Sarah never mentioned anything like this."

"I do not know if he discussed it with her," Ramsey

said. "But later that month we were in London with Lord Drayton, and my wife saw him . . . courting another woman."

Robert kept his body still, although his every sense heightened. This changed everything.

Ramsey sighed. "I worried that Mistress Sarah might be hurt. But then he took ill, and I never had a chance to ask him what he'd decided to do about the two women."

Robert nodded. "Thank you both for your time."

They glanced at each other, as if surprised the interview was over so quickly.

"We are at your disposal, Sir Robert." Ramsey rose and took his wife's arm.

After they'd gone, Robert remained still, thinking. He knew Drayton had not asked Sarah to marry him, or she would have said so. Robert could not confirm a dead man's conversation with his cousin, but it wouldn't matter in the end, for Ramsey had already betrayed himself, Robert thought with satisfaction. Even as he knew he had to discuss this with Walter, he decided not to speak to Sarah of this new development until he had all of the facts. He didn't want to raise her hopes.

After supper, as the evening began to wind down, Robert at last found a moment alone with Sarah in the great hall. She seemed . . . melancholy, but the pearl brooch continued to shine by the light of the hearth, as if she wore it proudly, though he didn't believe that to be the case.

"How do you fare?" he asked quietly.

He thought her smile a bit forced, but it was still a lovely thing to behold.

"Well enough," she answered, "considering that everyone is now beginning to realize what I might have had reason to do."

"Do not think of it like that, Sarah."

She nodded, then glanced up at him from beneath her eyelashes. "I thought you might be angry with me."

He smiled. "Why would I be angry?"

"You did not seem happy to see me walking with Simon."

He opened his mouth, but before he could speak, she rushed on in a low voice.

"What we . . . shared last night was special to me, Robert. I could not continue to allow Simon to think that I favored him. It would be cruel."

He wanted to touch her, but could not. He murmured, "So what did you tell him of us?"

"Little, actually. He already guessed I favor you."

She hesitated, and he thought a faint blush touched her cheeks.

"He said that you would hurt me, that you were a man who favored the conquest, not what came afterward."

"He thinks to assume so much?" Robert asked with faint sarcasm.

"He was hurt, Robert. I don't know what he truly thought."

"Thank you for telling me," he said. He hesitated, then found himself saying quietly, "I admit, I experienced my first taste of jealousy over you and Chapman."

"Really?"

"Aye. I have never known a woman like you before, Sarah." He continued to stare down into her warm brown eyes, wanting her to believe his sincerity, in this at least.

At last she lowered her gaze, smiling, blushing. Robert thought this was good. He didn't want people to think he'd ceased his flirtation because Sarah was guilty.

"I have to retire soon," she said at last. "It has been a long day."

"For all of us," he said. "Good night, Sarah."

He watched her leave the hall, saw how she said good night to others, and they still replied politely. Robert took his own leave of the keep, and when he arrived in the guest lodgings, he found Walter waiting for him.

Robert dutifully sat down at the table opposite his partner. He imagined Walter wanted to know about the interview with Ramsey, but he wanted to save that until he had Walter's report.

"Do you have any news about the investigation?" Robert asked.

Walter arched a brow, but didn't protest. "I received a missive today, from our men investigating Sarah's background. They could not confirm any truth to the rumor that Sarah murdered her husband, but his family certainly believes so."

"She told me this. She said he fell from his horse when they were alone together, as I already told you."

"The Audleys were quite open about their dislike of her from the beginning."

"Were they open about cheating her out of her right to compensation at her husband's death?"

"Nay, they were not, although our men did press the point. The Audleys claimed that if Sarah's father was foolish enough not to fully understand the contract, 'twas not their fault."

"Coldhearted is what they sound like. What proof did they give for their belief that Sarah killed their son?"

"They said their son spoke often of his dissatisfaction with his marriage."

"He must not have told his parents that he beat his vulnerable wife."

Walter's frown deepened. "That is an ugly thing to do to a woman."

At least Walter did not try to say they only had Sarah's word. "Are they trying to claim that Sarah's inability to have a child was a motive for murder?"

"Nay. They claim that for a woman, she took too much pleasure in studying. They thought that proved she meant all along to rid herself of the marriage and then better her prospects. They implied that with her knowledge of herbs, she might have kept herself from having a child."

"This is all nonsense."

"Which is why they were unable to prove their beliefs to the local sheriff. They claimed the blow to their son's head could have come from Sarah, rather than a fall from a horse."

"Tiny Sarah, striking a blow that would kill a man?" Robert rolled his eyes. "Did the sheriff consider their case had merit, but just no proof?"

"Apparently not. Except for her husband's family, Sarah was well loved in the village. She healed and comforted many. She was pitied for having married into the Audley family."

Robert nodded. "Then her background alone does not make Sarah a suspect."

"Nay, it does not."

"And although Ramsey tried to implicate her during our interview, he failed."

Walter leaned forward, his eyes alert. "You think he did so deliberately?"

"Ramsey claims that Drayton told him he was going to ask Sarah to marry him."

Walter's eyes widened, which was practically a shout of emotion for him. "Interesting, yet it cannot be easily confirmed."

"True."

"If it could be confirmed, then Sarah's motive to kill Drayton is gone. How does that implicate her?"

Robert smiled. "Ramsey claims that before Drayton took ill, Lady Ramsey saw him courting a woman in London."

"Ah," Walter said, nodding thoughtfully. "You seem rather pleased, considering this might be another motive against Sarah."

"But it isn't." Robert rubbed his hands together. "She has never mentioned a marriage proposal to me—and before you say anything, I know that a guilty woman would not want this motive known. But she's too intelligent not to realize that it would come out. I don't believe she ever heard any of this."

"Are you saying Ramsey is lying?"

"Perhaps not about the marriage proposal. Drayton probably never got around to asking her to marry him."

"Before he met this other woman."

Robert slammed his hand onto the table. "And there's the solution to our dilemma."

Walter frowned. "What are you saying?"

"We cannot confirm what one man said to the other, but we already know Drayton wasn't courting another woman. The League investigated his every move in the months before his death. I read detailed accounts of his stay in London. The League never mentioned a woman, and you and I both know they would have."

Walter cocked his head. "Your memory is impressive."

Robert leaned back in his chair, stretching out his feet and crossing them at the ankles. "Did you think I wouldn't tell you something that could potentially incriminate Sarah?"

Walter's hesitation spoke volumes.

"You're my partner, Walter, and I take our mission very seriously. I know my duty, and I would never betray our brethren."

"Glad I am to see you are using League resources," Walter said.

That was as close to acceptance as Robert knew he was going to get. "Thank you, Walter."

"Yet we cannot condemn Ramsey based on one lie—or one mistake."

It wasn't a mistake, Robert thought, but he didn't say the words aloud. "I know. But it shows me I'm on the right path. I'll consider my options."

Chapter 19

To her own surprise, Sarah slept soundly, as if she'd used up all her worry during the day and her body needed to recover. Of course, she was even more tired because she'd stayed up far too late, hoping that Robert would come to her. He hadn't. Was all the evidence mounting against her swaying him?

She tried to go on with her normal day, going to mass, eating the morning meal, escorting Francis to the chaplain.

But she also saw the occasional long look from some of her friends, and then their haste as they turned away when they realized she'd seen them. It was difficult to feel optimistic in the face of that. She told herself that everyone would know the truth soon.

Of course, what was the truth? Who was truly guilty? And where was Robert?

Sarah didn't mind the light, misty summer rain that began to fall in the afternoon. The coolness felt good on her skin. She was accompanying Francis on the horseback ride she'd promised him. He'd been eager to leave the castle behind, and although some part of her felt uneasy, she could not refuse him. She had insisted they would not go far, and he'd pouted but agreed.

Francis rode slightly ahead of her on Lightning, and soon he turned his mount toward a path into the woods.

"This leads to our favorite stream!" he called. "Can we go?"

"Be careful. I will be right behind you."

With the renewal of his confidence the last few days, he'd proven a competent little rider. She watched him fondly, enjoying his eagerness.

But then he suddenly lurched to one side, and she realized his saddle was giving way.

"Francis!" she screamed.

He slid farther, even as Lightning pranced in confusion. But to her surprise, he caught the pony's mane and held on tightly. Sarah dismounted and ran to him, calming the pony while helping Francis slide to the ground. He collapsed onto his backside, staring wide-eyed up at his mount as raindrops freckled his face.

"Are you injured?" she cried, dropping to her knees beside him.

He shook his head. "My legs wouldn't hold me."

"Because you've had such a scare. How did you think to hold Lightning's mane?"

"Sir Robert taught me."

She closed her eyes, thanking God for Robert's forethought.

"What happened?" Francis asked, his voice becoming tremulous.

"'Twas not you," she insisted, briefly cupping his cheek. "You have become an excellent rider. Something is wrong with your saddle. Will you be well while I look at it?"

He nodded and scrambled back away from the pony.

There was a fear in his eyes she hadn't seen for at least a sennight, so she decided to take a chance. "Will you hold Lightning's reins for me? She might be afraid because of what happened."

Francis slowly got to his feet and went to Lightning's head. He started talking softly to the pony, petting her nose while holding the reins.

She breathed a little easier, then turned to the saddle, which had fallen to the ground in a heap. Had a buckle broken on the girth? But it was intact. She followed the strip of leather, and inhaled sharply when she saw that it had ripped in half. Then she peered closer.

Only part of it was ripped; most of it had been

neatly sliced by a blade. Her hands started to shake, and fear was sour nausea in her stomach.

Someone had wanted Francis to fall from his horse.

Frantic, she told herself that surely the saddle could have been used by anyone—but nay, it was smaller, for a young rider. And the stable boy would have examined the saddle as he put it on Lightning's back. This had to have been done *after* the pony was saddled, and the person who did it must have known whom it was for.

This was twice in several days that Francis had had an accident. His injury in the dairy shed from a cow that was suddenly spooked now flashed vividly into her mind. Had an actual person been responsible, rather than a cat? God Above, who could be cruel enough to wish harm on a five-year-old boy?

The same person who could slowly poison a man and watch him suffer until his death.

But why Francis? Was this unknown assailant trying to make *her* look like a monster who would kill a child? She'd been with Francis during both accidents—nay, she could not call such deliberate crimes accidental. It seemed as if this man wanted to make sure Sarah took the blame for *all* his crimes. But she couldn't care about herself, not when Francis was in terrible danger.

"What's wrong?" Francis suddenly asked, looking past Lightning's head to stare at her.

She swallowed hard, hoping her voice wouldn't shake and frighten the boy. "The girth broke."

"So it really wasn't me?"

She reached and tousled his hair. "Of course not, silly goose."

She felt a wave of dizziness hit her. If he hadn't caught himself, he could have hit his head in this rocky terrain, or been trampled by the pony's hooves. She shuddered.

"Stupid saddle, huh, Lightning?" Francis said. "Mistress Sarah, we can still walk to the stream before we go home, can't we? Lightning must be thirsty."

Part of her wanted to insist they flee, but she didn't want to frighten him. And after all, the murderer would have had no reason to follow them, had only to wait for the plan to succeed.

But she felt very vulnerable as they led their horses farther down the trail after throwing the damaged saddle across Lightning's back. She allowed Francis time to look for rocks for his collection, even as she nervously and repeatedly glanced around her. At last she said it was time to go. She managed to tie the saddle awkwardly onto the pony's back, then took Francis up behind her for the ride back to Drayton Hall.

"Do we have to tell everyone I fell?" he asked.

Perfect, she thought with relief. "Nay, of course not. We'll say we discovered the broken girth when we tried to tighten it."

"That's a lie," Francis said softly.

And now she had to feel guilty about this. "Do not worry. I'll talk to the stable boys. You won't be lying."

"Oh." That seemed to brighten his mood.

By the time they reached the courtyard, he tried to slide down so quickly she had to grab his arm to help. He laughed up at her, then ran off toward the boys by the tiltyard.

She froze, not knowing if she should call him back. But there were so many people that surely nothing could happen to him.

In the stables, she showed a groom the broken girth, innocently saying, "Could a spur or a nail have done this?"

He pondered the strap, frowning. "Aye, mistress, perhaps a nail on a fence. I'm so glad his little lordship wasn't hurt!"

"Do not worry that I will tell anyone of this," she said in a lower voice. "You should not get into trouble over an accident. In fact, why don't you bring the strap to me later, so no one will ever have to know?"

"Thank you, mistress!" he said, gulping, his eyes wide with panic.

Oh, that made her feel terrible, but it couldn't be

helped. She hoped fear would keep him from telling anyone what had happened. She could not let the murderer know she was on to his tricks.

Walking slowly toward the tiltyard, she hugged herself even though the rain had let up. She felt cold and damp and dazed with shock, unable to think what to do next.

"Mistress Sarah?"

She jumped with a shot of fear, then told herself to calm down. She turned to face Simon, who was carrying his helm under his arm as he obviously headed for the tiltyard. He looked awkward and uneasy, unable to hide his misery.

"Good afternoon, Simon."

"Is something bothering you?" he asked, studying her face. He spoke stiffly, as if forced to be near her. "You look . . . pale."

She called on every skill she'd once had to pretend her life was fine. "Nay, I just returned from a ride with Francis, and only now realized how cold the rain made me. I will change soon. Thank you for your concern."

As he nodded and strode away from her, she inwardly berated herself. Too much was at stake for her to lose her calm now. What should she do?

She sent a stable boy to find Margery, then waited perched on a bench, knowing if she rose, she'd start to pace. It seemed like forever before her friend appeared, walking too slowly. Sarah wanted to shout at her to hurry, but bit her lip instead.

She smiled to reassure Margery. "I am so sorry to send for you so abruptly, but Francis is enjoying himself with the boys. Would you mind staying with him for a while?"

Margery's smile gradually faded. "What is wrong, Sarah? Yer eyes look . . . haunted."

She opened her mouth to disagree, then suddenly it proved too much for her, and the story about Francis's "accidents" spilled out of her.

"Am I wrong, Margery? Tell me I'm wrong, that I'm being too suspicious."

Margery had covered her mouth with both hands while Sarah talked, and now she dropped them to say, "Ye're sure someone *cut* the girth?"

"Aye! I told the stable boy it could have been a nail, but it was too neat a slice. I know I'm not wrong. Someone wants to hurt Francis!"

Margery took her upper arms and gave her a little shake. "Calm down. He's here and safe out in the open. I'll keep a close eye on him. What will ye do?"

She hadn't even thought it to herself, but the words still emerged. "I'm going to Robert. I know not who else to trust. Later, I'll even be able to show him the damaged strap."

Her friend sighed. "Good. My thought exactly. He'll know what to do. But change yer garments first, afore ye catch yer death."

"Don't leave Francis alone," she said, hearing the break in her voice.

"I promise I won't."

She quickly turned away, forcing herself to walk with measured steps across the courtyard, splashing through a muddy puddle before she realized she wasn't even seeing the ground. In her mind the image of Francis starting to slide from the pony kept playing over and over.

In her bedchamber, she could barely pull the wet garments off her body because her hands shook so badly. Once she was suitably dressed, she returned to the great hall, but Robert still wasn't there. She groaned softly to herself, trying to think of where he'd be. He hadn't been at the tiltyard . . .

"Sarah?"

She turned as Sir Anthony called her name. "Aye, sir?"

"I just wanted to tell you how sorry I am about this investigation."

She blinked at him in confusion. Why was he apologizing to her?

He gave a faint laugh that wasn't amused. "I feel badly that such a terrible thing had to happen to my cousin. And now that I've spoken with Sir Robert, I understand how difficult being questioned is. I assume it was not any easier for you."

"Nay, Sir Anthony, I—I could not stop wondering who could do such a thing."

He nodded. "'Tis difficult for me to know that I have a stronger motive than most, as if I'd want my own cousin dead. I imagine you know how I feel," he said, patting her shoulder.

Of course he thought she had a strong motive, she thought bitterly. Like everyone else, Sir Anthony assumed she'd been Lord Drayton's mistress.

"I apologize if I've made things worse for you," he said.

Now she was truly confused. "I do not understand, sir."

"I had to tell Sir Robert about . . ." His voice faded away, and he gave a soft whistle. "You didn't know, did you?"

"Know what?" she cried, spreading her hands.

"I could not keep the truth from the king's man. I had to tell him that Drayton confided in me that he was going to ask you to marry him."

She stared at him, knowing her mouth had sagged open like a fish. She had always thought Lord Drayton was devoted to his wife's memory and might never remarry since he had an heir. But apparently he'd planned to trust her to be Francis's mother . . . Her eyes began to well up.

"Perhaps I should not have spoken," Sir Anthony said. "Do you have a handkerchief?"

She nodded, pulling it out of her sleeve to dab at her tears. "Forgive me, but this is so . . . unexpected. I had . . . no idea."

"Glad I am that you are touched by my cousin's words, but regretfully I must explain it all. We later heard that he'd begun to court a woman in London."

"Ah, so he never asked me to marry him because he'd already changed his mind," she said ruefully. She wasn't surprised. He could have had his pick of well-dowered noblewomen instead of the daughter of a poor knight.

And then she realized why Sir Anthony watched her with hesitation. He'd just explained that she now had *another* motive to have murdered his lordship.

And Robert hadn't told her.

Her dismay and sadness were quickly erased by a growing feeling of confused anger. Why had he lied to her *again?* Perhaps his attention to her was only so that he could find more proof that she was guilty.

Or was the only attention he paid her because she'd been *throwing* herself at him?

She wasn't sure of anything.

"Perhaps we should look for Sir Robert," Sir Anthony said as he studied her. "Last I knew he was with Lady Ramsey in the sewing chamber."

"The sewing chamber?" she echoed in disbelief.

Though she wasn't yet certain of her strategy for confronting Robert, she followed Sir Anthony through the castle corridors until they reached the large chamber that was Margery's domain. They found the maidservants all atwitter with laughter, Lady Ramsey looking amused and charmed, and Robert in the center of the adoring women.

Chapter 20

Robert had the faint feeling that something was wrong, just by the expression on Sarah's face—or perhaps it was the absence of expression. He was surrounded by chattering, flirting women in the sewing chamber, something he'd been taking advantage of. If people feared him, they wouldn't reveal things so easily.

But Sarah had accompanied Ramsey here—to find the man's wife? Lady Ramsey had been Robert's true reason for being here, of course. By knowing the wife, he might get to know the husband. But she'd been friendly and utterly guileless. He'd learned nothing new about Ramsey.

Ramsey looked down at Sarah with concern. Robert felt tense, worried about her, even as he forced a laugh and held a maidservant at arm's length.

"Thank you, Sir Robert, for brightening everyone's day," Sarah said, her smile obviously false.

"Oh, he did," Lady Ramsey gushed, coming to take the arm of her amused husband. "He was gracious enough to accompany me here." She lowered her voice. "I had avoided the sewing chamber after dear Lady Drayton died. It brought back too many memories. But now I believe that was a mistake, for memories of happy times can also bring comfort."

Robert smiled. "Lady Ramsey, glad I am that I could help you remember your way." He glanced at Sarah, his uneasiness increasing. "Mistress Sarah, how was Francis's first pony ride outside the castle?"

"He wants to tell you himself, Sir Robert. Would you care to accompany me?"

After promising to visit with the seamstresses again, he nodded to Ramsey and followed Sarah from the chamber.

When they were away from prying ears, she slowed and said in a quiet voice, "You seemed outnumbered there."

He chuckled. "I had things well in hand."

She didn't say anything else, just walked at his side.

"Lady Ramsey is very inquisitive," he began. "She's a little too interested in the investigation."

"Can you blame her? After all, you interviewed her husband as a suspect in a murder."

"True." She was walking almost too fast, and he

touched her arm. "Sarah? Is something wrong?"

"More wrong than it's been since you arrived?"

He frowned, even as she heaved a sigh.

"Forgive me," she murmured. "This isn't about you. 'Tis about me, and the pressure I'm feeling, and all the uncertainty. Are you any closer to discovering the truth?"

"Wishing I would leave?" he asked, still smiling but half serious.

Her eyes widened and she bit her lip.

"You do not have to explain, Sarah. I cannot imagine how you're feeling."

She began to tell him about Francis's pride in his horsemanship. But something was still wrong, and she didn't trust him enough to explain what it was. That frustrated him more than he thought possible.

After supper, Sarah found herself confronted by Margery, who looked over her shoulder at everyone else in the great hall.

"Ye look guilty, so ye didn't tell Sir Robert about the accidents, did ye?" the seamstress said in a low, stern voice.

Sarah sighed at how easily her friend could read her. "Nay, I did not. I've caught him in lies, Margery, and I'm not certain I can trust him."

Margery groaned and rolled her eyes.

Sarah leaned toward her. "Just because he and I
. . . feel something for each other, does not mean it's
anything more than lust. And perhaps his feelings are
all about keeping me close and proving me guilty."

"Oh, ye cannot believe such a thing!" she pro-
tested. "I have seen him watchin' you, and 'tis not
with suspicion."

"He is very good at masking his true thoughts.
And the plan from the beginning was to flirt openly
with me."

"Ye need to show him yer trust, Sarah. Ye need
help. Yer only other choice is to leave here, because
someone is tryin' to make you look guilty."

"I don't care about myself!" she hissed. "'Tis Francis I fear for. And I'm also not finished with Robert. I
have to know for certain if he trusts me, if he believes
in me, and it is not so easy to ask him."

"Sarah—"

"I'm still so afraid for Francis," she interrupted, her
eyes going to him where he played chess at the hearth
with Lady Ramsey.

"Ye've been watchin' him close, 'tis true."

"Will you—" She hesitated, afraid how this would
sound, but knowing she had no choice. "Will you
sleep in my bedchamber tonight, and keep the door
open between my chamber and Francis's?"

Margery's eyes widened, and although she was obviously full of questions, she didn't utter them. "Aye, Sarah. Ye can trust me."

Sarah nodded and left Margery. For the rest of the evening, she stayed on the fringes of the hall, watching over Francis, staying away from Robert. She saw his questioning looks that he covered with cheerful behavior. Was she really able to see beneath the masquerade?

But what kind of man was he?

The minstrels played for the crowd again, and he claimed a dance from her. She let him flirt with his eyes and his smile, as he did with every other woman.

And before she let him go on to the next, she leaned in and whispered, "I'll be waiting for you in the corridor beneath your lodgings after the stroke of midnight. Come down to me."

She felt his body tense, but then she turned away without looking into his face.

After midnight, Sarah wasn't even trembling as she waited below the guest lodgings. The candle flame burned steadily, her heart didn't pound. Somehow she was going to truly discover if Robert believed in her innocence.

He appeared at the bottom of the circular staircase, a shadow come to life, without his own candle to guide him. She inhaled sharply, startled, but she'd been expecting him, hadn't she?

He stood in front of her, that irrepressible smile gone. His eyes watched her, waiting, dipped down to the neckline of her gown, to the hint of cleavage. His nostrils flared.

She felt a wave of heat and trepidation shimmer inside her. She put a finger to her lips, saying nothing. Beginning to turn away, she glanced back at him over her shoulder. With her eyes she begged him to follow, and he did. He moved soundlessly, though she could hear her own steps. But she didn't look back again.

She took him farther along the corridor to the final guest lodgings, vacant now. She went slowly up the circular stairs, knowing he was watching her from behind.

She didn't stop on the first floor, but continued up to the second, to the largest bedchamber, as far away as possible from the chance of being overheard. She'd prepared a small fire in the hearth to warm up the cold stone of the castle. She set the candleholder down near a pitcher of wine and turned to face him. He watched her from the shadows, his blue eyes glistening, his faint smile reminding her that he was not like any other man she knew.

Words failed her in the face of the desire in his eyes. His gaze went past her to the bed, and she realized how all of this looked. He thought she'd planned an assignation.

Heat flooded her—along with nervousness and passion intertwined. She was frozen, desperate for the solace of his embrace. But he'd always resisted her.

Should she press her advance? Would he stop resisting?

Suddenly, he reached toward her and tugged at the laces at the front of her gown. She caught her breath. Freed, the bodice sagged open with the too bountiful display of her breasts beneath her smock. His chest rose and fell with his quick breathing.

When she trembled, it wasn't with fear. She felt . . . desired, and if she weren't careful, she would forget everything else that was important as she succumbed to the heady sensations.

This is what had been building between them for days, even as she'd stoked his jealousy, hoping to bind him to her. Should she stop it now, before it went too far?

The laces loosened farther, and the gown began to fall, baring one shoulder, the smock caught at her breasts. She watched, dry mouthed, as he loosened the laces on the front of his doublet, parting it so that she could see the fine cambric of his white shirt, gathered at the narrow band at his throat. The laces came free, the doublet parted, and it fell from his shoulders and down to the floor. The shirt covered him to his upper thighs, and feeling flushed, she wanted to see below.

She gasped as her gown fell to her feet. She wore not a lady's sheer delicate smock, but hers was a comfortable cut that hugged her curves.

He moved closer, until his body just touched hers. There was little between his chest and her breasts but two thin garments. The brush of him against her nipples made her softly gasp and half close her eyes as she swayed against him, feeling, experiencing. She'd never known how sensitive her body could be.

She took another step closer, flattening her breasts against him, pillowing his erection in the softness of her stomach. She let her hands slide from his hips and up beneath his shirt, feeling the rippling curves of muscle, the scattering of hair, all of it intoxicating her. Her hands went up his broad, smooth back until she reached his shoulders.

He leaned forward and kissed her with so much heat and need that her knees weakened. She held herself up by the strength of his body as she devoured him, tasting him with her tongue and lips, moaning into his mouth. He walked her backward until she hit the bed with her legs. She tumbled down and pulled him with her, spreading her thighs to take him even deeper against her.

He suddenly propped himself up on his hands and

looked down at her. She pulled on his shirt until it billowed over his head. He yanked it off and tossed it behind him. His powerful shoulders were tense above her, his arms like two giant columns on either side of her. She could have felt intimidated by all that strength poised above, but she wasn't.

He seemed to be hesitating, studying her, his smile long gone. Where was that playful man, the one who loved women? Was this the real Robert, and he was showing himself to her? Was there a serious side of this man, one he'd learned to hide because he'd had no one in his life to trust, no one to protect him? Had laughter been his shield?

Though she knew it might be hopeless, she ached to love him. She bent her knee and brought it up along his hip, feeling her smock slide down her skin. Her thigh gleamed in the candlelight, and she knew he was watching it, too.

She arched her body against his, felt his hips hard against the depths of her, his body far too obvious with its need.

He tugged at the laces of her smock, baring the upper curves of her breasts, even as the garment caught on the hardened peaks. His gaze was riveted on the display. She rubbed her hands along his arms, reveling in his strength. She caressed his shoulders and neck, then pulled his head down to her, those wavy dark curls fluttering through her fingers. He bent willingly, his open mouth on the skin just below her throat.

The laces parted further, revealing one breast to him. She gasped, barely able to breathe. Her body aflame, she lifted herself toward him. She wanted him to take her now, to make her forget—

So she could use him.

She was using him as her husband had used her, though the reasons differed.

She tensed, dropping back onto the bed, even as he held himself above her.

This wasn't the way to solve her problems. She would never know the truth of their relationship if she let him take her like this.

She covered her face with both hands, ashamed of herself. He slid off her and rested at her side, still touching her, sharing his heat. She felt him gather the laces of her smock together to cover her.

She rolled into him then, burying her face in his chest. His arms came around her, comforting her, though she did not deserve it.

What was she going to do now? Being intimate with Robert didn't mean she could trust him to care for Francis, to believe in her.

She dropped back onto the cushion, looking up at him with beseeching eyes. Why was he keeping important secrets from her? She always felt he had things he didn't share, and now that she knew some of them, she could only imagine that other secrets might be worse.

He smiled as he gently brushed a stray curl back from her forehead. "Sarah, I am weakened in the face of your charms."

She tried to return his smile, though she felt her lips tremble. "I can hardly believe that. You have women flaunting themselves at you."

His fingertip dipped down to her cleavage. "Remember, when I was a child, I had no woman to hug me as you do Francis. I think I grew up starved for a feminine touch."

"I think you've more than made up for that," she said dryly.

He chuckled. "You know 'twas not the same. Those sorts of women are nameless, soulless in the sense that I knew nothing about them. We didn't care about each other's thoughts, were only using each other for pleasure and companionship and to get through the long nights. 'Tis not the same with you."

Using each other, she thought despondently. People who used each other lied to each other.

She wanted to tell him of her fear for Francis, but it all froze in her throat. Every man in her life whom she'd trusted had let her down in the end, even her beloved father. She didn't know how to cross the line and trust with her whole heart. After all, he was here to find a murderer.

Robert could sense Sarah's pain. He wanted her body with an ache he could barely ignore—but he wanted her trust more, and he didn't have it.

They lay still, not speaking, as he freed her hair from its ribbon so that he could comb his fingers through the soft, red curls. The outside world, the danger and uncertainty, seemed so far away.

But perhaps that wasn't true for her, he thought, watching as her gaze focused on the candle, whose flame glimmered deep in her worried brown eyes.

Did he want to spend every night like this with her? He'd spent these last weeks focusing on the League, on tightening his grip of it before it could slip away from him. He hadn't thought beyond it to his real life, the one he'd have fifty weeks of the year when he wasn't on his yearly assignment with the League—should they choose to keep his membership.

What had he planned to do with all that time? Linger in London, lying with women, feeling only an eagerness for the next drink, the next bed? It seemed so empty to him now.

Or could he have Sarah every night?

He didn't know, for he was uncertain what her behavior tonight meant. She was hurting, obviously confused about what she wanted. Hell, he was confused. He'd been resisting her appeal since the moment he'd arrived, and tonight . . . Tonight, he hadn't been able to keep himself from touching her. Yet he wanted her glad surrender, not this wild need that seemed forced.

This must truly be love on his part, because he could easily have seduced her this night, but he hadn't.

I love her, he thought letting the back of his hand caress her cheek as the words sank into his mind. *I love Sarah.*

But she didn't love him. Or if she did, it was buried beneath her fear and mistrust. He would have to be so patient to win her. It would be worth it.

"Let me take you back to your bedchamber," he whispered.

Her eyes returned to him, searching. Then at last she lowered her gaze and nodded. Though he knew it was for the best, he felt an ache of disappointment.

Sarah kept Francis at her side all the next morning and into the afternoon, always staying near crowds of people. She canceled his lessons with the chaplain, who frowned but did not question her. Francis was thrilled to have her constant attention, and wanted her to play games with him, to chase him out in the lady's garden, to help him sort his rocks.

But she had not forgotten how his father died, how the little boy was now in grave danger.

For meals, she told him she was teaching him to understand how a lord's food was prepared. They invaded Cook's kitchens, so she could teach Francis where to find a plate, how to choose his own loaf of bread and slice a piece of meat from the lamb roasting on a spit. The scullery maids looked at her as if she had lost her mind, but she didn't care.

As the day wore on, she felt more and more fearful, knowing she, a mere woman, could not protect him forever.

During a mock melee on the tiltyard, where numerous knights fought for Drayton or for Ramsey before a small, cheering crowd, one man suffered a bloody cut beneath his arm, where the armored plates separated. She was almost glad, for at least now she had something to think about other than her fears.

When she went to fetch her tray of herbs and potions, she took Francis with her, much to his disappointment. She pretended she didn't hear Lady Ramsey's offer to watch him. As she marched through the corridors, holding his hand, her mind raced—Robert wasn't at the tiltyard. Where was he? He was so competitive, so talented—would he not compete in such a melee?

In her bedchamber, Francis stomped about, pouting. She uncovered her tray, checking for crushed yarrow leaves. She would have to boil water to make a poultice to draw out any inflammation. Was there enough? She spread wide the tiny sewn bag to better see the contents, then something gave her pause.

The crushed herb seemed to be mixed with another substance. She went to the window, held it up to the light and saw a white powder.

Her breath seemed to stop in her throat. This hadn't been in the yarrow the day before, when she'd seen to a stable boy's cut foot. She attempted to smell it, but it seemed to have no odor, for she could only smell the yarrow.

She went still, her heart thumping loudly in her chest. Arsenic was a white powder. If she'd used this on the injured knight—how ill would he have become? Was it a lethal dose?

The chamber seemed too small, the air too confined.

"Mistress Sarah, there is something in my wine," Francis called from his bedchamber.

"Do not drink it!" she cried, dropping the tray onto the table and rushing through the door connecting their chambers.

Francis held up the goblet to her.

"Did you drink it?" She snatched it from his hand.

He shook his head, staring at her uncertainly. "I was going to, but do you see, there is something sticking to the sides. 'Tis dirty."

She stared into the wine she hadn't poured, that Francis didn't have the strength to pour. A few small lumps floated on the surface, and dried powder clung to the sides, as if everything hadn't dissolved.

Who had left this lethal poison for a child?

And she'd thought she'd protected him so well all day. She felt cold and clammy. She trembled so violently, it was difficult to smile at Francis even as she dumped the wine down the privy.

She had no choice; she could not remain here and put Francis in any more danger. They had to flee. The only man she knew with the power to protect them was Lord Morton, her father's liege lord, who'd been so kind as to recommend her services to Drayton years before. Surely he would take them in.

Chapter 21

Late that night, Robert decided that he couldn't leave Sarah to face her fears alone. He would have to coax the truth from her. He hadn't had a chance to speak with her before heading outside the castle to leave his report for the League that afternoon. In a way, it was for the best. He hadn't wanted to fight in the melee, having to choose which side to battle on, having to hide even more of his skills.

He silently left his lodgings and began to move through the castle corridors, keeping out of sight. He reached her door and didn't bother to knock, not wanting to alert anyone else to his presence. The room was dark, of course, but by the light of the torch in the corridor, he could see that Sarah's bed was empty. Though the bedclothes were rumpled, as if she'd just gotten up, he couldn't seem to stop the slow rise of tension. The door was open into Francis's bedchamber. Surely she was there.

Silently, cautiously, he moved into the boy's chamber, and although the light from the corridor had now lessened, he could tell instantly that no one was here. Francis was gone, too.

Moving quickly now, he searched the privy, the master's bedchamber, even the solar beyond that. He found nothing. Where else could they be in the middle of the night? He wouldn't let himself think of the implications until he was certain of the facts, but anger and betrayal welled up inside of him regardless. Had she been playing him all along? Perhaps the League was right to question his membership, if he could be taken in so easily by one woman.

Back in Sarah's bedchamber, he lit a candle from the torch in the corridor, then closed the door to begin a thorough search. Since he wasn't sure of her belongings, he could not tell exactly that things were missing, but her cloak was gone from the peg by the door. Other pegs were bare, and he remembered garments hanging there.

He stood in the center of the chamber, hands on his hips, and forced himself to slow down and think. If she were guilty of murder—and he didn't believe it—she would flee alone, not hamper herself with a child. The only logical reason she would have taken Francis . . . was to protect him from someone else, he realized with dawning understanding.

What had been going on these last days? Never in his life had he been as mistrusted as he had this last fortnight, first by the League, and then by Sarah.

He would not let this stand. He would prove his methods to the League—and he would save Sarah.

Moving silently, he went back to his lodgings and gathered supplies. He could not open the castle gates—she must have left before they were closed for the night—so he would not have a horse. But he didn't think he would need one. How far could she have gone with a child in the night?

He picked a corner of the battlements high above the keep, where the torches didn't quite reach the shadows. He waited for the night guard to move past, a chill wind clutching at his garments. Then he climbed down a rope to the ground below. The moon peeked out from behind the occasional cloud, so he held to the shadows as he moved along the castle wall. Out on the main road, he turned away from the direction of the village, assuming she would not go where she would be known. From his pack, he carefully removed the covered lantern with its lit candle braced inside. He had practiced many hours of his life learning to keep such a lantern lit.

Soon he found the imprint of a horse's hooves moving off the road and into the woodland. He began to run, maintaining an easy pace, keeping near the road but still well hidden.

Her encampment was too easily found. Much of his tension eased, though he still had to confront her. He remained within the trees at first. Sarah had built a small fire, and he could see the lump that was Francis curled up near it. Sitting at his side, she crooned softly to him, stroking his hair, kissing his forehead though he obviously slept. Robert watched the gentle touch of her hands, the sad, loving expression on her face as she looked down at her charge. No one who would treat a child with such tenderness could have murdered his father.

Robert stepped out from the trees into the firelight, throwing the hood off his head. She gasped and came up on her knees, then sagged weakly for a moment.

"You frightened me," she whispered.

"You frightened *me.*"

He came closer and she rose to her feet, taking several steps away from Francis.

"You know this only makes you look guilty," he said flatly.

She nodded. "I imagine you would think so."

He snorted. "Why did you run away?"

"Because I can't trust you to protect us," she said coldly. "I was taking Francis to my father's liege lord, because you weren't even there today, when I needed you the most!"

"I was on the tiltyard all morning, trying to understand the way the Ramsey household works," he countered with fury. "In the afternoon, I was fulfilling my duties, sending word to the king. Now tell me what happened!"

"You've been lying to me!"

He inhaled deeply. "To protect you."

"Keeping me in the dark, confused, is protecting me?" she said fiercely, throwing her arms wide. "I disagree! You didn't tell me that Lord Drayton considered marrying me. I had to hear it from Sir Anthony."

"Then he must have told you the rest, his belief that Drayton was courting another woman, another motive that possibly implicated you."

She frowned. "Possibly? Of course it implicated me."

"It didn't. I already know he's a liar."

She covered her mouth. "How do you know this?"

"Because I know every move Drayton made in London. There was no other woman. I believe Ramsey is trying to cast blame on you."

"But why?" she cried.

"To keep it from himself. Walter says we cannot convict a man on such a statement. I wanted all the information—and the solution in hand—before I told you."

Such welcome news should have calmed her. He thought he even saw tears glimmer in her eyes.

But instead she said coolly, "That's not all you're hiding. I can tell there is more."

"This one is mild, and is part of my investigation. Walter received good news that no one suspects you in your husband's death except his family, and they are not a credible source."

"As if I didn't know this. My friend Maud wrote to tell me that men were asking questions about me, so I already knew what you were doing."

The mysterious missive, he thought, relieved.

"Nay, there is something else," she continued, "something that worries you, that seems to bubble up inside you as if trying to break free."

He caught her upper arms and drew her closer, feeling frustrated. "I am not your husband, Sarah, who misled you for no other purpose than to have what he wanted from you. When I arrived here, I had a duty to perform, and I'm still doing it. I have discovered the murderer. You are innocent, and I will never allow you to be charged in this crime, even if I have to flee my duty and my family to see you protected. This is all I have, all I can offer."

"You can offer the truth, Robert!"

He let her go, knowing that this was the moment that would decide their future. And he felt as if he had none without her. "If I tell you what I've sworn never to tell, if I betray all I've known for you, will you tell me what you're keeping from me? Will you trust me?"

She nodded without hesitation.

He ran a hand through his hair. "I am on a mission from the king, but he did not grant it to me personally."

Her eyes went wide, her expression wary.

"He asked it of the League of the Blade, of which I am a member."

"The League of the Blade?" Her face showed disappointment and disbelief. "What is this you say, Robert? The League is a story told to children when they cannot sleep."

"Legends often come from fact. The League is real, and exists to help the innocent, the weak, or the unjustly accused." He arched an eyebrow.

Feeling uncertain and exhausted, Sarah stared at Robert, half his face in the firelight, the other half in shadow, as if he were two people.

The League of the Blade?

She wanted to scoff; she wanted desperately to believe. After all, he had finally professed his own belief in her innocence.

"Although we do not officially work for the king," Robert continued, folding his arms over his chest, "he does call upon us in times of crisis. The mysterious death of a nobleman can be such a time, but in this case, there was also another reason. Drayton was a Bladesman. We would never let one of our own go unavenged."

"A Bladesman?" she echoed weakly. "Lord Drayton? How could he have kept it from so many people?"

"The same as we all do. After the initial period of training, we are only called to duty for a fortnight each year. And by the time you knew him, he had already risen to our Council of Elders, an esteemed post. We investigated his death to see if it pertained to his status as a Bladesman, but could find nothing. 'Twas determined that the motive had to be more personal, so Walter and I were sent here."

She looked about, beginning to believe, yet still wary. "Should we not speak . . . softly?"

"No one followed me, I am certain of it."

The truth was finally beginning to sink in, and she stared at him as if she'd never known him. He had another life he could never talk about with anyone—yet he was sharing it with her.

"How did you leave the castle?" she asked slowly.

"I used a rope."

She gaped at him, and her vivid imagination let her see him clinging to stone high above the ground, the wind buffeting him. And then she thought of his skill on the tiltyard, the praise about his abilities as a horseman while the men had been hunting.

She stared at him, at his calm expression, the way he just . . . waited for her next move. What should it be? Since learning of his lordship's murder, she'd been questioning herself, losing confidence. Terrible things had been done by others, while she'd been punishing herself for naiveté.

Yet she'd spent two years of a bad marriage honing her instincts, trying to understand how people thought, educating herself. And since Robert had arrived, her every instinct had been to trust him. She could not ignore that anymore.

"Someone is trying to hurt Francis," she said in a low voice, glancing at the sleeping boy. Could it really be Sir Anthony, his own guardian?

Robert's expression grew harsh and angry, the change so shocking from his usual cheerfulness. She almost felt afraid, even though she knew his anger was for another.

"Tell me everything," he commanded.

So she did, explaining about the startled cow, the sabotaged saddle, and then the worst of all, the arsenic in the wine goblet in Francis's bedchamber.

"In my herbs, I found arsenic that hadn't been there yesterday. I could have—I could have used them on that poor knight today." She hugged herself to fight the trembling. "How could I let Francis remain in danger?"

"You should have come to me," he said in a low voice.

"I was on my way to do just that—and then Sir Anthony decided to commiserate about our motives to have killed Lord Drayton."

"His is a good one," Robert said. His voice was soft, yet dangerous. "He'll control all of Drayton until Francis's eighteenth birthday. And who is to say the boy would even live that long, especially given what's happened these last days."

Though her mind was racing, she forced herself to slow down and think as he put more wood on the dying fire. Flames crackled and rose higher, illuminating the sleeping boy.

When he returned to her, she said, "But . . . Francis was hurt in the dairy shed *before* the Ramseys arrived."

"I do not assume he is working alone."

"He has help?" she asked in disbelief. "How many men could want a child dead?"

"There are some men who believe they are owed the best in life, and will stop at nothing to have it."

A wave of grief battered her. "I suspected early on, you know," she whispered.

He said nothing, although his expression softened. It gave her the strength to go on.

"When Lord Drayton's illness went on and on, I began to fear it truly was poison of some kind. But I was alone and vulnerable, too afraid to speak up and be banished again. And who would have believed me? Even Margery did not."

"Sarah—"

"You have no idea what it was like to be so afraid, to be a woman no one listens to."

"I know what it's like to be ignored," he said quietly.

She ached, remembering his lonely childhood.

"Ramsey made a critical mistake targeting Francis," he continued. "There would be no reason for you to want the boy dead, even if you'd killed Drayton. But Ramsey has a powerful motive—with Francis dead, he would have all of the estates *and* the title. Perhaps he'd planned Francis's death from the beginning."

She shuddered, her gaze helplessly lingering on the sweet, sleeping boy.

"You're being framed for this out of desperation, and desperate men make mistakes." He gave her a penetrating stare. "We know the truth, and we will soon be able to prove it, I swear to you. You don't have to do everything yourself. You have me now."

Since this afternoon's terrible revelation, she'd been

too frightened and frantic to cry, but now the tears welled up and spilled down her cheeks.

"I trusted other men, Robert, from my father to my husband. No one has ever taken care of me. I have had to become strong and do it myself."

Gently, he said, "Sarah—"

"You must listen to me, to the rest of the truth! I didn't think I could trust you. I—I was using your attraction to me to save myself."

Where was his anger, his disbelief? His expression only showed compassion, and it was almost her undoing.

"I didn't want to care about you, but I couldn't help it." Her words ended on a whisper.

He smiled, a bit grimly, but it was there. "I vow to show you that your instincts about me aren't wrong. I want only what is best for you. There is one way to prove it once and for all. You tell me what you want me to do next."

"What?"

"Whatever you think our next move should be, I will abide by it, even if it means leaving this place and living a life in secret."

"But . . . but . . . you have family, you have the League!"

"But I want *you,* Sarah." His voice was gruff. "I will do anything for you."

The words she'd been desperate to hear now tugged hard on her heart. He was trusting her with his future—with all of their futures. He believed in her. His belief restored her own. She could not let him down.

"We cannot risk Francis's life by trying to do this alone," she said at last, her voice steady. "We need Sir Walter's help."

Robert slowly smiled.

Chapter 22

Robert enjoyed Francis's delight when the boy woke in the morn to find that he had joined them. Francis was gleeful when they cloaked themselves to reenter the castle, mingling with all the servants who lived in the village without revealing their identities. Robert insisted people only saw what they wanted to, and as he predicted, no one imagined that Sarah and the little Lord Drayton would be *entering* the castle at dawn, leading a single horse.

They did not head for the chapel, where many filed to attend mass, nor did they return to the viscount's chambers. After taking the horse to the stables, they went directly to the guest lodgings and surprised Walter as he came down the stone stairs to the courtyard. He looked impassively at the three of them, then led them back up to the first floor.

Once they were alone in the outer chamber, Francis grinned up at Walter. "We slept out of doors!"

The gruff man smiled and patted the boy's head. "What an adventure you had. Do you understand that it must be a secret adventure? Those are the best kind."

"No one is to know?" Francis asked hesitantly. Then he glanced at Sarah. "Like when I fell off the horse?"

She nodded.

"Very well," he said, his little voice sounding mature.

"And now we adults need to talk. Come with me."

Walter led the way to the inner chamber, and Robert watched through the open door.

"I have parchment and quill," the Bladesman said. "Surely you can write words and sums for me."

"I can!"

"Then occupy yourself until we return for you."

"By doing my studies?" Francis asked in disbelief.

"Then draw me pictures."

Relieved, Francis glanced at Sarah, who nodded her permission.

When the door had closed behind the boy, all three adults stopped smiling. Walter looked directly at Robert, no emotion visible.

Sarah hastily said, "I ran away with the boy, and Robert had to come find me."

"The explanation will surely prove interesting," Walter said dryly. "Let us sit."

Robert watched Walter's face as he and Sarah took turns explaining everything. He saw the moment Walter realized that Robert had committed the sin of revealing the presence of the League of the Blade. But he couldn't care about his own future now. All that mattered was the safety of Sarah and Francis.

When Robert reiterated that there was no reason for Sarah to want the boy dead, Walter looked right at Sarah as he spoke.

"You could want to punish the whole family because the viscount rejected you."

She gaped at him.

Smoothly, Walter continued. "But I do not believe that."

She hung her head, her shoulders trembling. Robert tensed, wished he could comfort her, but knowing her best chance with the League lay with his detachment.

"Ramsey does have the stronger motive to want both Francis and his father dead," Walter continued. "And he has the resources to command or pay for the loyalty of an accomplice. And we know he has lied to us. Therefore I will remain with young Lord Drayton at all times. He will only eat what I see prepared before me, or what one of you prepares for him. Mistress Sarah, you need never fear for his life again. Everything else I will leave in Sir Robert's hands."

Robert nodded. "I have been thinking much about the way to prove that Ramsey is the murderer. The only way to do so is to trap him so that he's forced to admit to his crimes."

He laid out his idea before Sarah and Walter.

Walter considered for a moment, and then nodded. "'Tis a good plan."

"Sarah?" Robert said.

She licked her lips, her hands clasped before her. "Aye," she said in a low voice. "We can do this."

"I will send for more Bladesmen," Walter said.

Robert cocked his head in surprise.

"I am concerned that Ramsey could turn loose his armed guard upon the household."

"That would betray him just as clearly," Robert said.

"Perhaps, but we should not take the risk."

"Will I need to prepare chambers for these guests?" Sarah asked.

Robert smiled. "I don't think they will allow themselves to be that obvious."

"Let me keep Francis here with me this morn," Walter said. "I am rested, and the two of you are not. Send for me when all is ready, and I will bring him secretly to his bedchamber."

Sarah looked at the two of them, and Robert could see her mind working. She hadn't known them much beyond a sennight, yet now she had to trust them with her very life. For the first time in days, he sensed no hesitation, no secrets. He only hoped she sensed the same thing in him.

It was difficult to leave Francis with Sir Walter, Sarah thought, even though she knew the boy would be protected.

As they hurried down the corridor beneath the guest lodgings, she glanced at Robert. "Surely you can tell me if Walter has experience with children."

"I know not, although at his age, I would imagine it plausible. Remember, Sarah, our lives are as secret as the existence of the League. I know nothing at all about Walter—except the most important thing of all: that he was deemed worthy to be chosen a Bladesman. That is enough for me."

She would have to take him at his word.

"Follow me," he said, leading her through the rear of the keep.

They saw no one, as she knew Robert had planned, because it would have been difficult to explain why all of her belongings were in bulging satchels.

Together they searched each chamber in the viscount's lodgings, but could find no evidence that anything had been disturbed during the night. Sarah unpacked, returning all to its proper place. When she left Francis's bedchamber and returned to her own, she found Robert standing at the hearth. He'd made a small fire, and she smelled the odor of burning yarrow leaves. He was taking care of the last of the evidence against her.

"Do not inhale too much of it," she warned.

She came up beside him and silently looked into the fire. Their shoulders brushed, but it didn't feel awkward. It was a companionable moment, as if this ordeal might actually end soon, and well.

"The League of the Blade," she murmured, shaking her head.

He looked down at her, that faint smile on his handsome face.

"What great deed brought you to the attention of such warriors?" she teased.

He chuckled. "No great deed, as I'm certain Walter performed. I was part of an experiment that the League conducted from the time I had four years."

Her amusement faded and she wrapped her hands about his upper arm. "I don't understand."

He covered her hand with his. "I was not lying to you when I claimed to have been raised without the presence of women. But my home was not a monastery. I was hidden within the League fortress because my parents were killed, and the murderer had not been brought to justice."

"That is so close to the details of Francis's life," she murmured, her heart aching for Robert and his lost childhood.

"My brother Adam is the earl of Keswick, and our family name is Hilliard."

She felt a stab of uncertainty, of coming sadness. He was the brother of an earl, while she was only the daughter of a poor knight. Her hopes for a future with him no longer seemed so bright.

He smiled wryly. "Since our parents' murderer wasn't caught, the League was concerned that Adam would be the next target, so it was determined that only the League could keep us safe. We could not return home. We were orphans and someone wanted us dead. I understand Francis's life too well."

"So . . . what was the experiment?"

He drew her to the edge of the bed and sat down beside her. "The League usually recruits members from adulthood, but our arrival gave them a new opportunity to train Bladesmen from childhood."

"But surely that does not seem a fair thing to do to a child."

"Our foster father, Sir Timothy, who brought us to the League, agreed with your sentiments, but the

Council voted and he was overruled." He smiled down at her. "Do not look as if this was the worst thing imaginable. I've had a good life. My brothers were my playmates, and I was taught all the things young men should learn. I was tutored in everything from the classical sciences to sword fighting. Nothing was left to chance—except our ability to be like normal people."

"I don't understand." She leaned closer, and was glad when he put his arm around her.

"There were some disadvantages. My younger brother, Paul, always suspicious, knew something was wrong with our lives. I thought he took things too seriously. All I wanted was to enjoy myself."

"Then you and I were much alike in our youth."

"I knew we were kindred spirits."

He was so close, so warm. He was her protector. Their smiles faded as they looked into each other's eyes. She could feel the long, lean length of him all the way down her body.

Hastily, she said, "There was a problem with the experiment?"

"By the time I escaped to find girls, Adam was already participating in the occasional mission for the League. This was when all realized that they had not prepared us well enough for entry into a society we knew nothing about. Oh, they taught us to play instruments, to wait on noblemen, as every squire learns. They even gave us dancing lessons."

"With no women?"

"I thought the whole thing amusing. But I truly wanted to fit in out in the real world, for it was my turn to work for the League, to do what I'd spent my life training for. And I'm good at it, Sarah."

There was a passion and urgency in his voice that called to her, but she would let him explain it in his own way.

"Yet it was brought home to me every day that I was very different from other men. A Bladesman is trained to hide himself among others, but I found this more difficult and challenging than did the regular Bladesmen. The League realized that their attempt to train Bladesmen from the cradle was fraught with a different kind of problem. They declared that their experiment had failed. I have never been the sort to worry over a past that could not be changed, but Paul felt used and mistreated. He left the League, left us."

She felt a pang of sympathy at his loss. Another family member gone from his life. "Have you seen him since?"

Robert shook his head. "Nay. He simply . . . vanished."

"How terrible for you."

"I do not fear for him. He is as trained as a man can be." He sighed. "And soon Adam left without telling me. He knew the identity of our parents' murderer, and was determined to bring the man to justice. I followed and refused to leave him. We traveled the length of England, kidnapped the murderer's daughter—"

"What?" she cried in alarm.

"Adam promptly fell in love with her, and they are happily married." He smiled. "We defeated the villain and were at long last able to declare ourselves the missing heirs. That was a year ago. Since then I have spent months enjoying London as a man set free might do."

"Enjoying?" she echoed, raising an eyebrow.

He gave her a lascivious smile. "Though we tell others that we grew up in a monastery, I am no monk." He set his hand on her thigh. "Now you know everything about me, Sarah."

She looked down at his hand, the tips of his fingers just touching her inner thigh. If she let herself be swayed now, she would never hear it all. They didn't have much time.

"What is the problem between you and Walter?" she asked, thinking of the strange tension between the two men.

He gave an exaggerated sigh. "That is a difficult

matter. You see, the League is displeased with my behavior in London this past year."

"I assume you did nothing illegal," she said
lightly.

"Of course not. But there was a young lady who did
not want to remain a virgin . . . I didn't know she was
soon to be betrothed to a powerful man."

"Ah, and the League did not appreciate your willingness to help this young lady," she said.

Though he grinned at her, she sensed that their disapproval bothered him most of all.

"I have performed every assignment given to me.
They have no cause to question my service. But there
are those within the League who believe that my upbringing is not conducive to true, untarnished service.
The fact that I enjoyed myself at the king's court, sam-
pled the delights of willing women, somehow made
the League believe that I am not a serious Bladesman." He turned his head so that their gazes met. "I
have not deserved their mistrust. I have spent my life
in service to them, through no choice of my own. Yet
now they are evaluating me."

"Walter is evaluating you for them."

He gave a stiff nod. "When I arrived here, I told
myself that the League was all I knew, that I had to be
very careful not to ruin my future. But as my doubts
about the true murderer rose, my all-accepting belief

in the League suffered. I knew they were wrong about their chosen suspect—you—and I did not agree with their orders. So I've done what I've needed to."

Sarah stared at him with a growing tenderness, saw the way he'd risked himself for her—with a murderer, and with the League. "But you let me decide what we were going to do. If I would have chosen to flee, it would have been the end of your life with the League. Everything you've done for me endangers you in this way."

He turned to face her, taking both her hands. "I have told you everything about myself, Sarah. I want no secrets between us. The League means nothing if I cannot have you."

Her heart spilled over with tenderness. How could she deny to herself any longer that she'd fallen in love with him, that she trusted him with all that was most dear to her, her body and her soul? Yet . . . he was so above her in station that these last days might be all she ever had of him.

"Robert," she murmured, leaning forward to kiss him.

The touch of his mouth to hers felt like the answer to every question she'd ever had about herself, about her life. She deepened the kiss, wanting to take him inside her any way she could.

Between kisses, she whispered, "I have no doubts,

no fears, Robert. Make me yours. Make love to me."

With a moan, he lifted her and draped her across his lap. She clung to his neck, covering his face with kisses, feeling his hands caress her back, her hip. He cupped her breast through her gown.

It was her turn to moan as he kneaded her, playing with her nipple. She felt the pleasure shimmer there and throughout her body. It made her move and arch and gasp.

"You have too many garments," he said hoarsely against her mouth.

She smiled. "So do you." She sat up and straddled his lap, reminding her of their earlier intimate encounter that had shaken everything she thought she knew about the pleasure involved in lovemaking.

Her hands unlaced his garments, tangling with his hands as he roamed her body to do the same. He pulled her gown over her head, she yanked on his tunic until he was forced to half rise so that she could pull it above his hips. She grabbed for his shoulders, laughing, as he pretended he might drop her. Under his tunic was his shirt, and she made quick work of that.

Then their smiles died as they looked into each other's eyes. He had professed no vows of love, she had not spoken her own. Right now all that mattered was being one with him, this man who would give up everything he held dear just for her. Even if he didn't say the words, that was the meaning of love to her.

He slid her smock up her body, and she lifted her arms to ease the way. She felt the air on her open thighs, her belly, then her breasts, and when the smock dropped from his fingers and she could see again, she watched his heavy-lidded eyes take in her nudity. He kept her arms high, her breasts thrust forward as she loosened the ribbon from her hair. It cascaded down around her shoulders, red curls tumbling, her breasts half hidden.

"Sarah, how beautiful you are," he whispered.

His blue eyes seemed to glow with an admiration that warmed and eased her. Then he turned and laid her back on the bed. Her hair tumbled across the coverlet. She felt beautiful, voluptuous, desired. She was glad she had waited to give herself to him, because now she had no other motive but love.

She kept one knee raised, legs slightly parted with a brazenness she enjoyed feeling. Robert stood and removed his breeches. In the light of day, she could see the perfection of his muscular body, the scars that showed his determination. When he joined her on the bed, she tried to pull him over her, needing to feel him, but he only laughed and lay beside her.

"Let me enjoy this before we have to face the world," he murmured.

But she was the one who found great joy. He explored her body with his hands and mouth, trailing moist kisses between her breasts, dipping his tongue into her navel. She moaned and moved restlessly, as if the pleasure within her soon would not be contained. She felt like she'd come full circle, come back to the woman who could celebrate life.

Her legs parted to accommodate his body as he moved ever lower. And then he was pressing delicate kisses to her inner thighs, leading upward at such a slow pace that she was stiff with disbelief at what he might do, and desperately hoping that he would.

He raised his head briefly to give her that wicked grin she loved, then he bent and gave her a most intimate kiss. She groaned and convulsed with the fierce pleasure that surged through her body. He'd shown her once what a woman's desire could bring, and now she knew there were so many other ways to experience it. He licked and suckled her, taking the little button of her flesh into his mouth, invading her with his tongue. Her breath came in gasps between small cries, and at last she gave herself up as that need within her once again burst free, uncontained, showering her with pleasure and surprise and fierce joy.

No sooner had she collapsed, languid and spent,

than he rose above her. All her passion returned in a rush at the way he looked at her, as if he could no longer wait to claim her. And he did, thrusting home, so deeply and fully. There was no discomfort, no fear on her part, only gladness that he was able to join her in learning the true meaning of intimacy.

Chapter 23

"**M**y God," Robert whispered.

He held himself above her, looking down into her precious face, her eyes heavy with satisfaction, her mouth curved into a smile that was . . . wicked.

The depths of her body were hot and welcoming, so tight around him he thought he might lose himself without taking another stroke.

Everything in him strained for release, but he fought for control, even as he pulled out and sank in again.

She arched, her lips parting, her eyes shutting. He wanted to bring her ecstasy again. As he rocked inside her, he bent his head to take her nipple into his mouth. She cried out, clasping his head in her hands, touching his shoulders, his chest, caressing his nipples in the way he'd done to her. His breathing was ragged as he surged into her over and over, and when he felt her climax overtake her, he gave in to his own, mindless with the rushing pleasure.

With a groan, he collapsed against her side.

She only laughed, her arms high above her head, her body arching. "That was wondrous!"

He could barely move. "Glad I am that you think so," he ground out.

"I wish we could do that again."

He snorted a weak laugh. "Give me a moment to recover."

She shot him a teasing glance. "It will take you that long?"

"When you look at me like that, 'twill take no time at all." But he came up on his elbow, his look serious. "But we cannot linger . . ."

"I know. Francis is cared for, but only temporarily. We have to ensure that he will be safe forever."

"Though he may be an orphan as I was, I promise you he will have a better life than mine."

She gave him a soft smile, rubbing the back of her hand against his chest. "I know. For now, my thought is that he's too young to know what happened to his father, what almost happened to him."

"Aye, there will be time in the future to tell him such things."

They both rose and dressed. He watched the graceful moves of her body, and enjoyed the fact that she watched him as well, even as she blushed.

When he was ready to leave, he drew her against him. "Do you have any concerns, any fears, about what we will be doing?"

She shook her head. "Nay, 'tis a well thought out idea—although I should not praise you much, for fear it will go to your head."

He laughed.

Her smile faded. "But perhaps, without parents, you have not had much praise in your life."

"Nay, my foster father took care of that. And much as I did not take everything about my training seriously, I always worked hard to earn his praise."

"Then you have *my* praise," she said, coming up on tiptoes.

He met her lips in a kiss that he wished could go on forever.

They broke apart with great reluctance.

"I will depart through the lord's solar rather than be seen leaving your bedchamber."

"Thank you," she said. She touched his cheek. "Tell me we will be together again soon."

"Aye," he murmured, turning to kiss her palm. He left before the urge to do more overwhelmed him.

* * *

When Sarah reached the great hall, the morning meal had long been finished. She headed for the kitchen, for she was ravenous.

Margery hurried to walk at her side, whispering, "I was worried when ye did not come down to mass or to eat. What is wrong?"

And so the lying had to begin, even to her dear friend. "Francis is not feeling well. It began yesterday." It was easy to appear concerned, to show a hint of fear, when she knew how close another poisoning had come to fruition.

"The poor mite! Is it a fever?"

"Aye, and he can keep nothing in his stomach. But he thinks he is feeling better this morn. I am sure he will be well in no time."

Margery patted her arm with sympathy.

By the midday meal, more than one person had asked about Francis's illness, so Sarah hoped the news spread far—so that Sir Anthony could wonder if his arsenic was beginning to work.

At dinner, Robert began to distance himself from Sarah. He flirted with the other ladies, and made it obvious that he did not include her among them. Sarah saw the confused glances people cast from Robert to her, and could only lift her chin and ignore the rare sympathy—and the more prevalent suspicion. Sir Anthony was one of those who treated her solicitously, and she wondered if he was mentally rubbing his hands together over the success of his plan to implicate her. It was difficult to be near him without vividly thinking of what he'd done to Lord Drayton, what he'd tried to do to Francis.

After the meal, Margery cornered Sarah, who was forced to lie again, confiding her fears that Robert's intentions toward her had changed, that it might be only a matter of time before she was accused. Margery consoled her, promising that she would help her escape if need be.

At supper, two weary travelers requested a night's comfort, as did a messenger on his way to Gloucestershire from London. Sarah would have thought nothing of three strangers needing shelter—if she hadn't remembered Walter's promise to recruit more Bladesmen. Were they already arriving? Why didn't this make her feel safer?

Nothing would ease her until the truth was revealed.

To her surprise, Simon was one of the only members of the household to speak to her, offering to play a game of chess, when it was clearly so difficult for him to be near her. She accepted, her memories of being an outcast in the Audley home resurfacing until she felt so alone.

As they bent over the board, he spoke stiffly. "I do not believe these ridiculous rumors."

She was surprised, considering the way she'd had to reject him. With a sigh, she said, "You are kind, Simon."

"As I assumed, Sir Robert was only trying to befriend you to find a way to accuse you of murder." His voice was laced with misery.

She winced at his accusation. "I know not what to think anymore."

Simon defeated her at the game.

She was almost relieved as she rose to her feet. "I fear I was not much of an opponent this night. But now I must go see to poor Francis."

"He is still feeling poorly?"

"A bit. But he is on the mend."

Behind her, Robert suddenly said, "I will accompany you."

She heard the gasps and whispers, even as she turned around to face him. Though he wore a smile, his eyes were cold, and he could have easily frightened her.

"Why is that?" she asked coolly.

"You might need help carrying everything."

But everyone would now think she couldn't be trusted alone with the little boy.

Simon stalked past Robert, brushing his shoulder hard, deliberately.

Robert only inclined his head.

* * *

As midnight approached, Robert paced his bedchamber waiting for the lateness of the hour, all the
while reliving Sarah's white-faced performance of im-
pending doom. She was so believable, so brave, when
even her own life was at risk.

At last he could no longer deny that he needed to
see her. To minimize the risk to their plans, he once
again used a rope from the top of the keep, swinging
onto her window ledge, where he squatted and carefully pushed open the shutters.

Bathed in candlelight, she stood on one towel,
another wrapped around her, as she poured heated
water from the cauldron into a basin. He remained
motionless, openmouthed, as she dropped the towel
and began to wash herself. He followed the path of
the wet cloth with intense fascination as she leisurely
soaped her arms and shoulders, and then began to
circle her breasts.

She suddenly lifted her gaze to him and smiled.
"Are you going to crouch there all night?" she softly
called.

He dropped swiftly to the floor.

She put a finger to her lips, and then motioned to
Francis's bedchamber—where Walter was.

He had totally forgotten about his partner. It was
amazing he could function at all when looking at her

naked. She gave him that slow, wicked smile that twisted his insides. He was out of his garments in a flash. In utter silence, they bathed each other with soapy hands until the wood floor was a mess. Having to be quiet in some ways made the encounter all the more passionate.

He couldn't get enough of her kisses, hot one moment, sweet the next. And when she touched him, took his cock in her hand to explore, he shuddered with bliss. He lifted her off the ground, and with one thrust he was inside her. Her eyes went wide, she gave the tiniest gasp, and then she sagged against him, quivering, rubbing her breasts to his chest in a way that surely pleasured them both.

They strained against each other, their gazes locked, their bodies slick. Every time he lifted her, her breasts bounced, dazzling him. When she stiffened and shuddered in his arms, he gave himself over to the pleasure.

They dropped back onto the bed and just breathed, looking at each other, grinning.

Then she got up—God knew he probably couldn't—and brought several towels to dry themselves. Then they crawled beneath the coverlet and she came into his arms, her head resting on his shoulder.

"This might have been the worst day of my life," he murmured.

She hugged him tighter. "I know what you mean. But the goal is all that matters."

"Ramsey demanded to know what was going on, but I said I was still gathering evidence and couldn't speak. I hinted that I was close to making an announcement."

"Let him stew on that, wondering if he's safe at last." She looked up at him. "Do you remember Emma, our lady's maid who served the Ramseys when they were in residence?"

He nodded.

"I almost collided with her when I was coming up here earlier this evening. She cringed away from me, the first person to do so."

"I am sorry, Sarah," he said, caressing her arm where it lay across his chest. "Perhaps 'tis not just about you. Mayhap she has another reason to be afraid."

She lifted her head. "You think she knows something?"

"You've assigned her to Ramsey while he's here, and she's served him before. We think he might have had help."

"But using our servant rather than his? That seems very risky."

"I will talk with her on the morrow."

They both quieted until at last he could not deny the inevitable. "I must go."

She nodded drowsily. After he dressed, he bent to kiss her one more time.

"Be careful," she murmured, looking toward the window through which he would depart.

"I am always careful. Tomorrow is the day, sweetling. By the evening, it will be all over, and you'll be free."

She tried to smile up at him, but worries shadowed her eyes.

Sarah dreaded the morning, and for good reason. At mass, only Margery knelt on the cold stone floor beside her. In the great hall, when all went in to break their fast, servants obeyed her without meeting her eyes.

Master Frobisher approached her where she stood near the kitchens. "Mistress Sarah?"

She nodded but could not summon a smile.

"Are you . . . well?"

He looked uncomfortable and apologetic and sad. Somehow it made her feel better. Not everyone believed the worst.

"You can imagine how I'm feeling, Master Frobisher. I know not what is happening, nor why."

"It does not seem fair. I wanted you to know that I do not believe what Sir Robert is implying."

She bit her lip and nodded. "Thank you. That

brings me peace. I can only trust in my innocence, and that the truth will come out."

"The boy is well this morn?"

She gave him a smile. "Better."

"Good, good."

They stood silently, awkwardly for a moment, and then he cleared his throat. "I received some disturbing news after mass."

She raised her eyebrows and waited.

"One of our maidservants has disappeared."

That wasn't what she'd expected to hear. "Who is it?"

"Emma, the lady's maid."

The maid Sarah herself had assigned to the Ramseys.

"The servants who share a bedchamber with her claim that this morn, she said she was too ill to attend mass."

Sarah stiffened, worried that arsenic had been employed on someone else.

"When the maidservants returned, she and all of her possessions were gone."

Had Robert been correct? Was Emma involved and too frightened to remain?

"And no one knew a reason she was upset?" Sarah asked.

"None," Master Frobisher said, shaking his head.

"She might have taken some fancy into her head, or been led astray by a man. We may never know."

"Have the maidservants tell us if they hear word of her in the village."

"Aye, mistress." He put a hand on her shoulder. "Take care this day. I've seen Sir Robert's face, and though he smiles, I think he has made his decision."

As the servants left the hall by ones and twos to begin their day, Robert called people to his side: Sarah, the Ramseys, the steward and treasurer, Father Osborne, Simon, and Margery—the last of whom was a surprise, unless he wanted Sarah to be comforted by her only true friend.

"I have grave news to relate," he said as they all watched him in silence. "But now is not the time."

She could hear a ripple of sighs and murmurs.

"I invite you all to dine in the viscount's private solar at noon."

Sarah felt eyes on her, and saw Sir Anthony watching her sadly. She looked away.

And then began another long morning of suspicion. Each hour dragged slowly. She spent much of it with Francis, but only after Robert privately assured Sir Anthony that she would never be alone with him. The poor boy was restless and confused, although he'd found many hours of satisfaction with a skill Walter was teaching him—how to use his knife to make wooden figurines. Sarah was impressed at the graceful statues Walter created, especially the pony with a little marking carved in its forehead just like Lightning. She thought the Bladesman might even have blushed as she praised him.

Francis said she looked sad, so he wanted her to wear his mother's brooch to cheer her up. She let him pin it on her, smiling, so that he would know he'd helped.

At last it was time to attend their private dinner. Sarah felt nervous and afraid and relieved all at the same time. She straightened her shoulders, facing the door to the lord's chambers. She was surprised to feel a hand on her shoulder.

Walter looked down at her. "The plan is sound. It will not fail."

She nodded her gratitude, not trusting herself to speak. She entered the solar from the lord's bedchamber to find Robert already there. They glanced at each other, but said nothing. Worried that her eyes would give her away, she looked about the chamber. As planned, she saw individual silver plates overflowing with food on the cupboard along one wall. She hastily looked away.

Soon the rest of the guests were assembled. Robert seated Sir Anthony at the head of the table, his wife at his right. The rest filled in the empty spots, leaving the far chair for Robert. Sarah gave Margery a grim smile, and the seamstress responded in kind as they sat beside one another.

As one, they all turned to face Robert, who remained standing, hands clasped behind his back. "My announcement will be better accepted on a full stomach. Allow me to serve you," he said, setting plates before each of the guests.

They all continued to exchange confused glances.

"I was hoping young Francis would be well enough to join us, but he is not," Robert said casually, lifting the last plate. "The kitchen sent up his plate as well. I brought it here." He set it down before Sir Anthony. "No point in wasting a good meal."

Even as the steward and treasurer began to eat, Sarah watched Sir Anthony, waiting for him to ask for another plate, or to refuse to eat, incriminating himself. All day long each plate sent to Francis had been examined, and Walter had told her that evidence had been found of arsenic. Sir Anthony had continued to try to kill the boy. They didn't descend upon the kitchen, preferring to keep the villain in the dark.

Instead of refusing to eat, Sir Anthony picked up his knife and stabbed a piece of lamb. As he brought it toward his mouth, Lady Ramsey suddenly slapped it away.

Chapter 24

Sarah could not control her gasp. Robert stepped forward, his expression grim. Lady Ramsey gripped the table, her eyes closed.

Sir Anthony only looked confused. "Caroline?"

"Oh, how clumsy of me," she cried, her voice unsteady.

She bent to pick up the knife. The meat had landed somewhere else, and she looked at the empty tip of the knife as if confused.

"Clumsy?" Sir Anthony repeated. "Were you reaching for something?"

Robert opened his mouth, but it was Simon who spoke.

"'Twas no accident," he said impassively.

Sarah gaped at him where he sat across the table from her. His face was white with strain, his eyes haunted with sadness. Lady Ramsey blinked as if she didn't understand.

" 'Tis Lady Ramsey who wants the viscountcy for her beloved husband," Simon continued, his words dripping with sarcasm. "And there is probably enough poison in that poor boy's plate to make sure she succeeded at last."

The table was silent as all stared at Sir Anthony and his wife. Sir Anthony's mouth opened and closed several times, as if he didn't know what to say, his face as gray as death.

"Do not look like that, Anthony," Lady Ramsey exclaimed. Then she gave him a beatific smile. "You deserve only the best. And since I could not give you a child, I had to give you something else to make up for it. A viscountcy is perfect, do you not think?" she asked, clapping her hands together.

Sarah felt a sick sort of pity that she and Lady Ramsey had barrenness in common.

"Caroline, nay—" Sir Anthony began, his voice strangled and harsh.

Sarah glanced at Simon, who sat unmoving, his shoulders stiff, his stare concentrated on Lady Ramsey. What had he done for her, all the while he'd been courting Sarah?

"Emma didn't understand how important this was," Lady Ramsey said of the Drayton maid. "She would no longer obey me."

"She fled rather than continue to serve your evil,"

Simon said flatly, "as I should have fled. But I was . . . trapped."

"How is that?" Robert asked.

Simon continued to stare at Lady Ramsey with bleak eyes. "I was protecting my foolish sister, Isabel. She was once Lady Ramsey's lady-in-waiting, and had committed an indiscretion with a married man. Lady Ramsey threatened to reveal it all if I did not assist her." His gaze shot to Sarah. "I could not let her life be ruined!"

Sarah stared at him helplessly, angrily, unable to give him the understanding that he seemed to crave. A man had been murdered!

Whatever Simon saw on her face made him slump.

"What is he saying?" Lady Ramsey trilled, staring back and forth between her silent husband and the knight she'd blackmailed. "I do not understand!"

"You understand," Simon said. "I helped you frame poor Sarah, I helped you get the poison where it needed to be."

Then he lurched to his feet, and before anyone realized his intentions, he ripped the jeweled pomander from where it hung at Lady Ramsey's waist. He smashed it open on the table, and white powder leaked out instead of fragrant herbs. Robert caught him from behind, but Simon did not struggle.

Sarah had thought Sir Anthony was guilty, never seeing the truth in two people who'd masked their evil well.

Lady Ramsey slowly rose to her feet, staring wide-eyed at the arsenic scattered on the tablecloth.

Simon seemed distant, almost blank, as he said in a monotone, "Then she started in on the poor young lord. I couldn't—I just thought we were scaring him, startling the cow. But she wanted more. She wanted his saddle damaged and I refused."

"So *you* cut the girth, Lady Ramsey?" Sarah demanded, her hands clenched into fists.

"She tried to hurt Francis?" Margery cried. "Why?"

Lady Ramsey only gazed at her husband, her eyes shining with adoration. "Do you not see, Anthony? *You* are the one who deserves to be the viscount, not a little boy. I couldn't let Drayton marry Sarah and have even more children standing between you and the greatness you deserve."

"Caroline, how could you?" Sir Anthony buried his face in his hands.

Sarah rose swiftly to her feet, coming around the table to face Lady Ramsey. Her body trembled with the effort of restraint. "Only a truly evil woman would harm a child to get what she wanted. But Francis is safe. He was never poisoned. We foiled your plan, so *he* will remain Viscount Drayton."

The change in Lady Ramsey's expression was immediate. Rage rose like a storm in her gray eyes. She ripped the viscountess's brooch from Sarah's gown.

"Everything will soon belong to my husband!" she screamed. "You cannot stand in my way!"

"I already did!" Sarah said triumphantly.

Robert rounded the far side of the table to come to her defense. Simon followed him. Robert half turned as if he wasn't certain that Simon might defend his mistress to the end.

But Simon grabbed Lady Ramsey. "This bitch has ruined enough lives!"

She was no match for his strength. As Sarah watched in horror, Simon lifted the screaming Lady Ramsey and jumped through the mullioned window. In the silence that followed, all she could hear was the tinkling of glass, then distant screams from the courtyard below.

Robert ran to the window and looked out, the others crowding beside him. Sarah stood frozen in disbelief. Her gaze found Sir Anthony, who continued to stare at the broken window as he slowly sagged into his chair. He looked at Francis's tainted plate of food. She hastily took it away.

At last he seemed to see her. "Have no fear, Sarah," he murmured. "I am no coward to take the easy way out."

Was Simon? she wondered, grief mingling with her

anger and outrage. Or had Simon simply felt that both he and Lady Ramsey had to pay for their crimes? She would never know.

Robert stared down at the broken bodies in the courtyard below, watching as a frightened crowd gathered. No one appeared to have been injured below. And now Francis was safe, he thought with satisfaction.

The steward and treasurer started to pepper him with questions, but he lifted both hands. "Not now. I will explain everything later." He sent Margery to Francis so that Walter could join them.

He saw Sarah standing motionless at the table, watching over Ramsey. The man must be devastated, knowing that for his sake, his wife had killed his cousin.

Robert approached him. "Sir Anthony, I am saddened at the way you had to discover the truth."

Sarah looked from Ramsey to Robert, tears beginning to overflow her brown eyes. Walter stepped into the chamber, taking in the shattered window.

Ramsey slowly raised his head as if he were an old man instead of in his prime. "You have nothing to apologize for, Sir Robert. I knew her barrenness caused her great grief, but I never thought . . . You must believe that if I would have known it had damaged her mind—"

"I believe you, sir," he said gently.

"Did you see the truth from the beginning?" Ramsey asked in a bewildered voice.

He shook his head. "Nay. In fact, I thought this dinner would incriminate *you*."

"Ah," Ramsey said heavily. "It makes perfect sense. For my motive would have been the same as . . . my wife's." He lowered his face into his hands, his shoulders shaking.

Walter nodded to Robert. "Let us go below."

Robert saw Sarah glance sadly at Sir Anthony as they left the solar. "Should I have someone stay to guard him?" he asked.

She shook her head. "He is strong. But he will need time to come to terms with what has happened."

As they walked down the corridor, Walter said, "Well done, Sir Robert."

Robert eyed him. "My thanks, but I deduced the wrong villain."

"As did the League. 'Tis the end result that matters. Your method succeeded in avenging Lord Drayton's murder. That will not be forgotten."

By the time they reached the courtyard, the crowd around the dead had grown. As Robert approached, conversations died to murmurs, and they all separated to allow him access.

He heard Sarah gasp. He took her shoulders. "Stay

here, Sarah. There is no need for you to see this."

She nodded, hugging herself. Master Frobisher put his arm around her, and she leaned into his shoulder.

Lady Ramsey and Simon Chapman were dead, of course, their bodies broken. Robert would never condone what Chapman had done on his sister's behalf, but he could pity the man.

"What happened, Sir Robert?" called Cook, where he stood encircled by his scullery maids. Some trembled and looked away, others craned their necks with curiosity.

Robert spoke in a raised voice. "Lady Ramsey is the villain who killed your lord."

Gasps and cries of surprise and outrage rose around him.

"Sir Simon was blackmailed into assisting her. Their deaths bring this terrible tragedy to an end."

He saw several guilty stares granted to Sarah, and then one by one, people went to her. How would she feel, since they'd all suspected she might be guilty?

He noticed that there were several new strangers mixed among the Drayton servants, besides the three travelers from the previous night. Bladesmen all, he knew. He saw the profile of a man dressed in the simple breeches and shirt of a farmer, but in a startled moment, he cared nothing about what he was wearing.

"Adam?" Robert called.

His brother turned to face him, grinning. They shared the same height and dark coloring, even the same cleft in their chins.

Robert lowered his voice as he approached. "Can this be the earl of Keswick in such simple garments?"

"I've come to assist my little brother, but I see you have things well under control."

To Robert's surprise, Adam enfolded him in a hug.

"Well done, Robert," he said, his voice gruff.

Robert nodded, feeling embarrassed, even as it seemed a little difficult to swallow.

"Aye, brother," said another voice, "you have far exceeded my expectations."

Robert's breath caught, and at last he looked at the man with Adam. Their brother, Paul, lowered the hood from his head.

"Paul?" he said with astonishment.

He had not seen him in well over a year. He looked none the worse for wear, except that his face was thinner, his shoulders broader, as if he'd worked hard to support himself. There was no demonstrative smile of greeting, not from Paul. He'd always been a serious young man, but now he looked . . . dangerous.

Robert didn't care about any of that. He laughed and crushed Paul in a hard hug. Paul hesitated, then patted his back.

"Where have you been?" Robert demanded, as he

stepped back and held his brother's upper arms.

"France and Germany. The tournaments were my livelihood."

"I am certain you did well," Robert said dryly. "How could you not?"

"I was successful." Paul shrugged.

Adam laughed. "An understatement, I am sure."

"Though glad I am to see you," Robert said, "why did it take you so long to return?"

Impassively, Paul said, "'Twas time. And then I returned only to discover that you and Adam had successfully revealed the identity of our parents' murderer. With no help from the League."

"The League was invaluable at the end," Adam said.

Robert didn't quite agree with that, but it no longer mattered.

"I would say that you have proven yourself to the League, Robert," Adam said.

Paul said nothing, his brow furrowed, but Robert wouldn't allow his brother's bitter feelings to tarnish his own. "Adam, I think I proved something to myself, and that is even more important."

Sarah heard the well wishes, the apologies, the concern in the voices of the people she'd spent the last two years living with. But it all seemed so distant compared to the bloody death she glimpsed between milling servants. Simon . . . her suitor . . . her betrayer. It was all so terribly sad.

She closed her eyes briefly as she turned away. She saw Robert with two strangers. Bladesmen? she wondered. She didn't want to interrupt him, but she didn't seem to know what to do with herself. She couldn't seem to stop crying. His assignment at Drayton Hall had ended with success. But was this the end of their relationship? Would he go back to the life of a nobleman's son?

And then he was coming toward her, his face full of concern and tenderness. Her love for him ached within her heart.

He put an arm around her. "Come, Sarah, let us leave here. Others will do what needs to be done."

She nodded and let herself be guided into the keep and up to her bedchamber.

She took a step toward Francis's door. "I must tell him *something*, Robert."

"We will, but not now. Margery is with him."

She nodded, staring up at Robert helplessly. And then he enfolded her in a fierce hug, and she clung to him, grateful for his strength and his warmth.

"Thank you," she whispered, then repeated those important words in a louder voice. "Thank you. You saved my life. You saved Francis's life."

She looked up at him, and though he smiled, she thought he was a little embarrassed. It was endearing.

"What will you do now, Robert? You are a success in the eyes of the League. I know there are plenty of Bladesmen here to witness it."

He grinned. "Including my brothers."

She felt like smiling at last, when she thought she might never smile again. "Those two men—how did I not see it? They resemble you greatly. And one of them you have not seen in . . ."

"Over a year. Paul is home now, although I don't know for how long. We can hear the story of his adventures later."

She was happy for him, but he still had not answered her question. "So that is what you'll do next, go with your brothers?"

He took her cold hands in his warm ones. "Nay, next I am going to marry you."

She could only blink, stunned. "But . . . but you are an earl's son."

"Should you not cry out with joy and hug me?" he asked playfully. "I always thought a woman should be happy at such times."

She bit her lip, trying not to let happiness rise up within her, when reality could ruin everything. "Robert, I am but a knight's daughter—"

"Say that not again, sweetling. I would not care if you were a dairymaid. I love you," he said in a low, urgent voice.

The tears started again. "You love me?"

"I do. And I vow to spend every day of my life proving it to you. Never had I met a woman who captured my heart and soul, until I met you."

Hope blossomed within her, even though her tears didn't stop. "Oh, Robert, I love you, too. I was afraid to tell you. I always thought I was a failure as a wife, and it has taken me some time to realize that all men are not like my late husband. You've shown me such trust, such goodness—" She broke off, her throat tight.

He brought her hands to his lips and kissed them, his ready smile full of tenderness.

Her voice strengthened. "I let my old self be buried under doubt and misery. But I am finding my happiness again, and I owe it all to you."

"I should have known from the start what kind of woman you are, Sarah," he said earnestly. "You could never hurt another to better yourself."

"And I wouldn't hurt you either, Robert. I would never think to stop you from doing good works for the League, no matter the danger. You care about people enough to risk yourself helping strangers. You—and the League—saved Francis and exonerated me. I won't forget that. But I know you are still conflicted about the League's purpose in your life."

"Nay, I am through with doubts. Regardless of what the League thinks of my methods, it was worth going against them to make a difference in people's lives. With your blessing, I want to pursue a future with the League, even if I have to force them to take me back."

She cupped his face with both hands. "You don't need my blessing, but you have it, my love."

He grinned even as he kissed her, and she knew she would always associate his kisses with merriment.

"Until you win over the League, what will you do?" she asked.

"Take my bride to my home, of course."

She smiled with pleasure, though she felt she had to ask, "Your brother's wife will not mind?"

"Not his home, mine. I have my own manor, my own inheritance from my parents. I've never been there, of course, because it wasn't home to me then. I never had a true home. As long as you'll have me, Sarah, we can make a home together."

She came into his open arms and kissed him, knowing that two lonely people had at last found each other, found love.

Epilogue

That evening, everyone gathered in the great hall felt as if a spring wind had blown away the last of a bitter winter. There was no great rejoicing, for death had been too close, too deeply felt, but a new beginning was promised to all.

Robert watched Francis's glee after being freed from confinement. The little boy chased his friends about the hall, skidding through the rushes as was his wont. He had not really understood what had happened to Lady Ramsey and Simon Chapman, except that an accident had taken their lives. In the way of young children, after momentary grief and confusion, he'd let himself enjoy his freedom.

Robert had taken great pleasure in introducing his brothers to his future wife. Walter faintly smiled through it all as if he'd helped bring them together.

The celebration faded when Robert noticed Ramsey

enter the hall. He moved steadily, his face a grim mask, his eyes quiet and grief stricken. People stared and whispered, treating the man as if his wife's crime were his fault.

Ramsey approached them. "Sir Robert, I have a boon to ask of you."

"Ask, Sir Anthony, and I will do what I can."

"Would you assume guardianship of young Lord Drayton?"

Robert exchanged a surprised glance with Sarah. "I do not think my willingness will matter to the king, whose decision this is."

"He will listen to my recommendation. You *are* the son of an earl. You would be a good father to the boy, who already worships you. He should never have to live with me, the widower of the woman who killed his father and almost killed him."

"No one blames you, sir," Sarah said, reaching to touch his arm.

"I blame myself. I have to find some way to understand how I did not see the evil sickness in the woman I loved. Did I take her devotion for granted, as something due me? How did I not see that it was twisted with jealousy? I do not know, and I must come to terms with it. Will you do this for me, for Francis?"

"Aye, Sir Anthony. If the king approves I would

gladly oversee Lord Drayton until he reaches maturity."

Ramsey nodded, then turned and made his way out of the hall.

Robert felt Sarah clutch his arm, and he could see the happiness shining in her eyes. "You are pleased, sweetling?" he asked.

"Aye, my love, how could I not be? I dreaded telling Francis that I was leaving him. Now he will be able to spend time here, and at our new home."

Walter cleared his throat. "I do not wish to interrupt your happiness, but Sir Robert, I have something that needs to be said."

Robert nodded, even as his brothers gathered defensively behind him. Sarah took a step closer as if she'd throw herself between Robert and Walter.

He chuckled as he patted her hand. "Aye, Walter, say what you need to."

"I think your work was exemplary on this assignment."

That caught Robert by surprise and he couldn't help saying, "You do? I know the case was solved, but my methods did not exactly endear me to you."

"Believe me, Sir Robert, the League will be satisfied with you. They wanted to make sure you could think for yourself, that your upbringing hadn't made you bow to everything the League proclaimed. They gave you one suspect in Drayton's murder, but they actually wanted to see if you would broaden the investigation, not follow every order rigidly. You followed justice, Sir Robert, and that is all the League could want from any Bladesman."

Robert felt almost dazed as Sarah hugged him. Adam clapped his back, grinning, and Paul shook his head, a smile tugging one side of his mouth.

Robert clasped Walter's hand. "My thanks for your assistance, Walter. You were invaluable." Then he turned to Paul. "Does this not make you want to rejoin the League, brother?"

Paul clasped his hands behind his back. "I am only here to help you, Robert. Do not expect more."

Walter turned to give Paul an appraising look. "There is an important mission for which the League has been searching for just the right man."

"The League has distorted my life enough," Paul scoffed.

Walter shrugged. "'Tis a vital mission, to protect King Henry himself."

Paul inhaled sharply, opened his mouth, then said nothing.

Robert laughed, even as he pulled Sarah closer. For three brothers who'd known only the League of the

Blade since childhood, both he and Adam had found love and a real home. He prayed that his brother, Paul, could find the same peace and contentment.

He looked down into Sarah's beautiful face and for just a moment, he was speechless with gratitude and joy.

But he was never one to remain silent for long.

*Next month, don't miss these exciting new
love stories only from
Avon Books*

My Darling Caroline by Adele Ashworth
Lady Caroline Grayson is perfectly content to remain a spin-
ster, and Brent Ravenscroft, Earl of Weymerth, has no intention
of taking a bride. But when a matter of business binds them
together, even the best laid plans fall away...

Embrace the Night Eternal by Joss Ware
When Simon Japp awakens from a mysterious half-century
sleep to a devastating new world, he sees a chance to escape
his dark past and join the forces of good at last. But undercover
and posing as lovers with the stunning Sage Corrigan, Simon
finds that, sometimes, even a changed man can only be so
good...

Charming the Devil by Lois Greiman
Faye Nettles has a mission—to find out the truth, no matter
the cost. Brawny Scottish soldier, Rogan McBain has far more
on his mind than fighting. When the truth is revealed and passion ignites, will the beguiling beauty or the charming devil
be the one to cast the final spell?

Bound by Temptation by Lavinia Kent
Clara, the Countess of Westington, is one of the *ton's* most
scandalous women. Jonathan Masters has spent his life striv-
ing to be one of its most respected members. Of all the beds in
London, she had to wind up tied to his...

Unforgettable, enthralling love stories, sparkling with passion and adventure from Romance's bestselling authors

At Avon Books, we know your passion for romance—once you finish one of our novels, you find yourself wanting more.

May we tempt you with . . .

- **Excerpts** from our upcoming releases.

- Entertaining **extras**, including authors' personal photo albums and book lists.

- Behind-the-scenes **scoop** on your favorite characters and series.

- **Sweepstakes** for the chance to win free books, romantic getaways, and other fun prizes.

- Writing **tips** from our authors and editors.

- **Blog** with our authors and find out why they love to write romance.

- **Exclusive content** that's not contained within the pages of our novels.

Join us at
www.avonbooks.com

An Imprint of HarperCollins*Publishers*
www.avonromance.com